WOOD'S HOPE

STEVEN BECKER

THE WHITE MARLIN PRESS

―――――

Join my mailing list
and get a free copy of my starter library:
First Bite

Click the image or download here: http://eepurl.com/-obDj

MAPS

If you're interested in following along with the action or the locations it the book, please check out the Google map here:

https://www.google.com/maps/d/edit?mid=
1Fs3yUloYpyah7hFKPQoL9ax49xivhwF8&usp=sharing

WOOD'S HOPE

STEVEN BECKER

A MAC TRAVIS ADVENTURE

WOOD'S
HOPE

Wood's Island, Florida Keys

"You can go after her."

Mac glanced across the porch at Mel.

She met his gaze. "At least stop moping around and do something about it. You know where she is. You know how to recover her. What's stopping you?"

Mel was referring to *Ghost Runner*, Mac's forty-two-foot steel-hulled trawler that had been wrecked in the Bahamas. Mac knew Mel was right. There might not be a better time to recover the boat. He couldn't wrap his head around his reluctance, though. Part of the reason was that the boat being submerged in twenty feet of water was actually saving him money. Since she sank last fall, a series of disasters, both natural and manmade, had crippled the commercial fishing industry in the Florida Keys.

Barreling through the Middle Keys only weeks after the lobster season opened in 2017, Hurricane Irma's storm surge had reworked the ocean bottom, scattering the lobster that survived the storm. Six weeks later, when the stone crab fishery opened, it suffered the same fate. It took two years for nature to heal her wounds, and the 2019 season started well enough—until the lobster fishery was decimated again by the tariffs imposed as a result of the trade war between the US and China. In recent years, the Chinese had become the main exporter of crawfish from the Keys. The increase in demand had driven up prices. The political posturing cut them in half. Now, with news of a new virus about to run rampant through the country, prices had halved again.

The Keys' fishermen were faced with hard times ahead. Mac didn't rely on the fisheries for his income, only to supplement it. But Trufante, his wayward deckhand, did. Sometime over the last quarter century, Mac had adopted the trouble-prone Cajun. If he decided to run his string of traps, Trufante would be the main benefactor. Mac wouldn't admit it to Mel, but he felt responsible for his friend's income. There had been other times when, for one reason or another, Mac had paused his fishing career, forcing Trufante to work for Commander, the local bait magnate. Somehow, that arrangement had gotten both Mac and the Cajun in trouble. Trufante's unemployment had proven detrimental to Mac's health.

Faced with a choice of ending his fishing career, at least as he had been working it for the past few decades, or recovering *Ghost Runner*, he knew he should choose the latter. He just couldn't get himself to do it. Deep down he loved the boat, but he also knew that it would be a financial mistake to salvage her.

Over the years, Mac had raised dozens of wrecks, but not one of his own. If he were to think about it on a personal level, that might be the reason he had shied away from the project. If he were deciding on a financial basis if it would be better to salvage *Ghost Runner* or buy a new boat, repatriating the wreck would be the wrong decision. But, on an emotional level, the boat was a part of him.

He was torn.

"Mac?"

He realized he hadn't answered her question. "Why? I just don't know."

"Well, you better do something before you drive me crazy. This sitting around is not good for either of us."

Mel had "retired" from her position as an organizational lawyer several years ago and returned to the Keys. She had grown up here, but like many kids raised in the insulated community, had wanted nothing more than to get out. Her father, Bill Woodson, known locally as Wood, had bought the island where Mel and Mac now lived in the late eighties. The original structure he built had been firebombed by a rogue CIA agent several years ago. Mac had rebuilt the home. In place of the old wood pilings elevating the house, he had poured concrete columns, as well as a concrete deck. The structure had been built to the latest codes, which was fortunate, because everything below the ten-foot level had been taken out by Irma a few years ago.

The second rebuild following the hurricane was mostly cosmetic. The final touch was the addition of satellite internet, which had sealed the deal for Mel. She had moved back home permanently.

Now, Mac had to admit he was bored. The small island grew wild and didn't require much maintenance aside from clearing the brush from the area where the house and a shed were located, and the trail to the small beach and docks. Green leaves had finally replaced those that had been blown off by the storm. The remaining foliage, brown and gray for the last two years, was also finally showing new growth. But that was nature's work.

Mac still had a standup board, a kayak, his twenty-four-foot center console *Reef Runner*, and the Surfari motorsailer. None of the craft held much interest for him right now, though he used the kayak and board for exercise. Those sessions were usually limited to an hour or two at most. The center console was good for running around and some local fishing, which he did little of right now. That left the Surfari.

He'd come into possession of the boat after an adventure in the Dry Tortugas. It was an exceptional craft, able to use sail, motor, or a combination of both to cruise, but there was a taint left from its previous owner that Mac felt every time he climbed aboard.

That left a lot of daylight with nothing to do.

"I can't bear to see what she looks like." Mac finally put words to what had been bothering him these last few months.

"It's only work, Mac. You've refurbished her before."

Mac had repowered and fitted out the boat with the latest electronics a few years ago. *Ghost Runner* had been just the way he wanted her, and that was where the problem lay. Seeing her ruined, and having to repair and replace everything, was daunting. He felt like any mistake he made would ruin the rebuild of what had been his perfect boat.

"Yeah. Just not ready yet."

The answer wasn't good enough for Mel, who knew him too well. "Figure out the logistics. I'm going to start the paperwork."

Mac finished his beer and set the empty bottle on the rail. He stared out at the emerald water glistening in the sunlight. He wasn't offended or hurt by her ultimatum; actually, he was relieved that the decision had been made for him—as Mel had known.

"Don't know how the Bahamians work this kind of thing," he said, finally accepting that *Ghost Runner* would again see the light of day. Having been aboard when Trufante had driven her aground, on his own orders, Mac knew exactly what to expect.

His question didn't deter her. Mel was already furiously typing on her laptop. "For starters, you own the boat, so there'll be no question of rights. We can skip the maritime laws. Looks like we just need a permit."

In a foreign country, that was often more difficult than it sounded, but the economy of the Bahamas relied so heavily on US tourism that whether they liked it or not, they had to be friendly toward Americans. Mac knew there were many Bahamian government officials who would have it otherwise, but the fact remained.

Mel's decision was like a key being turned in the ignition of a race car. Mac suddenly had purpose. His first task was to find a weather window, and he left the porch and entered the house. On the water he relied on the NOAA reports over the VHF, radar, and more recently, apps on his phone, but if he had the choice, he preferred to see the raw data rather than the summaries. Grabbing another beer, he sat at the table and opened the screen on his computer.

It was March, a hit or miss weather month, but then they all were. Lingering cold fronts were a problem this time of year. The lines of squalls dropping down from the north were only the start of what was generally anywhere from a few days to a week's worth of unfavorable winds. If he could find a window, though, it would be an opportunity. The winds and seas during the summer months were more reliable, but the daily thunderstorms were an issue to a boat at sea. NOAA had everything he needed, and he was pleased to see the next week appeared to be good.

The next question was which boat to use. Despite his hesitation, he'd thought through the logistics of the recovery many times since the past summer, and knew how he wanted to raise the boat. With his salvage boat the one under water, Mac had devised a plan to float the wreck with air bags. Done properly, this would eliminate the need for a winch or crane. He wasn't happy about it, but the logical choice was bobbing on its anchor just past the dock.

It wasn't the boat itself that bothered him, just the bad *juju* associated with it. There might be a way to handle that, though, and he needed to see if Trufante was up for the trip, anyway. Despite the trouble the Cajun had caused him over the years, this was still the Florida Keys, and as Wood had said, you took what (or who) you could get here.

The Keys were a unique chain of islands, extending almost two hundred miles from the southern tip of mainland Florida. Though only one hundred twenty miles of them were accessible by vehicle via a sometimes two-lane road, the island chain served to create Florida Bay and divide the Atlantic Ocean and the Gulf of Mexico, before the two finally merged below the Dry Tortugas and became the Caribbean Sea.

Grabbing the keys to the center console, Mac drained the beer and walked onto the porch. "If we're going to do this, I need to see about Tru."

"Figured there wasn't much choice in that matter. Just so you know, I'm going with you this time." She paused. "Hey, you hear anything about this virus in China?"

"Only thing I hear about China is them all bitching about the tariffs and the price of lobster. Don't those things usually die out over there?"

"Usually, but there's some concerns about this one. Seems it's already sweeping through some of the European countries. Italy seems to be the worst right now. There are already cases out west. It's coming."

We're gonna need a bigger boat, was all Mac could think as he walked downstairs, crossed the clearing, and made his way to the dock. Climbing aboard *Reef Runner*, he started the engine and released the lines. As was his habit, the bow was facing out, and he nudged the shifter slightly forward until it clicked in the idle position. Mac passed the Surfari, giving her a long look. Somehow he would have to make peace with the boat.

Cutting the wheel to avoid the rock that stood sentinel over the narrow channel, Mac set a course toward the southeast and Marathon. As he traveled over the shallow flats, he started making a list in his head of provisions he would need. Even knowing these waters as well as he did, Mac still watched the color of the water for the telltale signs of the ever-present shallows and sandbars. *Brown, brown, run aground* was etched in every boater's brain. They all knew it, but any boater who said they hadn't run aground was either a liar or hadn't done it yet— eventually everyone did.

The Seven Mile Bridge soon appeared on the horizon, and Mac turned slightly to port in order to line the bow up just off the eastern end. Several miles later, he passed a shallow sandbar marked with a piling on one end and adorned with the latest boat to misread the water and ground. Once clear, he steered a course that would take him under the fourth span of the bridge. *Reef Runner* cleared both the old and new bridge easily. The entrance to Boot Key Harbor came up quickly to port, forcing him to dodge the boaters entering the passage between the Atlantic and the Gulf. It was a little like making a left turn on a busy highway—only it had no lanes—and few knew the rules. Once past the channel, he steered a wide birth around Boot Key itself, respecting the shallow water that showed the ignorance of the tourists, who tried to cut through the muddy flat and either got stuck or marred the sea bottom with their propellers.

Once around the Key, Mac spotted the red number-two marker and changed course again, this time avoiding West Sister

Rock. The small island had been easily visible before Irma, but was now only a foot-high hump sticking out of the water. Before the marker, Mac cut the wheel to port and entered Sister Creek. Keeping the green marker to his port side, he entered the channel and dropped down to a fast idle.

2

Marathon, Florida Keys

RELIEVED THERE WERE NO GUNSHOTS LIKE THE LAST TIME MAC had been here, he pulled up to the dock at Pamela and Trufante's house. Glancing quickly around the landscaping, he noticed the plants were thriving, a sign that Pamela had somehow exterminated the local iguana population. He could only hope no one else was injured in the process. If anyone asked, Mac would rank the green iguana third on the invasive species nuisance list in South Florida and the Keys. The top spots were taken by the lionfish and Burmese python, in that order. Both species had been released into the wild as unwanted pets. With no natural predators, they thrived.

Trufante was outside, hosing down his cast net. Seeing Mac, he draped it over a chaise lounge, and with his obligatory beer in hand, headed to the dock. His long strides had him ready to help Mac just as he pulled up.

"Hear about that corona thing?" Trufante said, showing Mac his Corona beer bottle. "Figured this'll give me some kind of immunity."

Mac suspected the immunity would be in the alcohol, not the name. "Mel mentioned something."

"Goddamned governor's talking about shutting shit down, Wuhan-style. I ain't worried, but Pamela's got her panties in a wad about it. Told her to chill and smoke a doobie." The Cajun laughed.

Mac was starting to worry now. Pamela was an enigma. Trufante had "found" her several years ago just off Duval Street in Key West while she was fighting a losing battle with a three-wheeled purple suitcase. She had claimed she was looking for her car, which was never found. Mel had done some digging on her, but her background was every bit as fuzzy as her personality. The only clue they had to follow was a hopped-up credit card, which with her and Trufante's wild spending habits was usually maxed out around the twentieth of every month. Then it was usually up to the Cajun to scrounge up enough work to cover the last ten days of the month's bar bills. Mac was thankful today was early in the cycle.

Over the years, Mac and Pamela had settled into a brother-sister relationship. She had gained his trust and had shown herself to be a badass in the course of their adventures. She still had her quirks, though, and one of those was her prescience. Among other things, she had known the path of Hurricane Dorian before the storm itself did. If she was worried about this corona thing, he knew he should be concerned.

"Where's she at?" Mac asked.

"Like I said, told her to smoke some weed and chill. Probably upstairs reading her crystal ball." Trufante finished his beer and held up the bottle. "Want some of this-here medicine?"

Mac nodded, and secured the center console while Trufante walked over to a full-size refrigerator sitting underneath the covered porch. He followed the Cajun, thankful for the shade. The T-top had been "removed" from the center console by a low bridge during a chase several years ago. Mac liked the way the boat rode without the weight and had never replaced it. But there were days when there wasn't a cloud in the sky, and he would have liked the shade.

"Thinking about heading over to salvage *Ghost Runner*." Mac still felt a little awkward calling his boats by their names. Until a few years ago, when Pamela had named them, he had always referred to them by what they were: the trawler, or the center console.

"Might be a good time, if what's coming down the pike is as bad as they say. Commander's brother's worried too."

"No word from Commander?" Mac asked. The bait king of Marathon and Trufante, with Mac's help, had sought refuge from the law in the Bahamas after a shooting last summer. Commander had not been back since, though there were rumors he had returned. There was enough shady business going down in the hurricane-ravaged islands to keep a guy like that busy for years.

"Nah, sure he's up to some shit. How's old Pip doing?"

A longtime friend of Mac's, Pip had sheltered the two refugees. "Wife almost got her claws back into him. Him and a carpenter buddy of his went back to rebuild his house."

"You mean Pip'll be supervising and the carpenter'll be laboring."

They laughed, then like most fishermen found themselves staring at the closest body of water, which in this case was the canal.

Both men drank.

"When're you thinking 'bout heading over?"

"Right away. Got a good enough weather window this week."

"Float bags?" Trufante asked.

"That was my thinking."

"Sure she's worth salvaging? Engines and all the electronics'll be ruined. Most folks that try it end up wishing they just bought a new boat."

Mac found it odd that Trufante was being the rational one. He'd thought this through too many times, though. *Ghost Runner* was a part of him.

As if reading his mind, Pamela called down from the second floor balcony. Mac couldn't see her from underneath, so he stepped outside and looked up.

"Thought I felt your vibe, Mac Travis. You're doing the right thing."

Mac knew her too well to ask how she knew. "Thinking about taking Tru over."

"Fine by me. Don't know if he's got enough lives left for this virus. They're saying the high-risk folks are going to have a hard time with it. Tru's as high risk as they come."

Mac laughed. He was pretty sure the Cajun was on his second or third set of "nine lives." "You really think it's going to be that bad?"

"Been studying up. It's already here. Only a matter of time before this turns into Italy."

Mac wasn't sure what she meant, but he knew that by the time he went to bed tonight, he would be up to date on the virus. It wouldn't change his plans. "So, you're good if he goes?"

"Sure as shit, Mac Travis."

"What the hell, Mac?" Trufante said. "I don't need no permission from no one to do nothing."

Mac didn't answer. He saw it more as himself asking permission to take Tru, not Trufante asking permission to go. There was a difference, and it never hurt to have Pamela on his side. "Day after tomorrow."

"What boat're we using?"

Mac hesitated. "Surfari. The plan's to fix the leak, float, and pump her. Then we can tow her to Chub Cay."

"You sure? That boat's got bad *juju*."

Mac found he was looking up at Pamela despite his efforts not to.

"Might be a way. How's your karma, Mac Travis?"

Mac shrugged. He had no answer for that question. He always tried to play it straight and do the right thing, but the gods weren't always with him. If he was to be honest with himself, there was nothing wrong with the Surfari—it was all in his mind.

"I'm going to make a few stops in town for provisions. I'll give you a yell later."

Mac was back aboard the center console and pulling away from the dock before Pamela could divulge her plan to exorcise the boat. With the supply list building in his head, he transited the canal system and reached Sister Creek, where he entered the Atlantic for the ride around Boot Key. Once on the Gulf side, he pulled into an open slip at the Marathon Yacht Club and tied off the boat. After checking with the dockmaster, Mac left the key in case it needed to be moved, and walked across the grass lot to his old truck.

The talk around town was all about the virus, and Mac absorbed all the information he could, though he graded each tidbit based on the source. The Keys were home to a unique bunch. The indigenous residents, or Conchs, were hardened, conservative, and prone to conspiracy theories. They'd skirt the law in a hot second if it was in their interest. The non-native population was almost the opposite, though they fell into two distinct groups: the lost and lonely crowd, and the retirees. Both demographics tended to lean left, and though they were often flamboyant, they more or less followed the rules.

Mac filed it all away to compare against what Mel gleaned from the internet. As he continued filling the truck with the necessary recovery gear and provisions, he couldn't help but form an opinion. By the time he reached Publix, the grocery store scene confirmed it: people were scared.

He was almost glad to be leaving home when he saw the empty shelves in the toilet paper aisle. This had the appearance of a hurricane on steroids. The residents of the Keys were used to the violent storms and knew how to prepare. This coronavirus threat was new, or as the media was calling it, novel. It was certainly the kind of thing outside of his wheelhouse.

The Surfari was well equipped as a cruising boat. The desalinator allowed Mac to pass on buying any bottled water. If they ran into trouble, it was only an hour's run into Chub Cay, though that was a last resort. Passports were a problem. He and Mel had theirs, but Trufante's only form of ID was an expired driver's license. The procedure for entering the Bahamas required them to check in with customs within twenty-four hours of entering the country. He would need to circumvent that.

Mac's plan was to head directly to the wreck site, raise *Ghost Runner*, and tow her into Chub Cay. He planned on checking in then. At that point, they would be on their way out of the country. He hoped to find a forgiving official who would let the mate's lack of documentation slide. If it all went according to plan, they would be in compliance, at least with the time limits, but Mac knew, especially with Trufante along, that was impossible.

With the truck bed and cab full of supplies, Mac pulled into a gas station to top off the tank. It was standard hurricane procedure, and he was surprised the station was empty. The talk of stay-at-home orders had made gas a nonessential item. The best news of the day was its price. It had been longer than he could remember since gas was this close to two dollars a gallon. The size and restrictions of *Ghost Runner* and the Surfari forced him to fuel at a marina, where he expected prices to be higher, but even then if he had to pay a dollar more, it was still cheap.

Mac retraced his route back to the marina, loaded the center console, and parked the truck. He was surprised by the boat traffic at the public ramp and on the Gulf. Apparently, the tourists hadn't gotten the message that there was a pandemic setting its sights on America.

Despite the swerving jet skis crisscrossing in his wake, being on the water lightened Mac's mood. Once he was a mile or so into the Gulf, the boat traffic almost disappeared. There were a few lobster boats out trying to salvage their seasons, and he waved to several captains he knew. After the third or fourth mile, he was on his own.

He saw the bright orange kayak well before he turned into the small channel. Mel, a diehard gym rat in her past, was now forced to do online yoga classes, swim, and paddle. Watching the blades of the paddle dip rhythmically in and out of the water, he envied her strength and flexibility. Even without a barbell in hand, she was a badass. He was still strong, but his joints often felt like rusted gears.

She waved and followed him into the channel. Instead of going to the dock, Mac pulled up alongside the motorsailer and offloaded the supplies that he could maneuver across the gunwales. Despite being awkward, it was better than doing it twice. When he finished, he was that much closer to being ready.

Now that he was past the point of no return, a calm fell over him. Though the feeling was sometimes elusive, he'd felt it many times in the past. It meant he was ready for the challenge.

3

STEVEN BECKER

A MAC TRAVIS ADVENTURE

WOOD'S HOPE

Marathon

OVERNIGHT THE NEWS HAD GOTTEN WORSE. THE VIRUS, NOW officially being called a worldwide pandemic, was on everyone's mind. That is, with the exception of Mac. Mel was wrapped up in the talking heads on TV pontificating on every angle that might entice a viewer to buy another package of the all-important toilet paper. Mac watched some, but he knew that there were few true experts on anything, and even less he trusted.

Mel could be almost bipolar with things like this. Her legal background and years of work for the ACLU had given her both a keen interest in political affairs, as well as blinders. She'd risen high enough in the ranks of the organization to be able to pick her cases. That might have been the only thing that made the job palatable for her last few years there. Though its founding principles were honorable, the organization's latest business plan, catered to the twenty-four-hour cable-news cycle, was to throw anything and everything at the wall and see what stuck. Topics ranged from placing tampon dispensers in men's rooms to the latest suffix in the LGBTQXXX cause.

It wasn't that Mac didn't have empathy for the "common man"; he did, after all, support Trufante. He believed that the life choices one made were more responsible for their personal and familial outcomes than the government. The networks were already screaming about people being evicted and starving in the streets. He would have liked to examine those people's monthly expenditures and see how many had iPhones, a half-dozen streaming service subscriptions, and a car payment. It was pretty well known in certain circles how easy it was to get food stamps. The programs were now disguised by initials like EBT or SNAP, supposedly to avoid the old "welfare" terminology. The stigma of being on the dole had been removed by the issuance of debit-type cards, with recipients being able to buy anonymously. You had to work hard to starve in this country.

Mac turned away from the screen. The more he watched, the madder he got. "Not going to be much left of our rights by the time they shut down the country."

"Sometimes you have to do things for the common good," Mel said. "Did you know there are only fourteen ICU beds in the Keys? Once they are full, anyone else gets transported to Miami, and if this is like everything else there, it's gonna be a shitshow."

They had already seen the boats lined up on top of each other at the sandbars. "I'll just go ahead and do the social distancing thing."

"You've been training for that your whole life," Mel said.

The tension eased slightly and dropped another notch when she closed the cover of her laptop. "Weather still good?"

"Looks like a stellar week. Almost too good to be true."

"Tru ready?"

"Called him a little bit ago. He'll meet us at the Thirty-third Street ramp in two hours."

"Might want to lock up good here, in case things get ugly."

"You think it's gonna come to that?"

"You saw those pictures of the sandbars and beaches. People are just idiots."

Mac took the next half hour to square away the house and shed. He left the hurricane shutters for last to keep the house cool. Fortunately, it was a comfortable night; living off-grid, there was no air conditioning. Despite being in Florida, they rarely missed it. The original house had been built using a passive solar design. With its large windows and living spaces oriented to catch the prevailing summer winds, and the roof of the wraparound porch to shelter the house from the subtropical sun, the interior stayed remarkably cool. Powered by an array of solar panels on the metal roof supplemented with batteries for nighttime and the rare cloudy day, they generally had enough power for their needs. When they didn't, there was a generator by the shed. Propane powered the stove, refrigerator, and the on-demand hot water system that was backed up with two large passive solar panels and a tank on the roof.

Mac took one last look around the shed and locked the door. All that was left was to fasten the hurricane shutters. They slid over the windows on barn-door tracks, and within a few minutes they were in place and locked. With the exception of the front door, the house was secure.

Mac had calculated and plotted their route a dozen times. With the forecast for one- to two-foot seas, and the Gulf Stream running at four knots, they could use the current to their advantage. Often when the seas were up and the river plowing through the middle of the Atlantic in excess of eight knots, many boats followed the coast of the Keys to Anglefish Creek, by Key Largo, before crossing. In poor conditions, spending as little time in the Stream was the best approach, but with the benign weather forecast Mac planned a more direct route.

Mac had plotted a course running east-northeast. It was a

straight line of two hundred miles out of Marathon. He had no worries about crossing on a calm, clear night. The Surfari was equipped with radar, as well as a metal reflector in the rigging to increase the boat's visibility to others. He planned to run at twelve knots, which was the best tradeoff between speed and fuel efficiency. If things held up, which he knew they seldom did, they would arrive sometime before sunset tomorrow afternoon.

Once on site, he would first dive to evaluate the wreck. Again, daylight wasn't an issue. Some work was best done in natural light, but to inspect the damage, he would need an underwater flashlight in either case. After that he didn't speculate. Depending on how badly Trufante had plowed into the coral head, it could take anywhere from a few hours to a few days to float *Ghost Runner*.

"Ready?" Mac asked.

"Sure thing." Mel had two bags. One held her personal effects, the other her computer. Using the interface on the satellite phone, she hoped to be able to access the internet to keep an eye on the developing crisis.

Mac grabbed his small duffle, and after locking the door behind him, followed her down the stairs. He took one last look around the clearing before heading down the trail to the water.

The Surfari was at the dock alongside the center console. Mac loaded their bags aboard and fired up the engines while Mel freed the dock lines, bringing them aboard in case they needed them. Mac stood with his back to the wheel and dropped the throttle to reverse. Once the boat was past the dock, he continued in reverse until he was clear of the rock at the end of the channel and cut the wheel to bring the bow toward Marathon.

The house might have been locked tight, but the rock was the island's primary security system. In order to reach the island itself, you had to know the waters. For years, a single pile set by Wood when he dredged the channel had been the only evidence that the island was occupied. He had gone to great lengths to ensure his privacy. The only boat at the time was a small skiff he used to run back and forth to the mainland and his construction yard, where the work boats were moored. Two concrete runners embedded in the narrow sand beach were the only visible evidence of the boat storage. A winch set in the clearing behind a near-invisible gate woven with mangrove branches was used to haul a trailer back and forth.

Mac had finally built the dock and out of respect had incorporated the old pile in the design. The approach might have seemed straightforward, but Wood had set a large boulder dead center of the channel. Submerged at all but the lowest of tides, the hazard had proven effective. At one time a winch had been secured to it with a wire running across to the pile to act like a boom. Mac might have kept the security measure had it not deteriorated in the harsh environment.

Once he was into Harbor Channel, and "sailing" at eight knots under power, Mac refamiliarized himself with the controls. The yacht was a semi-custom build with twin eighty-horsepower Yanmar diesels, which gave the boat a cruising speed of twelve knots, which Mac hoped to supplement with the sails. The cockpit was set forward and under cover, but where so many sailboats had multiple levels and obstacles built in, the Surfari's deck space was wide open all the way to the transom, which lowered like the tailgate of a pickup truck. Though not as large, especially in the beam, it reminded Mac of *Ghost Runner's* wheelhouse and cockpit. Mac had decided against towing a dinghy and had brought two paddleboards, which were fastened to a pair of runners built into the hard cover.

Mel came up beside him and sat in the adjacent chair. Mac remained standing. He was used to riding higher aboard *Ghost*

Runner, where he had been able to slouch in the captain's chair and steer the boat with his feet. The Surfari had a 360-degree view from the wheel, but only when he stood.

Running the Gulf side of the Keys required vigilance. Even knowing the waters like the back of his hand, it was too easy to make a mistake and ground. Small islands, or keys, lay everywhere. Many were merely extensions of shoals and sandbars, and barely visible at high tide. Boat traffic was all funneled through narrow, often poorly marked, channels with little room for error.

A few miles into the trip, Mac could see the lights of Marathon. The center span of the Seven Mile Bridge, and the trio of radio towers on the mainland, were the first lights to come into view. They cleared the last of the small keys and exited Harbor Channel. Here the Gulf was wide open, and with the exception of the shallow bank near the bridge and a handful of other spots, easily navigable.

On reaching open water, Mac turned east and steered toward the Thirty-third Street ramp, where he hoped the Cajun would be waiting. Located at the end of the street, the ramp had only a half-dozen parking spaces, though on weekends the school parking lot next door provided overflow parking. The ramp serviced a mix of the local commercial guys who ran smaller trailer-able boats, and tourists. As he turned between the red and green markers identifying the small channel, he saw the brake lights of a truck dropping a boat in the water.

This time of night, he expected it was a commercial fisherman. They were generally adept at dropping and pulling boats, so he paid little attention to them—until he heard two men yelling at each other. It was less than a hundred yards to the small pier placed adjacent to the seawall, and Mac steered toward it. Before he reached it, he recognized Trufante's lanky frame, and then realized he was one of the men in the argument.

Mac had planned on spinning the boat to face bow out, but the scene playing out in front of him made him head directly for the dock. Glancing over at Mel, who was in the process of placing fenders against the port-side gunwale, he caught an "Already?" look, which he dismissed.

Dropping to neutral, he coasted up against the steel piles.

"Just loop a line. I'll be right back," Mac said, jumping off the boat and onto the narrow dock. He crossed to the small concrete retaining wall that formed the ramp and walked its length to the truck.

"What the hell?" Mac yanked Trufante away from the driver's side window. He half-expected to see Commander, but knew it could be any of a hundred lowlifes here. The unkempt man had a phone to his ear.

"Easy, Mac, just got some business to settle."

"Settle it on your time. He calls the cops and we're not going anywhere." Mac glared at the fisherman in the old pickup, daring him to put the phone down. Mac exhaled a pent-up breath when he lowered it.

"Your friend here owes me five large."

Mac turned his glare to the deckhand.

"It ain't like that, Mac."

Mac didn't need Mel, who had come up behind him, to tell him it was *always* like that.

4

Marathon

MAC PULLED TRUFANTE AWAY FROM HIS CREDITOR AND DRAGGED him to the Surfari. To make an already difficult situation worse, Pamela was in the cockpit. Mac steered Mel away from the dock before she could see. The women weren't enemies, but neither were they friends. Frenemies wasn't the right term, either. Mac didn't care what they were, as long as he could get going. Pamela might be described as a "flake" in some circles, but she had proven to Mac that she could handle herself.

"Pamela's aboard."

"Shit."

"Not my doing."

"After watching you put out that dumpster fire, it might be better to take her. Keep Boy Wonder's head in the game."

Mac was glad she had acquiesced. If there was trouble brewing for the Cajun here, it would be better to have her along. The Surfari was equipped with two master staterooms, so there was plenty of room, though he was a little creeped out having to spend time in close quarters with the couple.

Together, he and Mel walked towards the motorsailer. Mel had looped the dock line around the steel piling so it could be released aboard, though he did linger a moment longer by making a show of untying an imaginary line to allow him to keep an eye on the driver of the pickup.

In many ways, the Keys embodied the last vestiges of the Wild West. Instead of horses and bandits, they had boats and fishermen, many of whom were part-time smugglers. It might seem odd, but the similarities were many. Starting with resentment for the law, at least as how it was prescribed to them, and a distaste for bureaucracy dictated from afar, the outlaw mentality prevailed. This lawless attitude made Mac wonder how the virus would affect them.

Dropping to the deck, he ignored his guests and went straight to the helm, where he called to Mel to release the single line holding them to the piling. Having docked bow in because of the argument, he motored slightly ahead into the turning basin in front of the double ramp. In the tight quarters, the value of the twin engines came in to play. The basin was too small for the forty-eight-foot boat to make a sweeping turn in forward, but by easing the shifters for each engine into forward and reverse simultaneously, he was able to spin the boat on its axis. In thirty seconds he was bow out and idling away from the ramp.

Trufante and Pamela, guessing they were on shaky ground, moved forward and sat on the foredeck. A few minutes later, even before they had crossed under the Seven Mile Bridge, Mac saw a puff of smoke. Seconds later, the smell of weed wafted back through the open vents in the windshield. Mac shook his head. He'd been around enough unstable people over the years to draw some of his own conclusions about pot, and he knew for some people it was beneficial. He wouldn't touch it himself, but for both Trufante and Pamela, it took the edge off their personalities. Of course, that came with a loss of motor control and a host of other issues, but compared to the two of them together in spin-out mode, it was worth the tradeoff.

Mac called out for Trufante to keep an eye ahead. One of the pitfalls to traveling at night was the chance of hitting something in the water. The Gulf Stream was like an express train, bringing all manner of flotsam with it. Once some of those items found the current's edge, the tide brought them right toward the bridge, which acted like a funnel. Though the tidal range was a modest two feet, but with the only access between the Atlantic and Gulf was under the bridges, the current often smoked through the pilings at several knots.

Having chosen his course, Mac headed to the west of the Sombrero Lighthouse, figuring he would harness the power of the Gulf Stream instead of cruising Hawks Channel on the inside of the reef. The ten-knot breeze would allow him to motor sail, something the boat excelled at. Having the wide-open ocean and being dozens of miles from the deadly reef would give them plenty of leeway to sail.

They had just crossed the reef when Mel came beside him. Mac hoped her lawyer brain was off and her mind wasn't churning away. A quick glance told him he was wrong. For a couple to survive the captivity of a small boat, they had to communicate. Had they been on land, Mac just would have found something to do to avoid her, but on a boat that wasn't possible, so he uttered the dreaded words: "What's up?"

Her hesitation was telling. If it was about Pamela, she wouldn't have waited. She had been on her phone since they had crossed under the bridge and had only just put it down, when he knew reception started to get sketchy.

"This is happening fast, Mac. They're talking about shutting stuff down tomorrow morning, starting with the restaurants and bars. Then they're going to come up with a list of what they're calling 'essential' businesses."

For the mental health of many of the Key's residents, bars were essential. "Can they do that?"

"They'll be lawsuits for sure, but they're going to try. Governors have a good deal of power, but there are almost no precedents."

Spoken like a constitutional attorney. Mac liked the fact that Mel had no party allegiance or agenda. He suspected she was still a registered Democrat, as any card-carrying member of the ACLU was required to be, but he'd noticed a marked change since she'd left the organization. She was as objective as they came.

The ocean tugged his attention away, and when the depth finder told Mac they were in two hundred feet of water—well clear of the reef—he cut the wheel twenty degrees to port and hit the button to unfurl the jib. If he didn't hate the boat so much, he'd love it. The Surfari was a pleasure to sail. With all the controls—many of them automated—available without leaving the wheel, she could be sailed single-handedly in all but the worst conditions.

Once the jib had caught the wind, with the push of another button he "raised" the mainsail. A pregnant pause followed while the sails grabbed enough wind to propel the boat. He soon felt the surge. Had they not been crossing the Stream, he might have shut the engines down. One of the most exhilarating feelings a sailor experiences is the change when going from power to sail. But with the time constraints he had set, he needed the engines to hold their course.

Once the boat had settled in, he turned to Mel. "Tourism takes a dive here, there's gonna be some interesting shit going on."

"Especially now. It's been one of the best seasons in recent history. Irma's all but forgotten except for the people who lived through it. It's been busy, and with spring break and Easter coming up, it'll kill the economy if they shut stuff down."

That wasn't exactly what Mac was worried about, but she was right. His concern was the fishing community. With lobster prices already halved from previous seasons, losing the lucrative stone crab season would be devastating. The hard-shelled crab lived up to their name. The succulent meat was protected by a shell that took a hammer to break. The claws could be frozen with minimal effect if done properly, but much north of I-4, they had never really caught on. The season coincided well with the tourist influx, and most were sold locally.

Fishermen would milk the system for what they could get, but they weren't the stay at home and live off the meager government check types. With the unlimited range of illicit activity available to them in the Keys, shit was gonna happen.

With the aid of the current, the sails, and the twin 80s, Mac found their speed over ground at near sixteen knots. Figuring the Gulf Stream was running faster than predicted, he retrimmed the sails and changed course to stay within its bounds. With the current conditions, the straightest line was no longer the fastest route.

The boat became quiet. The predominant sound was the hull cutting through the waves. The engine noise had been reduced to little more than a vibration.

"Might as well set a watch schedule. What's your preference?" Despite the visibility provided by the design of the boat, with four aboard it only made sense for one to remain with the helmsman, a job Mac would not give up.

"I'm tired of staring at computer screens. I'll take the last one."

"Can you tell them before you go down?" Mac asked.

"Sure thing."

Mac was relieved when Mel entered the cabin. The companionway was yet another of the features unique to the boat. Most monohull sailboats required four or five steps down to access the cabin. The main level of the Surfari's interior was flush with the deck. Again, he couldn't help thinking if he didn't hate the boat. . . .

With Mel below, he allowed himself to relax. She first had been spun out by the pandemic news and now, out of cell range, she was shut out. The best thing for her was to rest.

Somehow, Pamela must have sensed his mood. Leaving Trufante alone on the bow, she made her way around the rigging and dropped down into the cockpit.

"You thinking what I'm thinking?" she asked.

A pit formed in Mac's stomach.

"Come on, Mac, I'm feelin' it too."

Mac wondered how much she had smoked. He'd already seen this show. What was coming was inevitable. To delay, he checked every gauge in the cockpit—twice.

"I know what you're doing, Mac Travis."

Once again, the confines of the boat worked against him.

"What do you have in mind?" There was no reason to state the question. It was most certainly about the Surfari.

"You're making a face like I took your popsicle away."

Mac tried to ease the pained expression he knew he wore. "Okay. The boat's got bad *juju*."

"And then some, but let's start with what we have."

Mac and Pamela had done this dance before. With a hurricane bearing down on Key West and Trufante missing, they'd had a surreal moment when she had named his boats. Somehow over the years a connection had grown between them. Though she was attractive, it wasn't sexual or romantic, but he had to admit on some kind of cosmic level something existed. He'd fought it off for years—until that night in Key West when he had finally given in and accepted it as his fate.

"An exorcism might be a good start." Mac was engaged now that she had brought the fear in his mind out into the open. It was a problem to be solved, though—nothing more.

"I hear ya there, but I think you're gonna have to earn this one. You and this boat are going to have to go through something together. Some kind of experience that will bond you or break you."

He'd hoped she would just smoke a joint, say a prayer, and blow some smoke around. The thought that this was going to plague him until some unforeseen event happened was disheartening. "Maybe just a name would help?"

Pamela sat on the port-side bench and stared, dull-eyed, at the ocean. Mac knew better than to bother her and busied himself checking and then rechecking the gauges and chartplotter. Slowly she started to rock back and forth, in tune with the waves like a rider on a horse. Mac almost gave up on her. It wouldn't be the first time she'd lost focus.

"Runner, runner, runner, runner." She repeated the suffix of his other boats, *Ghost Runner* and *Reef Runner*. She started to add prefaces, but only one stuck—*Sea Runner*.

5

A MAC TRAVIS ADVENTURE

WOOD'S HOPE

The Gulf Stream

MAC WAS BOTH SURPRISED AND RELIEVED THERE WERE NO spiritual connotations in the name, but Pamela had made it clear that he would have to break the boat—or the boat would break him. Over the next dozen hours, the four quickly fell into a routine, each taking watch and trying to stay out of the other's way the rest of the time. Mac continued at the helm, liking the feel of the boat, but wondering when the crucible would come.

It was late afternoon when they arrived on site. Mac and Trufante, having done this more times than either could count, took care of anchoring the boat. The forecast had been correct, and despite the turmoil on land, the boat swung with the current on placid waters.

With daylight waning, Mac decided to dive the wreck. It was shallow enough to free dive, but he wanted the ability to examine the damage without limitation, so he grabbed a tank and his gear from the starboard storage locker built into the deck. The water temperature might not have required a wetsuit, but Mac knew better than to work around a wreck without protection. He donned a three-mil full suit while Trufante fit the buoyancy compensator over the tank and hooked up the first stage and low-pressure hose.

Mac took his fins, mask, and light to the transom, which had been lowered flush with the deck and water. Sitting on the edge with his feet in the water, he slipped into the BC and arranged his hoses. After slipping his fins on, he sprayed the mask with a diluted mixture of baby shampoo and water, rinsed it out, and placed it over his head. Strapping the lanyard for the light around his right wrist, he gave a thumbs-up to Trufante and pushed himself off the platform.

The sixteen pounds of weight in the pockets of the BC took him straight to the bottom. It was four pounds more than what he used for a recreational dive, but there was no need to maintain neutral buoyancy while on the bottom. Because he had to inspect the entire wreck, he used fins, but once the work started he would generally go with just his heavy neoprene booties.

Despite the low light, the water was crystal clear. Mac had chosen this site to ditch the boat because of its remoteness and the large coral heads projecting within feet of the surface. Trufante had dutifully driven the boat onto one. At the time it had seemed the only way. Mac's original plan had been only to disable *Ghost Runner*, not sink her. The Royal Bahamas Defense Force had other plans, and the wake from one of their cruisers responding to the incident had lifted the damaged hull from its resting place and sent the wounded ship to the bottom. Mac knew a storm could have done the same. The RBDF had accidently done some of his work for him. Had the vessel remained stuck on a coral head, a salvage vessel with a crane would have been required. In *Ghost Runner's* present condition, Mac hoped to simply repair the damage and float her.

The coral reef was already a lively fish habitat, but the addition of *Ghost Runner* had made it more so. Small schools of tropicals, mistaking him for a predator, scattered as Mac swam past. The moray eels and lobster were nonplussed, merely retreating an inch or two into their holes for protection.

Mac finned around the wreck. He noticed that the paint was barely visible through the first layer of algae that had started forming minutes after the boat was submerged. Brushing his gloved hand against *Ghost Runner*, he was able to remove most of the growth easily. It was a relief there were no barnacles yet.

Having anchored the Surfari in the sand off the deep end of the reef, Mac had started his survey from *Ghost Runner's* stern. Working his way toward the bow, he saw the gaping hole where the coral had torn away the steel hull. Turning on his light, Mac scanned the perimeter of the opening. Thankfully, the jagged edges were facing in. He had feared the wake that had lifted the boat might have left some metal protruding outside the hull.

He'd imagined the damage many times since the boat had grounded, and was relieved that it wasn't the worst-case scenario. It was far from good, though. Running the light around the edges reinforced his plan, which was good, because staging the operation from the Surfari was a far cry from having a proper salvage vessel, like *Ghost Runner*, as a working platform.

Mac flashed the light inside the opening to scare off any lurking predators. His effort was met by a surge of water as a large fish swam out. He popped his head above the level of the deck to see what it was, but was met by darkness. Panning the light back and forth, Mac inspected the interior of the ship. The coral had missed the engine compartment, not that it mattered. Both diesels would need to be replaced, as would all the electronics.

As he continued around the hull the costs started to add up in his head. He'd been through this exercise before and knew it would likely cost more to rebuild *Ghost Runner* than to replace her, but his decision had been made. This was his boat.

The other problem with raising the ship was the environmental impact. It wasn't likely, judging from the location the coral had penetrated, that the fuel tanks, oil reservoir, or hydraulic equipment were damaged. Just because they were intact now didn't lessen his concern. A punctured line or tank would have long ago spilled its fluid into the ocean. He was worried about what might happen during the salvage operation.

Checking his air, he saw only 500 PSI remaining. Satisfied he had covered what he needed to, Mac finned back to *Sea Runner's* anchor line and ascended toward a star-filled sky. Even through the fog in his mask, he could make out several constellations and even see the blur of the Milky Way.

Inflating his BC, Mac turned onto his back and kicked to the dive platform, where Trufante and Mel were waiting to help him with his gear.

Mac unbuckled the BC and did a somersault in the water, which allowed the inflated vest to bring the tank and regulator to the surface. Trufante reached a long arm out, snagged one of the shoulder straps, and easily lifted the gear onto the deck. Mel took Mac's fins, and he climbed aboard.

"Looks pretty straightforward," Mac said, regretting the choice of words as soon as they were out of his mouth. Nothing was ever straightforward with this crew.

MARATHON

COMMANDER POLISHED off his latest beer, placed the can on the ground, and with a swift strike, crushed it with his flip-flop. The ease with which the can folded had nothing to do with his strength; rather, it was the flimsiness of the packaging. The four other men gathered around the empty wire spool, which served for a table, ignored him. When he rose to get another beer, they suddenly seemed to wake up.

Commander crossed the gravel yard to the old upright refrigerator, which was working harder than it should against the modest heat. Grabbing a six-pack, he returned to the group and handed out beers, keeping the last two for himself. Simultaneously, all five cans cracked.

"Shit's gonna get real, bro," one of the men said, tipping the fresh beer back. He grimaced and glanced at the label. "Yo, dude. Expired PBR—really?"

Commander turned the can of Pabst Blue Ribbon in his hand to see the date stamp for himself. "That's all some hipster BS." Commander showed his disdain for the concept that beer could go bad by taking a long sip from his. "Anyhow, we gotta cut back the operation. This free shit's gonna end."

The men around the table looked down. They had known it was coming. With the panic in full bloom, nobody was going to be wanting fresh ballyhoo. Commander had cornered the market, allowing his "friends" a cut of the action. It was a full-time gig that conveniently fit into the off months in the Keys. The crawfish and stone crab seasons might be winding down, but it was spring break, and with No Vacancy signs everywhere —the market for fresh bait was hot. Commander saved the shoulder seasons, when the other fishermen were after mahi or were setting traps, for himself. Though he still sold some fresh bait during the slow seasons, the surplus went in the freezer. Handled properly, the frozen bait was every bit as effective as the fresh, and the convenience allowed him to expand his market share.

"Lobster's down, and it's too early to fish mahi. Without no tourists, don't matter about the rest of stone crab season. Bait fishing's all I got," one of the men said.

The rest drank and nodded in agreement.

"Uncle Sam's gonna cover this shit. Always does," Commander said, trying to reassure the men. If the men themselves didn't know how to get their hands on the many handouts available from the state and feds, their girlfriends or wives were experts. The problem wasn't generally income with this group; expenses killed them, and not for fuel or bait. Drugs, specifically coke, were expensive. These men, as did many of the folks working manual labor jobs in the Keys, had a tendency to burn the candle from both ends. There was nothing like a little bump to get things going in the morning—or extend the night.

The men kicked at the gravel. Though each one knew the other was probably taking handouts, none would admit it. "Y'all'll get by. We seen worse shit."

"Hey, where's Trufante?" one of the men asked.

The Cajun was a regular at these meetings.

"Ain't seen him," another man said.

"Went by the house to get some weed from his old lady. Wasn't no one around."

Commander wasn't going to speculate on the whereabouts of one Alan Trufante. He knew if he wasn't here, he was probably doing something with Travis, and oftentimes that meant opportunity. "Y'all should be out buying toilet paper and shit, not sitting here drinking my beer."

One of the men got up and slammed his beer. The others quickly followed and left. Once Commander was alone, he walked to the dock and hopped aboard his center console. Leaving the canal behind, he navigated the city mooring field in Boot Key Harbor and headed toward the Seven Mile Bridge. He was already up on plane before he passed the last marker. Cutting the wheel to starboard, he crossed under the bridge and cut inside the bank. Half an hour later he cruised by old Wood's Island.

He didn't slow in case either Mac or Mel were home. Mac

had done him a solid last summer when he had been in trouble with the law and hid him with a buddy in the Bahamas, though Commander had to admit he had taken advantage of the situation. After Hurricane Dorian blew through, he had ditched Travis and Trufante, seeing the money to be made, and had stayed on with a gang on the island.

Commander didn't need eyes on the inhabitants. He could find out all he needed by seeing which boats were there. He knew Travis's trawler had gone down in the Bahamas, and he expected to see the motorsailer and the center console. To his surprise, the motorsailer was gone.

Thinking Travis wasn't the type to take his old lady on vacation, he started to speculate where they might have gone. Add the missing Cajun and his girlfriend to the mix, and he expected he knew the answer. He spun the wheel hard and turned one hundred eighty degrees to head back to Marathon. What he needed was cell phone reception. He had an idea who might be interested in what Travis was up to.

6

The Wreck Site

WITH THE CALMING EFFECT OF THE WAVES BRUSHING AGAINST THE hull and the salt-laden air, Mac often got his best sleep at sea. Though after having been up for more than thirty-six hours, he could have slept anywhere. Trufante, Mel, and Pamela split the night into watches to allow him some rest.

Mac wasn't worried about another boat colliding with them. *Sea Runner* was well lit, and with the masthead light fifty feet from the surface, easy to see from a distance. They were also sitting only feet from the reef, which was a known navigational hazard. What he was worried about were the authorities, which was where Trufante came in handy. The Cajun might not have been the best choice for a mate in some cases, but when it came to the law, he didn't need the boat's radar; he had his own, built in.

Trufante and Pamela kept the first two watches, with Mel taking the early morning shift. Mac slept through the night and needed a nudge from Mel to wake him at five a.m. Coffee was already brewing, and the two had the cockpit to themselves.

Since they had stayed up until two, Mac would let Trufante and Pamela sleep until they were needed.

Mac drained his cup. "I'd like to get in the water pretty soon."

"Want me to wake the Boy Wonder?"

"Nah. Just want to have another look. Had an idea about patching the hole last night."

"When you were sound asleep?"

Mac ignored the barb. Somehow, when he slept he could solve problems better than when he was awake. "Instead of making the repair from the outside, I was thinking that if I could jam a flotation bag inside, it would both patch the hole and help float her."

"You'd have to use one on the opposite side for balance. You only brought four."

Mel knew her boats and was almost as savvy about the salvage business as Mac. Growing up an only child with a single father had given her an education into everything Wood had done. She could line fish, spearfish, captain a vessel, and fix things as if she was born to it—which she was. From an early age Mel had accompanied Wood on all sorts of salvage operations and adventures.

"But if it works, the tow job'll be much easier." His original idea had been to repair the hole and then attach the flotation bags to the outside, float the ship, and then pump her out. It would add hours, if not days, for the recovery. By using the bags to make the repair, they would be inside the hull, allowing him to start towing as soon as the boat was raised. They would then be able to pump out the vessel while they were underway. It would be slow going at first, but without the large bags creating drag, if the weather held he could tow her across to Miami. Not having to deal with the Bahamian authorities would be to all their benefits.

Mel helped him gear up, and within minutes, Mac was back in the water. This trip, he had brought a speargun. Though illegal in the Bahamas, he had brought it as a defensive measure. Large predators often roamed the reef at dawn and dusk, and there was a fair chance there would be one or two now. He had seen one last night. Mac's concern was not something cruising for breakfast, but one that had made the interior of the wreck its home. Deep recesses appealed to the larger fish. They served as ideal ambush spots.

Mac had only caught a glimpse of the fish that occupied the wreck last night, but if it called *Ghost Runner* home, had likely returned as soon as he had left. Nodding to Mel, he slipped off the dive platform and dropped to the sandy bottom. To be able to penetrate the wreck, he had gone without fins this time. Although the conditions for both this and last night's dive were essentially the same, and would fall under the "night dive" category for those who kept logbooks, the feeling was much different.

There was something about predawn on a reef that he liked. It was as if the sea life had the same circadian rhythms as humans. Mac took several strides across the sand and flashed his light across *Ghost Runner's* stern. The dive platform appeared to be intact, but was covered with sand. Stepping across it, he climbed over the transom and panned the light across the cockpit.

It was much as he remembered it, and he had a gruesome flashback to his struggle with Zena, the Russian gunrunner. They had fought, and she had died right here. Fortunately, Mac expected the sea to have cleaned house and removed the corpse. Still, he wasted several minutes checking before he entered the forward cabin. Again, he shone the light around the compartment and finally approached the closed door to the starboard berth.

Mac took a few seconds to load the speargun. One at a time, as he braced the butt end of the gun against his abs, he pulled back on the thick bands until they reached the appropriate notch on the steel shaft. With both bands engaged, he would be able to shoot anything at close range.

Slowly, he opened the door, hoping whatever resided within would be spooked and exit through the hole in the hull. Instead of the empty berth he expected, two large, yellow eyes stared back at him. The goliath grouper just sat there, its tail and pectoral fins moving in synchronicity with the current, allowing it to stay in position. Mac wasn't surprised that it occupied almost the entire cabin. These fish, protected in most countries including the US and Bahamas, often grew to hundreds of pounds. This one easily weighed as much as he did—maybe more.

It was illegal to kill it, but if he did nothing, the fish would plague the entire operation. With jaws that could crush the shell of a stone crab and were part of the reason for that specie's demise, one bite could take off a human's appendage. Chasing it away would only be a temporary measure. It would return and likely become more aggressive. Mac hadn't thought to bring his powerhead down with him but, realizing it was the only way to "clean house," he stepped out of the cabin and closed the door behind him.

Returning to the surface took only a few minutes, and soon he was back, standing in front of the cabin door with the power-head, loaded with a twelve-gauge shell in place of the spear tip. He pulled back the bands on the gun that he had manually released before surfacing and slowly opened the door. It was no surprise the fish was there.

Bringing the speargun up, he took aim at the fish's giant head and pulled the trigger. A dull thud signaled that the shotgun shell had done its job. Mac backed up to the end range of the cord connecting him to the shaft in case the fish wasn't dead. He had seen game, both on land and in the sea, come back to life and attack.

Seconds later, the fish rolled onto its side and then its back. Mac's next job was to remove the body before the brain matter scattering in the water column from the shotgun shell attracted any sharks. He knew the task was harder than it appeared, but it had to be done. The gore from the shot acted like chum, and already small fish had started to invade the space—the larger predators wouldn't be far behind.

Mac figured the best way to extricate the fish was to pull it headfirst through the doorway. Trying to remove it by the tail would likely cause it to snag on the jagged steel. Removing the spent powerhead was easy, as it had obliterated everything surrounding the entry point. After a glance into the berth and, seeing an increasing number of fish attacking the flesh of the dead grouper, he exchanged the powerhead for a standard tip, reset the bands, and set the gun aside.

Though killing the fish was illegal, Mac felt no remorse. He knew from experience that, though the goliath grouper had once been endangered, it was now thriving. The rules were antiquated. Most wrecks he had dove on in the past few years had at least one resident goliath. The declining state of the stone crab fishery was another indication of their rebounding numbers. With few predators, the hard-shelled crab had prospered—until the restrictions were placed on fishing the humongous grouper. As evidenced by what he was seeing inside the cabin, the meat would feed the reef fish that the grouper typically preyed upon. There was some kind of justice in that.

Mac walked back to the cabin and, making sure the speargun was still within reach, he reached inside and grabbed the fish by its gill plate. Despite its weight, buoyed by the saltwater it came easily. Mac had the carcass almost halfway out of the cabin when he realized something was wrong.

Mac had never questioned why the fish had been facing him. But now, with the body partially extracted, there was enough of a gap between door jamb and fish to see into the cabin. As the dawn's light penetrated the water and backlit the hole in the hull, Mac saw what he had missed.

A trio of bull sharks circled the opening. They had cornered the grouper in the hole, which accounted for its position. Mac cursed into his regulator. Without the carcass, the sharks alone were just a nuisance and probably not dangerous. With several hundred pounds of fish flesh available, not only would they become aggressive, they would likely attract even more predators. Killing the sharks was an option, but not one he liked. Adding more blood and guts to the water would only attract more sharks. If there was a choice between shooting the "endangered" grouper he had already killed and one of the bulls, he would choose the grouper every time.

Mac released the fish and let it drop in the water column. He stepped back to think and instinctively glanced at his gauges. He had plenty of air remaining. Diving in twenty feet of water took decompression sickness and all the related maladies of deepwater diving off the table. Air consumption was also much more economical at this depth. Without too much exertion on his part, the single tank on his back would last over an hour.

The only way to deal with the fish was to remove it from the site. Hauling it up to the surface wasn't a viable option. If the authorities paid them a visit, the dead fish would only create more trouble. The best option was to haul it to the far end of the reef.

Having been in the water almost nine months had allowed quite a bit of growth to latch onto the exposed areas of the wreck, and Mac wondered how the items in the holds had faired. Moving back to the transom, he pulled on the port-side hatch in the deck. It was reassuring to note it took a surprising amount of effort to open it. Reaching into the hold, Mac removed a large, coiled line. There was some growth on it, but not nearly as much as on the exposed surfaces.

Unraveling the stiff rope, he tied one end in a bowline knot, and slipped the bitter end through the loop he'd just formed. Returning to the cabin, he worked his way inside. Brushing aside the small fish, he placed the loop around the tail of the monstrous fish and returned to the deck. The length of the line would allow him the distance he needed when the sharks attacked the carcass. Walking the fish away would be slow and cumbersome, but he had another idea. Setting down the line, he went to the other cabin, where he found the underwater scooter and brought it back to the cockpit. Even though it had been submerged for so long, it was made for these conditions. Mac squeezed the trigger and felt the pull of the propeller as it spun inside its cage.

With the free end of the rope in hand, he powered up the scooter and rode away from the wreck. The fish caught in the doorway, temporarily halting his progress, but he was soon cruising over the sandy bottom. A look behind told him the sharks had taken the bait.

7

STEVEN BECKER

A MAC TRAVIS ADVENTURE

WOOD'S
HOPE

The Wreck Site

MAC DROPPED THE SCOOTER IN THE SAND AND TIED THE LINE, with the carcass attached, to a coral head on the opposite end of the reef. He didn't wait to see if the sharks followed—he could almost sense their presence in the water. There was a distinct feeling when apex predators were nearby. Long-forged instincts kicked in.

Slowing his breathing, Mac grabbed the scooter and made a wide circle back to the Surfari. Years of diving in shark-infested waters had taught Mac to respect sharks more than he feared them, but that was under normal circumstances. A two-hundred-pound fish carcass in the water changed their other-wise predictable behavior.

Mac was clear of the sharks when the battery died. The scooter dipped and dropped to the bottom. Mac checked his gauges. He was down to 250 PSI, plenty of air to get back to the Surfari—unless something went wrong. With the sharks only a hundred yards away, he left the scooter and swam for the boat.

As he rose in the water column, Mac was wary. If there was

one moment where he was most afraid of the predators, it was when his head was out of the water and his body still submerged. There was no real reason for it, but it felt like purgatory.

Reaching the drop-down transom, he hauled himself up the ladder.

"Shark City," Trufante said. "Could see them fins circling."

Mac sat on the platform and caught his breath. He released the buckles on the BC and shrugged out of the gear. Trufante returned and hauled the gear into the cockpit. Mac followed, placing a hand to his forehead to shade the rising sun from his eyes as he scanned the reef. The disturbed water where he had left the grouper showed the sharks had taken the bait.

"Probably damned near out of air. Might ought to refill both tanks." He had brought a portable compressor aboard the Surfari to fill tanks and inflate the float bags. Trufante laid the tank with the partially inflated BC between the cylinder and the deck to protect the surface, and dragged a hose to them. After attaching the first stage on the end of the hose to the tank valve, he started the compressor.

Mac hated the noise, but it was necessary. The "tin can" compressor was much louder than the cast-iron version he'd installed on *Ghost Runner* and could fill only one tank at a time, so it would run twice as long.

Free of his gear, Mac moved to the transom and opened a small hatch, where he removed the freshwater wash-down hose and sprayed himself off.

Pamela emerged from the forward cabin, running her fingers through her hair to smooth out the bedhead. "What's with the racket?"

Mac didn't bother with an answer. He grabbed a water from the cooler by the helm and sat next to Mel at the table mounted to the deck.

"You got Wi-Fi?" Pamela asked.

"Yup. Sloan might have been a bad guy, but he knew how to setup a boat." Mel closed the screen of her laptop and set her newly acquired reading glasses on top of it. "Sounds like the Bahamas are starting to freak out. I'm not sure how they're going to deal with us."

"That is, if they know we're here," Mac said, as he scanned the horizon.

"Their radar'll work better than your eyes."

Mac was well aware the authorities could easily locate them without actually having eyes-on—they had done it before—after less than an hour. Mel was good at reading situations, and it worried Mac that a run-in with the authorities might be different under these circumstances. Some countries quarantined cruisers with little or no cause. In fact, the yellow flag they should have been flying, along with the US flag, was actually called a quarantine flag. The proper etiquette was to show the yellow flag along with the ensign of the ship's nationality when entering Bahamian waters. Once the ship cleared customs and immigration, the yellow flag was replaced with the Bahamian ensign.

"I'm going to dig around in the locker and see what we have. No point flaunting it." It was really a toss-up, but playing it straight was probably the best way to go. With a twenty-four-hour window to clear customs and immigration and with the Chub Cay Marina close by, they could conceivably come up with a story if they had to. By not checking in or flying the quarantine flag, the penalties would be more severe. On the bright side, there was a lot of water in the Bahamas, and a case could be made that no one would bother them.

Mac found the flag and brought it to the deck, where he attached the two spring-loaded clips already in the grommets to the port-side stay. The flag fluttered at head height, which would reduce its visibility. As far as Mac knew, there was no height requirement.

With *Sea Runner* semi-legal, he put on his ball cap and sunglasses and scanned the water. The activity around the dead grouper had increased to a frenzy, and he wondered if the boat might have been better named *Shark Runner*.

Marathon

Commander pulled into his canal and cut the throttles. He'd decided to wait on making the call until he had more information. Rudy had a history of violence and had patience issues. If Commander wanted this to pay off, he needed to respect that, and get his facts straight first.

Having dodged authority all his life, Commander had a good grasp of how things worked. If he had taken the time to think about it, he might have been better served to have cleaned up his act and taken a real job. If he was to add all the time and effort it took to remain at liberty while still living his lifestyle, he probably made minimum wage.

With the boat secured, Commander grabbed two beers from the over-worked refrigerator and headed inside. Setting the beers next to the computer, he tapped the space bar impatiently.

While he waited for the computer to wake up, he glanced out the window which showed the tourists' view of the Keys. The image presented in advertisements was merely a snapshot of the surface. The Keys had been featured in many books and movies. The latest cult hit *Bloodline* showed the seedy underbelly of the island chain. For many it was entertainment, and they probably didn't believe it, but Commander lived it. Anyone who had a stake here was exposed to greed, corruption, and backstabbing. Neither elected officials nor their appointed administrators were exempt.

The do-gooders often had more enemies than the criminal element. Travis fell into that category. Different than the whistle-blowers, rats, and snitches, he was actually held in high regard —unless, or until, his morals ended up hurting you. Commander had never suffered directly by anything that Travis had done, but he knew many people who had. There were a few who still sought revenge and were willing to pay for it. Rudy was on the top of the list.

Commander knew it was a long shot, but if Travis was up to what he thought, it might be an opportunity to bank some coin, and with this shitstorm of a virus he needed to be creative with his paydays. The old coconut telegraph that was now Facebook had been lit up for the past few days with talk about closing boat ramps and marinas. Yesterday, that had actually started to happen. Now the government was about to jump off a cliff and close US 1 to visitors.

Before he made any calls, he needed to do some research and that meant more beer. Heading back to the refrigerator, he noticed a steady stream of small boats entering the canal. They were mostly the one- or two-man commercial boats that the fishermen trailered rather than docked. The fine print of the closure allowed commercial boats continued access to the water, but Commander knew getting permission meant a face-to-face with a law enforcement officer at the ramp, something that all but the bravest—or stupidest—would avoid.

Taking the rest of the six-pack with him, he sat down at the desk and opened his web browser. The stereotype that the underbelly of society were Luddites was patently false. Commander might not know how to work a spreadsheet or put together a PowerPoint presentation, but he knew how to find what he was looking for online. Like many, it had started with porn, but he quickly discovered the value of the web for his business.

Learning how to analyze the satellite images showing water temperature and current had come quickly to him—especially because they put him on the fish. The reef fish were seasonal, and the bait and pelagic species that followed them were temperature sensitive. Knowing where the fish were saved gas and time, which translated into profits.

He sat back, draining another beer while he tried to figure out how to find Travis. If Mac were aboard *Ghost Runner*, it would have been easier. Commander had spent some time aboard and knew the VHF radio was equipped with AIS. The Automatic Identification Systems, which was on by default, allowed vessels to be tracked by satellite. They were invaluable to insurance carriers and corporate boat owners, as well as a worthwhile safety device that could broadcast a Mayday signal with the ship's position with the flick of a button. Commander expected that, if it were up to Mac, he would have disabled it, but Mel would have stopped him. He wondered if the missing motorsailer was similarly equipped.

Several websites tracked the signals in real time, so he opened maritimetraffic.com. A global map cluttered with icons representing ships populated the screen. He zoomed in on the local area and started hovering the mouse over the icons around the Seven Mile Bridge and Boot Key Harbor. Sipping another beer, he continued placing the cursor over the different icons. There were several colors and styles, but without the paid version of the program, he was unable to filter them.

Expanding his search, he moved on to Key West. If Travis had traveled through the Gulf, the end of US 1 would be the logical spot to provision. There was nothing resembling the Surfari between the Capital of Weird and the Dry Tortugas. Commander started to get anxious, but not because he was failing. After eliminating several of the likely destinations, he started to feel good about his intuition. After checking the Key

Largo area, he panned the screen to the Bahamas. The vast country was made up of seven hundred islands and many times that number of boats, but Commander wasn't interested in the whole area. He focused on the waters between the Abacos and the Keys. Right in the center was Chub Cay, in the Berry Islands. He moved the cursor onto an icon about ten miles away. A small window opened next to the blue dot that labeled it as a pleasure craft.

Commander felt he was getting close. Anyone in the Keys who had set foot into the dozen or so of the bars the commercial fishermen haunted had probably heard some version of the story about Trufante's heroic effort to save the world by crashing Mac's boat into the reef. The story had grown to almost epic proportions since, but the fact that *Ghost Runner* had been driven aground was all Commander needed to confirm Travis's location.

Casting a sideways look at the last beer, he forsook it and opened Google Earth in another window. Zooming in on the area around Chub Cay, he placed a marker in the vicinity where the blue dot had been displayed on the other screen. The satellite imagery clearly showed the shallow reef underneath the position of the boat—he had found his man.

8

STEVEN BECKER

A MAC TRAVIS ADVENTURE

WOOD'S
HOPE

The Wreck Site

WHEN THE COMPRESSOR FINALLY CUT OFF, A SENSE OF CALM FELL over the boat. While it was running, it was impossible to hear anyone unless they were yelling in your ear. Mac would have liked to stay in the shade of the open cabin, but the sound seemed to reverberate off the bulkheads and glass, making it even louder. Instead, he stripped off the wetsuit, put on a long-sleeved fishing shirt, and sat on the transom.

Mel joined him, and together they watched the sharks for a few minutes. He was well aware that the clock was ticking, and he wanted to get back in the water. Because of the shallow depths, he didn't have to worry about surface intervals, but the prudent thing to do was wait until the feeding party was over on the other end of the reef. By now, the action would have attracted even more sharks to the area. Once the smaller black-tips came in, there would surely be fighting among the sharks themselves, and when one of them was injured, the frenzy it would create could reach the wreck site.

"You're not thinking about diving with this going on?" Mel asked.

With the decision no longer his, Mac shook his head. He probably would have waited anyway, and there was other work that could be done. "I'll get the gear set up and wait them out."

"Anything I can do to help?"

"Nah, Tru knows what to do."

"And it's too early for him to start drinking," Mel said.

They both glanced over to the cockpit where the Cajun and Pamela were sitting to make sure there was indeed no alcohol in sight, before sharing a laugh at his expense. Mac got up and moved to the starboard-side deck locker. The Surfari had no aft cabin, which meant that the storage spaces were cavernous. They easily held the four float bags, as well as the miscellaneous gear he had brought. Pulling out the large rubberized polyester bags, he handed them to Trufante, who carried them to the bow and tied a weight belt to each one.

Mac's next task was to rig the compressor hose to fit the inlet on the bags. He'd installed a quick disconnect on the end of the hose before they left and now released the first stage, which was used to fill the tanks, and installed a fitting similar to the low-pressure inflator on a BC for the bags. Uncoiling the hose, he attached a four-pound weight to the end of the hose, and set it on the deck.

Hoping the shark extravaganza was over, he scanned the water. "Looks clear," he said, hoping that Mel wouldn't notice the action down-current. From the size of the dorsals breaking the water, it looked like blackfins. He expected the bulls were gone. The grouper was probably broken up long ago, and what remained had floated with the current to where the small group of sharks remained.

"I see 'em, Mac. But I guess they'll only drift further away."

That was good enough to get suited up. "You good to dive with me?"

Her look was enough. Mel grew up diving and in her teen years had won several spearfishing competitions. She was every bit as capable as him and had an ace in the hole—she was a middle-aged woman. Though on the lower end of that sliding scale, it was well known that women around a certain age used much less air than men. It was a bright spot on the aging matrix.

Mac called to Trufante, "Pull the anchor line and get us over the wreck, then drop the bags and let the slack back out." He noticed Mel was already in her wetsuit and slipped into his own. Already wet, he struggled with the neoprene, even further delaying him. By the time he had pulled up the zipper and secured the Velcro tab at the back of his neck, Mel was geared up.

Just as he buckled the BC, he heard the first splash. Looking over the side, he could see *Ghost Runner* sitting below them. Three more splashes followed in close succession. Once the float bags were gone, Trufante called to Pamela, who dropped the weighted air hose into the water.

"Ready?" He sat on the edge of the transom platform and donned his mask. Mel wore fins, but Mac was more comfortable without. The extra mobility would allow her to move around while Mac did the grunt work. She placed the regulator in her mouth, and with her right hand over her mask and regulator, slipped into the water. With the powerhead attached to the speargun and loaded with a fresh twelve-gauge shell, Mac followed.

Before starting work, and with Mel finning overhead, Mac walked around the wreck. Cautiously, he checked the forward cabin and was relieved to find it empty. The sharks must have spooked everything. There nothing larger than a few yellowtail snapper and small grunts left on the wreck. The flat bags had landed in a pile, and Mac started to move them into place while Mel retrieved the hose.

While he was working with the second bag, a shadow crossed over his head. His first thought was a shark, but when he looked up, he saw it was the shadow of *Sea Runner* sliding past as Trufante released the slack in the anchor line. It would have been more convenient to hold the boat overhead, but the memory of the RBDF cutter's wake sinking *Ghost Runner* was fresh in his mind. He could have anchored up-current and had the boat drop back on the wreck, but that didn't appeal to him. He wanted the anchor within reach of the wreck in case they needed it for a safety line.

With the bags set in place, he met Mel by the cabin, where the damage had occurred. His plan depended on that particular bag deploying properly, so he figured he ought to start there. It wasn't as simple as inflating a tire; the four bags needed to be filled in sequence. If one bag was totally filled first, it might unbalance the wreck. With all four filled in steps, evenly, Mac hoped the wreck would just float to the surface. It didn't have to bob like a cork. He only needed the gunwales to break free of the water to allow the pumps to work.

After completing the third round, Mac caught Mel's attention and tapped his air gauge. She checked hers and laid two fingers on her forearm, indicating she had 2,000 PSI remaining. A glance at his gauge told Mac that he had slightly less. Both had plenty to finish inflating the bags, but there was little point in one watching the other. Mac signaled to Mel that she should finish and made a kicking motion with his fingers, pointing to the reef. His intention was to retrieve the scooter and line from the other side.

She flashed him an OK sign. Mac turned away and started walking in the sand surrounding the reef, scanning the water ahead for any sharks as he went. With one-hundred-foot visibility, he could see the area where he had left the grouper before. From fifty feet away, he saw the loop of the bowline knot floating in the water. The fish was gone and with it the sharks.

Mac grabbed the end of the line, and coiling it as he went, he started walking back to the coral head it was secured to. With the line looped over his shoulder, and an eye out for the scooter, he started back to *Sea Runner*.

He knew firsthand how deceiving underwater features could be when viewed from different perspectives. Several years ago, before he moved to the island, he had secreted a cache of gold coins in a small cavern below three coral heads to the west of the Sombrero Key Light. The features were distinct, but he had never found the stash. After countless tries, he determined that an anchor had latched onto one of the heads and dragged it across the bottom. The destruction had opened the cavern to the tides, and he had never found the coins.

Mac had dropped the scooter over the reef, and as he walked by the edge, he realized there was no way he would see it. With the extra weight he carried, he was too heavy to swim, and without fins that would have been a laborious task anyway. Mac decided to return with fins, but continued to search just in case it should reveal itself.

With the coral for cover, the nearby fish had little fear and had all but forgotten the sharks. The shallow-water reefs in the Bahamas were famous for their tropicals, and this reef was no different. Schools of the tiny fish darted past him. Larger angelfish swam through the coral, undisturbed by the large man walking by. Mac noticed several overhangs hiding lionfish, and though he had the speargun, decided that if he had time, he would return with his sling to extinguish the invasive pests.

Without realizing it, Mac had moved into predator mode. Hunting brought a focus that he wouldn't normally have. Mac wasn't sure what it was, but there was some base-level instinct that kicked in whenever he hunted. In this state, he saw things differently—with more detail. Small holes and caverns appeared that he might normally have overlooked. Within them, he saw several sets of antenna protruding. He dismissed the crawfish, but something else caught his attention.

Straight lines rarely occur in nature, and Mac wasn't sure if what he saw wasn't just an illusion. Something looked odd, though, and he was intrigued enough to lay the coiled line down on the sand and examine the structure. At first, it appeared simply to be an overhang. These kinds of features were common on patch reefs. Surrounded by sandy bottom, the reefs were subject to the elements. Years of storms and currents usually eroded the sand from the coral on one side of the reef, creating ledges like the one where he had seen the lionfish. On the opposite side, the features were often filled in.

Mac stepped closer and carefully shooed the lionfish out of the way. The last thing he needed was to be stung by one of their venomous spines. The exotic fish had no natural predators in these waters and took their time as they moved away. Mac checked again to make sure there were no others hidden in the recess and started to examine the structure.

Wood had started Mac in the salvage business almost thirty years ago, and in that time he had seen many wrecks. The older ones, disguised by a cloak of coral, were almost indistinguishable from the reefs themselves, but there were usually subtle differences. Mac stepped back to get a better view. From ten feet away, he was able to see the big picture and, using his imagination, he stripped the structure of the coral growth. Beneath it, he saw the shape of an airplane.

Mac knew better than to get excited. With the extensive growth of the coral on it, it could easily have been just a reef, but he suspected otherwise. Moving toward it, he unclipped the dive light from his BC and turned it on. Figuring the underside of the structure likely had less growth, he got on his hands and knees and crawled to the overhang. Dropping to the sand, he slithered on his belly until his head was just under the ledge. He would have preferred to be on his back, but the tank wouldn't allow it.

Several chunks of coral lay in the sand nearby, and taking one, he smacked it against the coral growth. The sound was certainly different than solid coral, but he was still unsure. The only way to tell for certain would be to remove some of the coral. The powerhead, lying next to him in the sand, would certainly do the trick, but he was loathe to destroy the reef. Instead, he unscrewed the explosive head from the shaft and moved back several feet. Aiming at a small section, Mac fired the shaft at the coral. Pieces fell away, and it took a long minute for the sediment to be swept away by the current. When the water was finally clear, he saw the shaft had penetrated the reef—something that was impossible if it had been solid.

9

The Wreck Site

MAC STARTED TO JOG BACK TO THE WRECK, BUT THE TANK VALVE
kept slamming into the back of his head. He slowed to a walk,
hoping to reach Mel and return to the coral area before they
exhausted their air supply. It was odd, but he felt something had
drawn him to the site. He was skeptical of Pamela's *woowoo*, but
once again, she had been right. Deep down, he had known all
along that salvaging *Ghost Runner* was a fool's errand. Had the
wreck been located close to Marathon, it might have been a
different discussion, with probably the same result.

Mel was still filling the bags when he returned. Checking
their levels, he saw they were a little over half-full—not yet
buoyant enough to raise the hull. He caught her attention and
slashed his throat with his hand. Rather than hide her expression, the mask amplified it. Mac performed the signal again. She
might not understand why, but she removed the fitting from
the bag.

He checked his gauge, and saw 500 PSI remaining. Recreational divers were schooled to return to the boat with this much

air, but Mac knew it was sufficient to take the time and show Mel his discovery. He didn't bother checking hers—he was certain she had more than he did. One of the things he liked about being underwater was the ability to discuss anything was limited to a few hand signals. Since she couldn't question him, Mac started walking along the reef, leaving Mel no choice but to follow him. When he reached the spot where the shaft extended from coral, he stopped and waited for her to descend. She started to examine the hole, but Mac stopped her and stuck his hand inside it. He was up to his elbow when his fingers touched something odd. He grasped the object and pulled. At first, it didn't yield, and when it did it was with enough force to throw him backwards. When he recovered, he found he was holding a clump of electrical wire.

Mel's reaction was immediate, and she moved to the hole. Craning her head for a better angle, she shone her light inside. After a long minute she pulled back. Mac could see from her expression that she understood what he was excited about. He made a V-shaped sign with his two hands and pointed to the surface, indicating they should return to the boat. She nodded and started back, but not before circling the area of the reef. Mac wished he had her perspective, but without fins he would have to wait until they surfaced to see if she had been able to discern anything.

The second Mel's head broke the surface, she spat out her regulator. "I think it's a plane."

Mac was a second behind her, and heard only the word *plane*, but it was enough.

"What y'all been smokin' down there?" Trufante asked, as he helped Mel slide out of her BC. He took the gear into the cockpit while she climbed aboard.

The scent of weed drifted toward Mac. "Didn't I tell you there was more to this than the boat, Mac Travis?" Pamela said.

Mac ignored her, his brain already having shifted gears. He was on to what to do next, not why he was here and if this was some kind of cosmic kismet. "Let's have a bite and make a plan." He needed the time to fill the tanks and think.

Trufante handled the tanks while Mel and Pamela made breakfast. When he smelled the fresh coffee and bacon, his stomach started to grumble, informing him how long it had been since he had eaten a meal. He grabbed his insulated tumbler from the cupholder and filled it from the freshwater faucet. Taking it to the chart table inside the cabin, he opened up a large-scale chart of the area.

It was an easy decision to place the salvage of *Ghost Runner* on hold. With the unidentified wreck beneath them, there was no need to attract attention. Besides, he knew in his heart that it was better left in its final resting place. The Surfari wasn't the only boat that needed an exorcism. Zena, the gun-running Russian mobster, had died aboard *Ghost Runner* as the boat had gone down.

Mac's brain was finally engaged. He finished the water, set down the tumbler, and went forward to the anchor locker. Inside was a large red inflatable ball, which he moved to the side. Many fishermen used a quick-release anchor ball, but Mac wanted the site to remain his secret. With the hatch still open, he pulled the remaining rode out and fed it into the water. On the bitter end, a carabiner was attached to a large metal ring fastened to the hull as a security measure to prevent the line from leaving the boat. While he waited for the boat to drift back, he released the clip and secured it to a six-pound dive weight. In the event the authorities showed any interest in their activities, he would simply toss the weighted line in the water. If it was convenient, he could dive and retrieve the anchor when they returned.

They had been in Bahamian waters for only about twelve of the twenty-four-hour grace period, and Mac wondered if being anchored here actually violated any laws. The law was mainly for cruisers who put in at the smaller islands, where officials were not readily available. Knowing that the law was open for interpretation, in both directions, he decided it would be better not to attract attention to themselves. He moved to amidships, where he took down the yellow quarantine flag. Tucking it under his arm, he returned to the cockpit.

Breakfast was ready at the same time the compressor shut off, and they sat down to eat. Mac dug in and cleaned his plate before saying a word. Pushing it aside, he brought the mug of coffee closer and took a sip.

"We're going to abandon *Ghost Runner* and see if we can identify the plane."

"Thinkin' there's something to it?" Trufante asked.

The Cajun had voiced what was on all their minds. They knew there was a chance of finding treasure. Mac was less concerned about riches, which—if there were any and were recoverable—would likely be contraband. Countless drug runners had ditched their planes in an effort to evade the authorities. Mac knew from experience that cashing in someone else's ill-gotten gains was often harder than finding it. He and Mel already had a sizable reserve of gold recovered from a pirate ship in the Dry Tortugas. It was split between several caches— all above ground since the disaster with his cache on the reef. Mac had learned his lesson the hard way about stashing something in the ocean.

It was the history of a thing that drew Mac, and he wished Ned were here to share it. Thinking about the longtime friend of Wood's, Mac decided to take a ride to Key West to check in on him after they returned.

"First thing is to do a survey. Mel and I will go down and take some measurements. It'd be nice if we had a camera. Did you bring that waterproof case for your phone?" he asked Mel.

"I did. Thought it might be cool to get some shots of *Ghost Runner* seeing the light of day."

"Great. We should document everything."

Though he hated it, Mac knew the value of dotting i's and crossing t's. "Let's get back in the water, then."

Marathon

Commander hesitated long enough to finish his beer before he made the call. He knew his own boat could make the trip if he added some portable fuel tanks. It was tempting, but there was a better way—more power. With the seas down, the right boat could make the trip in several hours. It would cost some money in fuel, though, but he hoped that revenge would pay the bill.

The smuggler was waiting at the dock when Commander pulled up twenty minutes later. "You think they're trying to salvage the boat?" Rudy asked.

"Dude, you gonna trust me or what?" Commander was going into this on his terms. "AIS says they're there. I already checked the island. That fancy-ass sailboat's gone."

"So why don't we go trash the place instead?" Rudy asked.

"I thought you wanted a piece of him? Besides, money don't mean much to the dude." Commander knew it was boats that made Travis tick, and the trawler was something special to him. Being able to sabotage his efforts to recover it and inflict some bodily harm at the same time had to be worth something to Rudy. For himself, knowing that Pamela was with Mac only sweetened the pot.

"Shit. You know Travis. It's all about the boats. Besides, the Cajun's woman is with them." Commander didn't even like to call her by name. Several years had passed since she had scorned him, but the grudge remained. "Don't have to worry about that sheriff, either. He got no authority over there."

"Long as you kick in for some fuel, bro."

If this paid out, Rudy would owe him, and that was worth more than money. "Shit, got that covered."

Commander wasn't worried about the ask. Rudy was one of those guys who had his hands in a dozen pots, and so far he had been smart enough to keep all his fingers.

While Rudy fired up the quad outboards hanging from the transom, Commander walked over to the small store by the fuel dock and bought several twelve packs of beer. When he returned, Rudy smiled as he placed them in the cooler. Commander was aboard a minute later, and with the engines purring quietly, they made their way out of Boot Key Harbor.

Once clear of the last marker, Rudy turned to the south and pushed down on the dual throttles. Each lever controlled a pair of the three-hundred-horsepower engines. The boat lurched forward, and before Commander could even adjust his beer, the twelve-hundred horses had the boat up on plane. Rudy trimmed the hull before increasing power again. By the time Commander took his first sip of beer, they were past the small tower over East Washerwoman Shoal. Another five minutes and they skimmed over the reef.

"What are we gonna do about checking in? I got a passport, but I doubt your sorry ass has one."

Commander leaned next to Rudy. "Bro, I was over there after Dorian came through. They was givin' ID cards to anyone that asked. I'm what they call a dual citizen."

Rudy shook his head. "Long as we get that son of a bitch, you could be a freakin' terrorist, for all I care."

"Dude. This shit is perfect. They're sitting ten miles out of Chub. Ain't no one go there. Too shallow for shit besides snorkeling, and the tourist charters ain't runnin' no ten miles. We'll have them to ourselves."

Rudy grinned.

There was a whole lot more risk in this operation for Rudy than for him. His custom boat alone probably ran north of four-hundred grand, and Rudy had been smart enough to funnel his "winnings" into a small fleet of lobster boats. They were the perfect vehicle to launder money from his smuggling operations. Commander had "negotiated" some deals with him over the years and found him tough but fair. But Rudy's reputation said he was not a guy you screwed with.

The rumor was that when the price of lobster tanked, Rudy had needed to increase his take, but not from greed. Without the revenue from the catch, his business plan was upside down. Mac had turned in two of Rudy's boats for running illegal traps. Commander figured that Rudy had run them out by Travis's island, far enough away from the mainland that the FWC wouldn't check if they were tagged or not. Commander didn't care about the details. He was fine being a spectator to Travis's demise.

10

STEVEN BECKER

A MAC TRAVIS ADVENTURE

WOOD'S
HOPE

The Wreck Site

MAC KICKED EASILY INTO THE GENTLE CURRENT. AFTER TRUDGING around over-weighted, the fins gave him freedom to float over the reef. The top of the coral was less than twenty feet below the surface, and to get the perspective he needed, he stayed high in the water column. That close to the surface, it was harder to maintain neutral buoyancy, but it allowed him to see the bigger picture. It was strange, once he knew there was some underlying structure to the coral growth, how easy it was to visualize it. If he had simply dove the reef, he never would have seen the subtle lines.

Mel had been reluctant to experiment with her phone underwater, so Mac sacrificed his. A smartphone holdout at first and for longer than most, he had been a technophobe. If you were to stereotype a group who wanted to disconnect from society, it would be fishermen. They were the last to adopt smartphones, but when they did, it came as a tidal wave. Computer-driven chartplotters and color depth-finders were the reasons for their newly acquired tech savvy. Back in the day, Mac remembered the simplicity of Loran-C and paper bottom-readers. In the eighties and nineties, coordinates were given in a pair of numbers that represented the beam of a radio signal. Numbers starting with ones and fours were predominant in the Keys, as the signals were at nearly right angles to each other and more exact than the "six" line. The change from degrees and minutes to a random system of radio beacons had resulted in a time in ocean navigation when latitude and longitude were lost in some circles.

The ease and accuracy of GPS eliminated the Loran system overnight and forced a generation of navigators to relearn the meridian grid. Color was the next innovation, and when it was applied to depth finders, the fishing community jumped on board. Able to define hard bottom from soft and show actual fish in the water column, every serious fishing boat had at least one. The addition of the chartplotter, where the boat's position and route were overlaid on a digital nautical chart, as well as large high-definition displays and touch screens, sealed the deal. Once weather forecasts, ocean conditions, and navigation apps became available for smartphones, the flip-phone holdouts disappeared.

GPS didn't work underwater, though, which was where his phone's camera came in. Mac held the waterproof case steady as he gently covered the reef. When they surfaced, he would transfer the digital image and overlay his idea of the plane's position on paper.

Mel had the less prestigious task of adding proportions. Without a tape measure, she gauged the distance between the reef's predominant features by using a hundred foot line marked every ten feet, and recorded them on a waterproof tablet.

Mac had to guess the location of several of the features. The wings were evident, as was the nose, but the tail fin, which would have been easily identifiable, had been lost on landing or taken by the sea. Mac tried to gauge the age of the plane by the growth of coral. Hard coral grew slowly, and was probably a better indicator of age than the larger staghorn and elkhorn. By the degree of camouflage the coral provided, Mac guessed it was two feet thick in sections. Growing no more than an inch a year, and usually half that, his excitement grew as he realized the plane could be fifty years old.

That put the time of the crash in the sixties or seventies—directly in the middle of the Cold War. His stomach clenched as he remembered the discarded bomb he once had found from that era. Its origin covered up for decades, it had ultimately cost Wood his life. The history here could very well be dangerous. Still, Mac was fascinated.

He checked his air, realizing he had been down longer than he thought. Though he and Mel were technically "dive buddies," the reef was small enough that they had gone their separate ways to perform their tasks. Mac glanced around and saw her bubbles streaming toward the surface. He finned over to check on her and saw she had the same amount of air remaining. This was slightly gratifying—until Mac realized she had been working a lot harder.

He signaled to her that they would surface in ten minutes.

She was near the south end of the reef, where he suspected the tail section lay. Because of the coral growth, it was impossible to tell what had happened to the plane, or even how badly it was damaged. It could be intact, minus the tail fin, or in pieces.

When he held the phone up to resume his video, Mac saw the screen was dark. Awkwardly, he pressed the "home" button through the case, but nothing happened. There was something about mixing electronics and water that, even when protected, made them quirky at best and frustrating at worst. Looping the lanyard around his wrist, he decided to examine the wreck from the reef level.

Dropping to a depth of twenty feet, he was able to adjust the air in his BC to maintain a two-foot gap above the reef. Measuring his inhales and exhales both to conserve air and keep his buoyancy neutral, Mac studied the coral formations, even though he knew they were random and would yield no clues as to what lay beneath—until he saw a slight dome.

Several coral species, most notably brain coral, grew naturally in a dome shape. But this appeared different. On closer examination, Mac saw that it wasn't a single coral head, which he would have expected, but many smaller ones. There had to be some structure underneath to support them. With the grouper and sharks long gone, Mac had foregone the speargun on this dive and had only a knife. Removing it from the sheath clipped to his BC, he tapped a section of coral with the butt. Small pieces floated away. He waited for the silt to clear and continued.

After a few minutes, Mac paused to check his watch and saw he had only three minutes until the time when he and Mel had agreed to surface. As much as he wanted to see what lay underneath the coral, he stopped.

This reef appeared healthy, but many throughout the world, especially sections of the hundred-mile-long barrier reef in the Keys, weren't. A variety of maladies plagued the more sensitive species of coral, especially the staghorn and elkhorn that were thriving here. Some issues were naturally caused by rising ocean temperatures, while others were the direct result of man's activities. There was enough data to conclude that the damage caused to the reefs adjacent to sewage outflow pipes and areas where fertilizer and other chemicals were dumped into the water illustrated the effect of man.

In order to salvage the plane, Mac would essentially be

destroying the reef. He expected that Mel had the same thoughts. It was something they would need to figure out if they decided to proceed. Returning to the small section, Mac decided that the information his small excavation might reveal was worth the few square feet of coral it would harm. He'd already removed the large pieces with the butt of his knife. Now, he reversed it in his hand and used the tip to pry away the smaller pieces.

They came away easily, giving Mac the impression that this area was indeed different. After a few minutes, the tip of the knife skidded off something smooth.

Mac jumped when he felt Mel tap him on the shoulder. He had been so engrossed in his work that he had failed to see her approach. Once she had his attention, she tapped her watch. Mac checked his and realized he was five minutes past time, but he felt he was close to something. He checked his air and saw he had 200 PSI remaining. The needle was well into the red area of the gauge, but with no need for a decompression stop and the surface only twenty feet over his head, he flashed Mel five fingers. She shrugged, checked her own air, and gave him the okay sign.

As Mac continued to remove pieces of coral, the underlying shape began to appear. When a small section was mostly clear, he brushed the remaining pieces away with his hand. A round shape appeared. Mel was right next to him as he shone his dive light at the area. Instead of the decomposing metal he expected, it was transparent.

The Berry Islands

"So, what you gonna do when we get there?" Commander asked. They had already crossed the Gulf Stream and, according to the ETA on the chartplotter, they would be on site in less than an hour. He'd had second thoughts, especially after the beer had run out. "How 'bout we scout it and go into Chub for the night?"

"Screw that. If Travis is there like you say, I have a plan."

Commander knew Rudy would be reluctant to go into port. Aside from some firearms that he suspected were aboard and were required to be declared, along with a verified count of their ammunition on exit, there was probably nothing to worry about. That was, unless there was blood in the water. Then, it was better to get in and out like some Navy Seal shit.

Beer might be an issue, though. Rudy had dipped into Commander's twelve-pack to the tune of about four beers. He appeared to be sober enough now, but he was one of those drunks who got mean when the buzz wore off. That might help his immediate plan for Travis and company, but for the bigger picture, it was dangerous.

"Might be better to check them out after it gets dark?" Their ETA was five o'clock, and sunset was a little after six.

"Now you're thinking. We'll go dark and creep up on 'em."

With its masthead light high above the water, the Surfari would be visible from over a mile away. "Bitch got radar?"

"Shit. I got zoodar. Ain't nobody gonna see us coming. Shit is carbon fiber. Only radar signature on this bad boy's the engines, and they got heat sinks on them."

Smuggler's boats were of two varieties: the ones that were camouflaged to the degree that they could only be used on a run, or the more commonplace custom boat. Commander knew Rudy had his boat custom built, but was unaware of the degree, out of either necessity or paranoia of its owner, to use light-weight material over typical construction. Worried about how this was going to go down, Commander watched the purple dot that marked Travis's location inch closer at an alarming rate.

Half an hour later, he saw a single white light hovering over the water. If this were a Navy boat, the captain would have called for general quarters. Commander gritted his teeth and started to breathe deeply. He wasn't afraid of bloodshed or a fight—it was the prospect of Fox Hill, the notorious Bahamian jail, that rattled his nerves.

Rudy finally slowed when they were a mile out. He cut the navigation lights and turned the chartplotter display to night mode. With the red glow of the screen the only light aboard, they moved closer. He zoomed in the chartplotter and studied the contour lines, then shut down the unit. The boat had been designed for this. Instead of the glossy gelcoat finish and gleaming stainless steel most boats had, Rudy had opted for a midnight-blue graphite paint job and a black matte powder coat on the carbon fiber superstructure whose only function was to support the radar dome. Instead of reflecting light, the boat seemed to absorb it.

A half-mile away, Rudy cut two of the engines and dropped to an idle. With the lapping water against the hull louder than the hum of the engines, Commander braced himself for what was coming.

11

The Wreck Site

MAC LOOKED UP WHEN HE HEARD THE VIBRATION OF AN ENGINE. The source seemed to be far away, but it was impossible to tell direction underwater. Tuned into the sound, he guessed it came from multiple outboards, and from the increased volume, that it was approaching. Mel turned toward him and shrugged. She had heard it too.

They had gone as far as their air supply would allow and were heading back to *Sea Runner*. The excitement Mac had felt on finding what he guessed was a turret on the plane waned with the sound of the approaching boat. Suddenly, the sound died. Mac expected that wasn't good news. A passing boat, if anyone were foolish enough to run this close to the reef, would have kept going. The vibration was still there, only quieter, which meant that the boat had dropped to an idle. Whoever it was, the chance for a good outcome was nonexistent.

Mel would handle things if it was the authorities; if it wasn't, they'd have to play it by ear. In either case, they needed more information. With only hand signals to communicate, Mac took the lead. The keel of the Surfari was visible ahead, but the last place he wanted to be was on the surface. Mac pulled on the retractable cable that held his compass and took a heading before dropping back to the reef.

He continued on his course until the keel of the Surfari was directly above them. Mac stopped and waited for a minute to try and ascertain the position of the approaching boat, but it was still too far away. Glancing at his air gauge, he saw the needle pegged against the pin in the red zone. At this point, every breath could be his last. Mel had seen him checking and signaled that she still had 200 PSI remaining. Neither dove with an octopus, so they would have to share a regulator if they were to buddy breath. It wouldn't really matter. Between the two of them, they would suck her tank dry in minutes, certainly not long enough to outlast their visitors.

What felt like an hour was probably less than five minutes until the hull of the newly arrived boat appeared. Mac noted the overall length and shape of the hull, as well as the four lower units. ICE had some go-fast boats like this, but he didn't recall that the Bahamians did. Whoever it was, their visitor was not a tourist—another sign of trouble.

The boat stopped and was drifting about twenty feet from the Surfari. Mac signaled to Mel that he was going to have a look and started to ascend. He thought about motioning for her to stay while he checked things out, but knew she was going to do what she was going to do. He glanced back and saw her following. His intention was to come up on the far side of the motor-sailer in order to use the bulk of the hull to conceal them from the other boat. Figuring the new boat's attention would be focused on the cockpit, he finned toward the bow.

Mac surfaced and pulled himself behind the hull. He let the

regulator fall from his mouth and took several breaths while he waited for Mel to surface. He might as well enjoy the air because, if they had to descend again, he could tell from the way the tank bobbed behind him that it was nearly empty. Mel was beside him now, and just as he was about to stick his head around the bow, there was a loud blast. When a second shot fired, he knew it was his Remington shotgun. The twelve gauge was undoubtably in Pamela's hands.

Mac had no idea what the intent of the go-fast boat was, but Pamela's actions signified that it wasn't friendly. Another round chambered and fired. The intruder's engines coughed loudly, and the boat moved away. That gave Mac the chance he needed to peer around the bow. He knew immediately that it was Rudy, and it was no surprise to see Commander standing next to him.

"Who is it?" Mel whispered.

She was right behind him. "Rudy's boat, and it looks like Commander is with him," he said, without turning around. Mac continued to watch the boat as it moved out of range. Rudy was volatile, but cautious. He wasn't going to risk his custom boat to a lucky shot. Mac knew better—Pamela was a crack shot. If she had missed, Rudy was either out of range, or she had chosen to.

"What's the plan?" Mel asked.

They had two immediate options: either go back aboard *Sea Runner*, or stay in the water. Looking at Rudy's boat bobbing in the waves a hundred yards away, he decided on the latter. The only weapon aboard the Surfari was the shotgun. There was little doubt in his mind that Rudy had them outgunned. Mac was also confident the smuggler was after him personally, and if he wasn't aboard, it might keep Pamela and Trufante safer. That meant staying in the water but, without air, they would be like sitting ducks floating on the surface.

"There're fresh tanks on *Ghost Runner*," Mac said. He had

taken a pair of aluminum 8os to the Bahamas after Dorian. They were stashed in the forward berth.

"You're bobbing like a cork. I can go bring one back."

With only 200 PSI left herself, having to find the tanks, then drag one to the surface would leave her empty as well. Many wrecks were a tangle of metal and rigging, making it difficult to penetrate them. *Ghost Runner* was pretty clean, but stuff happened, and Mac wouldn't risk Mel being stuck inside the cabin and running out of air.

"We'll go together. Buddy breathe on your tank. There's probably a couple of sips left in mine if we get in trouble."

"What about them?"

"I'm thinking we have a standoff. Rudy's not going to risk his boat."

"What'd you do to him?"

"That story'll wait. Ready?"

Mel placed her regulator in her mouth and dropped under first. Mac took a deep breath, and with his hand on her tank valve, followed her down to the wreck. Without the opportunity to breathe up and prepare himself, Mac barely made it to the bottom before he tapped Mel on the shoulder. She took a breath and handed him her regulator. Mac could feel the resistance as he filled his lungs. It would increase with every breath until the tank was empty. They would have to work quickly.

Mac reached the cabin first and pulled himself inside. His fins were a hinderance now, but he was not going to lose his ability to bolt to the surface. He worked his way to the front of the berth and tugged on the lid. It resisted at first, but yielded with his second attempt. The tanks sat side-by-side next to an assortment of life vests and lines.

Pulling one free, Mac handed it to Mel. She passed him her regulator, and he took another breath before retrieving the other tank. With both cylinders on the deck, Mac motioned for Mel to turn around. She understood what he was doing and took a deep breath from her tank before dropping the regulator from her mouth. The easy way to swap tanks would have been for her to remove the BC but, without the weights in the pockets of the vest, she would struggle to stay at depth.

Mac grabbed the regulator to take a last inhale. Halfway through his breath, the restriction that had been building stopped the air flow. The tank was empty. Working quickly, he purged the last drop of air from the regulator and unscrewed the first stage from the tank. Opening the Velcro tab and clasp on the wide strap that secured the tank to the vest, he let the cylinder drop.

The first convulsion hit him as he was easing the fresh tank into the strap. For inexperienced freedivers, the body's instinctual response to the buildup of carbon dioxide would send them to the surface in a panic, but Mac knew if he controlled his mind, he was only at the halfway point in his breath hold. That didn't make things easier, and he fumbled with the regulator. The lack of oxygen caused a noticeable decline in his motor skills.

Mac knew he had only seconds until his body would override his will, causing him to gag and suck seawater into his lungs. Finally, with the knob tightened, he turned on the air supply. He'd noticed Mel had started convulsing later than he had and took the regulator for himself. A long, deep breath brought him back to life, and he handed the regulator to her. They took a minute to share the fresh air back and forth before Mac changed over his own tank.

Once Mac's heart rate lowered, he realized that he had lost track of Rudy's boat. Inhaling deeply, he held his breath to silence the sound of the incoming air and outgoing bubbles, and listened. An idling engine caught his attention. Mac looked up and saw the underside of the Surfari's hull, but other than the sound, there was no sign of the other boat.

Just as he was about to draw a fresh breath, he heard something. It was far off, but from the vibration sounded like a larger boat. Mac expected that they were in radar range of the Royal Bahamas Defense Force base in Nassau. An astute operator might have seen *Sea Runner* at anchor and watched the other boat approach. Considering the remoteness of the location, it could be a natural assumption that the two boats were involved in some kind of illicit activity. Mac glanced at his watch and estimated it had been a good thirty minutes from when he had first heard Rudy's boat approaching. An RBDF cutter on patrol could have easily reached them— especially if they were already watching the Surfari.

The noise from the large boat was now audible over his breathing. In the short term, it was probably a godsend. Though Rudy had been careful in moving the boat after Pamela shot at it, he clearly had the upper hand and could afford to wait out Mac's air supply until he surfaced, and then move in.

The RBDF would preempt Rudy from taking any action. Mac expected that if he were correct, Rudy would be watching his radar and was ready to run if a cutter appeared. That would take care of one problem, only to replace it with another. Surfacing quickly and getting underway was the best way to counter the authorities' position. *Sea Runner* would likely be boarded and searched, but an explanation that they had mechanical difficulties on their way to Chub Cay should suffice as an explanation. The worst he could expect from the RBDF was an escort to port. It pushed the rock down the road a bit, but once there, they would have to deal with their lack of documentation. At this point that was the least of their worries.

Mac signaled to Mel that they should surface. She acknowledged him and added a touch of air to her BC. Together, they floated up to the surface, kicking gently so they would emerge at the drop-down transom. As Mac removed his fins and climbed the dive ladder, he glanced over at Rudy's boat. He was still sitting where Mac had last seen him. Mac handed the fins to Trufante and climbed aboard, quickly moving out of the way to allow the Cajun to help Mel.

"Got trouble, Mac Travis," Pamela said.

STEVEN BECKER

A MAC TRAVIS ADVENTURE

WOOD'S
HOPE

The Wreck Site

MAC WENT DIRECTLY TO THE HELM TO CHECK THE RADAR SCREEN. Rudy's boat showed a light signature that appeared much smaller than the boat actually was. That wasn't what Mac was interested in, though; it was the cutter approaching from the south. He assumed it was the RBDF, and the radar screen confirmed his guess. The radar showed the boat crossing the one-mile loop on the screen.

Each time the screen refreshed the cutter appeared significantly closer. "Better ditch whatever you don't want them to find," Mac called out, looking at Pamela. She quickly dumped what remained of their weed supply overboard. Mac nodded, thinking there would be some happy fish here. There was no need to check; Mac knew she was as adverse to spending time in a Bahamian prison as he was.

Mac glanced over at Mel; he didn't need to check on her, either. In anticipation of being boarded, she had found the document case and was sorting the papers the authorities would want to see.

The cutter was a mile away and growing in size every few seconds. There was no need for the radar now. "We need to get the anchor up," Mac called to Trufante.

Trufante had other ideas. Freeing the anchor line from the clip, he tossed the weight into the water.

Mac smiled, and started to move away from the reef. Ditching the anchor had saved valuable time. As he turned, he was able to see Rudy's boat and the cutter on the horizon. Knowing the go-fast boat could outrun the cutter and be off the radar before a helicopter or a faster boat could be dispatched, Rudy waited to see what happened.

Mac took a chance and steered directly toward the go-fast boat. The motorsailer had no chance of evading the RBDF, so his plan was to bring them to Rudy. As the boats converged, Rudy must have sensed his intention.

Mac watched the rooster tails from the quad outboards as the boat sped away. He turned to the cutter, curious to see how the captain reacted to the fleeing vessel. As expected, its course remained the same. The cutter was heading directly for *Sea Runner*.

Mac used the shallow water to his advantage and was able to move about a quarter mile from the wreck of *Ghost Runner* and the reef holding the plane before the cutter finally hailed them to stop and prepare to be boarded. Because of the dangerous bottom, the deep-draft RBDF cutter was forced to stand off. Mac complied with their orders and watched as they deployed a RHIB, which quickly skipped across the water in their direction.

Mac and Trufante took their lines and tied the soft-sided boat to *Sea Runner*. He checked the faces of the four crewmen and officer aboard. There was something about the singsong Bahamian accent that made the officer sound cordial, though his perfect English made it seem that he was not.

"Good afternoon. Please allow us to inspect your vessel and documents."

"Of course," Mac said, extending a hand to help the first crewman over the gunwale. While one crewman remained aboard the RHIB, the others crowded the cockpit. The wide-open floor plan of the Surfari was uncomfortable with eight bodies aboard.

"Your papers, please. Boat documents and personal identification."

"We haven't cleared customs yet."

"A bit of a detour, then?" the officer asked, with a suspicious look on his face.

Although Rudy was probably twenty miles away by now, the crew of the cutter had surely watched the interplay of the go-fast boat and the Surfari on their radar screen. They had been too far away to hear the shotgun blasts and had no idea that the go-fast boat's intention was revenge, not smuggling.

"We had some engine trouble."

The officer nodded, but Mac sensed he didn't believe him. "Your port of call?"

"We were heading to Chub Cay," Mac said.

"Lovely island, but I'm going to have to insist you change your plans to Nassau."

"What is the reason for that?"

"Coral Harbor is the closest base."

"Are you forgetting that we have engine trouble?" Mel asked. "That's a long way for a crippled boat, and with this virus...."

Steering their destination away from Nassau was to their advantage. The officer moved away and called someone on the radio. A minute later, he turned back to them.

"You have permission to proceed to Chub Cay."

The compromise was as good as Mac could expect. He knew the economics of the islands. In order to collect the entry fees and whatever fines the authorities could dream up, they would have to be sent to a port. Mac tried to evaluate the officer without appearing to do so. Back in the day, many of the old timers were open to bribes, but this man was young, and by the way he carried himself, Mac decided against the risk.

"Our speed is limited to four knots. Maybe there is a yard in Chub that you could recommend?"

That got a smile. Mac had given him the opportunity to profit from the encounter without taking an outright bribe. The "recommended" yard would almost certainly provide a kickback to the officer, and with Chub having no base, he could allow Mac to dock there without repercussions.

"That can be arranged. Now, your papers."

Mel motioned him to the table where she had laid out all the documents. Mac would have liked to stand nearby, but he was forced to give the remaining crew a "tour" of the vessel. While he opened the large storage lockers by the stern, he silently thanked Mel for making him change the title and registration of the Surfari into his name. The inspection was cursory. Mac expected the crew were primarily concerned with contraband and weapons. A more thorough search would occur when they reached port.

"We've only got a powerhead and a twelve gauge aboard," Mac said, hoping to subvert the search. He had brought the shotgun with just this in mind. Handguns and many types of rifles were strictly regulated on land here, but were allowed on boats.

"I'll need to see the weapon as well as the ammunition aboard."

Mac retrieved the shotgun from the forward cabin, surprised that the crewman didn't check to make sure it was under lock and key, which was another requirement. The crewman accepted the Remington 870 and checked the chamber, allowing the round that was ready to fire to fall onto the deck. He continued to clear the chamber, noting that only four rounds ejected.

"You seem to be light by two rounds."

Mac shrugged. "I'll get the rest of the ammo." He returned with the partially filled box. The officer took the box, noting that a half-dozen shells were missing. He handed the gun and the box of shells to another crewman to document them. Mac knew this was standard procedure. He would now be accountable if any ammunition went missing on a subsequent inspection, not that it mattered, as the shotgun and shells were handed down to the man in the RHIB. In all likelihood, he would never see the weapon again.

"The boat papers are in order. I will leave the personal identification to customs and immigration." The officer rose from the table and radioed the cutter with his progress. While he did, Mac noticed one of the crewmen taking pictures of the boat and crew. Mac would have stopped him, but there was nothing he could do. Already worried that the Cajun might be identified, he listened to the conversation between the officer and the captain.

"Proceed directly to Chub Cay. Do you need the coordinates or any instruction?"

"I know where it is," Mac said. He did a quick calculation in his head. Feigning engine trouble, he would travel at four knots. It would take them almost three hours to reach the marina. He hoped that would give them time to make a plan.

"You can expect us in three hours."

The *thump thump thump* sound of an approaching helicopter answered Mac's next question. He had been surprised they were going to allow him to proceed without an escort, but that clearly wasn't going to be the case.

"Very well, we will see you then." The officer gave Mac the name of a boatyard and signaled his men to the RHIB. Mac watched as they headed toward the cutter. Once they were clear, Mac immediately moved to the helm and put the engines in gear. There was no reason to give the helicopter or cutter any reason to suspect he was not going to comply.

Mac had hoped the three-hour run would give him time to figure out his next step. Instead, once underway, his mind started to drift back to the wreck. The original plan to salvage *Ghost Runner* had been scrapped. Were it not for the plane, he had no reason to remain here—or return.

"Is the plane worth any of this?" Mel asked, reading his thoughts.

"That section was a turret. That would make it a military plane, probably World War II era. I'd say I'm curious." Mac didn't know aircraft like he knew boats, but he had a feeling he couldn't walk away from this. Stories of lost ships—sunk by storms, hazards, or foes, taking their treasure to the bottom of the sea—were commonplace. Similar stories involving aircraft were much fewer, and Mac knew several. He had no way to know if this particular craft was one, but the vintage was right.

With nothing to be done except steer the course programmed into the chartplotter, Mac left Trufante at the helm.

"Let's have a look at the video." Mac retrieved his phone from the waterproof case still attached to his BC and took it into the cabin. Mel grabbed the slate that she had sketched the reef and wreck on and followed him. Once settled, Mac waited while Mel uploaded the video onto her laptop in order to use the larger screen.

Pamela, sensing their excitement, slid in next to Mac, but remained quiet. Together they watched the video. As it played, Mel transferred the primitive sketch on her dive slate to a piece of paper. Every few seconds she pressed the space bar to pause the video while she updated her drawing. The shape of the plane started to emerge on the page. They reached the last minute of the video, where Mac had filmed the turret. Mel added the shape to her drawing, placing it just forward of the tail section.

He had been so involved in uncovering his find that he hadn't thought to use the location of the turret to identify the plane. Many planes had tail gunners. Most were located at the very rear of the craft. Very few, in fact only one that he knew, was located in front of the tail section.

"We need to get to Key West and see Ned."

Chub Cay

WHEN THE SMALL HUMP OF CHUB CAY APPEARED ON THE HORIZON, Mac was surprised how quickly they had arrived. A glance at the chartplotter told him they were only three miles away. These low islands gave little notice of their presence. Many Caribbean islands were volcanic in nature and had peaks visible from many miles. The Bahamas archipelago was actually the top of a large underwater plateau. The tallest natural feature, Mount Alvernia, barely cracked the top ten of the tallest buildings in the islands.

Mac hit the standby button on the autopilot and took control of the boat. Traveling between the wreck site and Chub Cay was not as simple as steering a straight line. With shallow reefs throughout, the Berry Islands were even more dangerous than the backcountry of the Keys. Many were visible at low tide, but were most dangerous when the water was higher and their deadly coral lay just beneath the surface. In order to avoid the hazards, their course had taken them east into deep water, and actually away from their goal, which lay to the south. Now, with the island in sight, Mac checked the chartplotter. He would have to navigate around almost the entire island in order to enter the riverlike inlet to the marina.

Mac felt Mel come beside him. "We need to get this over with quickly. I'm thinking we need Ned to help identify the plane."

"It would be a good idea to check on him, anyway. He's in the high-risk category that they're so worried about," Mel said.

"Has it gotten worse?" Mac asked. During the trip over, Mel had been buried in her computer. Mac had hoped she was working on identifying the plane, but apparently she was reading about the virus.

"They're starting to nickel-and-dime us. Restaurants and clubs are closed, and I saw something that they were going to repave Duval Street this week."

"Some good'll come out of it, then."

"I know this is dangerous, but we're talking about civil liberties here," Mel said.

"I hear you." Mac had more immediate things to worry about than getting sick. He picked up the VHF mic and hailed the Chub Cay Marina on channel sixteen. There were two official points of entry on the island, the airport and marina. Mac spoke to the dockmaster, asking if there was room at the fuel dock. Though it would be more expensive on the small island, passing up a chance to refuel was a bad idea. He also hoped not taking a slip would show the authorities that he was serious about heading back.

Mac entered the wide "S" curve that led to the marina and pulled straight ahead to the long dock.

"Youse the one who called?" the meaty Bahamian asked, with a smile.

Mac returned the friendly greeting. "We need fuel, probably about sixty gallons, and customs is expecting us."

"Where's your flag, mon? They be getting strict now."

Mac called to Trufante to raise the quarantine flag. While he did so, Mac took the fuel nozzle from the attendant and, laying it on the dock, unscrewed the gas cap. Using a paper towel to surround the opening and catch any overflow, he started the pump. Mac was grateful for not only the money saved by taking the efficient Surfari, but also for the shorter time his hands spent holding the nozzle. Marine pumps required that you manually hold the nozzle, so as not to discharge any gas into the water. With many boats taking on hundreds of gallons of fuel, this got tiresome, though there were plenty of workarounds.

Before the tank was full, Mac saw two uniformed men approaching. They exchanged a greeting with the attendant and walked to within a couple of feet of Mac.

"Youse the one the cutter sent?"

"We are, but I think there's a misunderstanding," Mac started saying. They had at least agreed on the trip over how to handle the interaction. Trufante took the fuel nozzle from Mac, freeing him to speak to the authorities, and Mel came beside him. They had decided that it was better for him, as captain, to do the talking. The fact that she was a lawyer and a woman had played into the decision. It wasn't that they were judging the authorities; it was just better to play it safe and show respect. Customs agents were notoriously hard to read, and they needed every advantage they could get.

"What kind of misunderstanding would that be? You are in Bahamian water, youse need to follow the law here."

This wasn't the start that Mac was hoping for. "No disrespect, but our plans have changed. We had some engine trouble and would like to return home."

"Plans, no plans, everyone has plans," the officer said, shaking his head.

He had probably heard every excuse over the years. With the

proximity of the islands to the east coast of Florida, many fast boats made the run for a day's fishing. Having to come into port and check in took hours from their trips.

"We'll be havin' a look at your papers all the same," the other man said.

Mac knew he had every right and was prepared. "Come aboard if you like."

The officers stepped onto the gunwale and then down to the deck. Used to the monstrous sport fishers that came through here, they paid little mind to the motorsailer. They sat at the table with Mac and Mel and accepted the coffee that was offered. It was all very civilized until they got to the personal documents.

"Who is this Alan Trufante?"

They had expected this as well. Trufante could have hidden below decks or even in the engine compartment, but that was a risk to all of them. It was better to show what documents he had rather than chance the ire of the authorities, who had the power to jail the entire crew.

Trufante lurked behind the console, until Mel finally went and whispered something to him. "That's me." Reluctantly he stepped forward.

The officer held up the driver's license and compared the picture to the man standing before him. Trufante had passed the first test, but there was no telling how the two men were going to play it from here.

"We'd be happy to pay your entry fee, but we still want to head back."

"That is possible for all of you except this man. We will need to take him for questioning."

Mac and Mel glanced at each other. Both knew that it was not uncommon for people to enter the Bahamas aboard personal boats without proper documentation. The airlines and cruise ships checked every passenger's papers before allowing them aboard, but there was no such check for pleasure boaters.

"On what grounds?" Mel asked.

Mac deferred to her. The threat of jail meant a lawyer, not a captain, should handle the discussion. The man shrugged and pulled a piece of paper from his pocket. He unfolded it and handed it to Mel.

It had the slick texture of old-school facsimile paper. Trufante's picture was clearly above the fold. It appeared to have been taken with a cell phone and showed him carrying a crate of guns onto the concrete dock on Green Turtle Cay. Below, it said he was wanted for arms smuggling.

Mac knew it could very well have been himself who was pictured, but Trufante was the one who had gotten caught. In the aftermath of Dorian, they had broken up a smuggling ring, but the picture was incriminating.

"We have a sheriff's deputy who can confirm that this is not what you think," Mel said. Deputy Garrett in Marathon had been involved in the recovery of the weapons. Though no law enforcement officials would claim Trufante an ally, Garrett would at least tell the truth.

"That may help, but all the same he must come with us." They led Trufante onto the dock. The officer turned around. "And there is a mandatory fourteen-day quarantine for all visitors now."

The Gulf Stream

Rudy kept the throttles buried until his chartplotter clearly showed he was in international waters. All four engines were pegged at sixty-two hundred RPMs and very near redlining, but reaching that magical and invisible point, twelve miles from the nearest land, was worth the risk. He had further confirmation that he had made it when the RBDF chopper that had been following him turned and moved away. They were sure to get a visit from ICE on the other side of the Stream, but he wasn't worried about that.

Commander had gone forward and sat on the cooler installed in front of the console. Rudy was angry, but not at the bait man. He had done what he had promised and led him to Travis. It was the wretched woman and her shotgun that had delayed his plan long enough for the authorities to arrive. Still, he knew that his showing up unexpectedly had put some measure of fear in Travis. It was some small consolation that Mac would be looking over his shoulder from now on.

Dropping his speed to conserve fuel, as well as not wanting to attract the attention of ICE on the other side of the Gulf Stream by running full out, he pulled back the twin throttles until the RPMs settled in at forty-two hundred. He was still running close to forty knots, but it felt like nothing. Enabling the autopilot, he released the wheel and pressed a small, unmarked button installed between the live well and the freshwater pump switches.

The inconspicuous button turned on the AIS beacon, allowing him to be seen. He always thought of his boat as a Romulan Warbird, and had even named it *Valdore*. The switch was his cloaking device. When turned off, and combined with the lack of metallic parts aboard, he was almost invisible to the authorities' radar. With no contraband aboard, the AIS beacon turned on, and cruising at a modest speed, he would likely be left alone. On this trip, he almost would have liked to be pulled over. There was every chance that Commander was wanted for something and would be taken into custody. That would get the bait man out of his hair.

Now that Rudy had time to think, he wondered what Travis

was up to. He had been there every bit of an hour, and there had been no sign of Travis or his woman. Rudy doubted they'd been hiding in the cabin. Travis generally didn't roll like that. That meant he was underwater, but he should have surfaced on hearing a boat approach.

The more Rudy thought about it, the more he came to believe Travis was hiding something. He'd built too many boats to think Travis was really interested in salvaging his trawler. By the time he raised it, got it across the Stream, and replaced everything aboard including the engines, he would be able to buy two boats.

As the boat cruised across the Stream, he thought about the possibilities. Retrieving something aboard the sunken ship was conceivable, and with the RBDF cutter approaching he probably wouldn't risk bringing it aboard. That meant it was still there. A return trip was in order, but not with Commander. Once they got back to Marathon, he planned to give the bait man a finder's fee and ditch him. This was between Rudy and Travis.

With the autopilot doing the heavy lifting, he was able to concentrate on the left-hand screen of his three identical displays. That particular unit was dedicated as the radar display. In his line of work, knowing who was around you and, more importantly, which direction they were traveling was priceless. The right-hand unit was dedicated to the chartplotter, leaving the center unit for a combination of different screens and zooms or just the depth finder.

He retraced the black and white dashed line, which was essentially a trail of breadcrumbs on the screen, back towards the reef. The easternmost point was where Travis had been anchored. Zooming out his radar, he observed the area was clear. That meant the authorities had ordered Travis to port. Looking at the screen again, he saw two vessels underway and moving away from the wreck site. One was identifiable by its signature and speed as the RBDF cutter. The other, heading toward Chub Cay, would be Travis.

STEVEN BECKER

A MAC TRAVIS ADVENTURE
WOOD'S
HOPE

Chub Cay

"Mac, if they're going to let us leave, we have to go. There won't be any good we can do if we're all quarantined for two weeks."

"Right," Mac said. He turned to Pamela. "You understand?"

She nodded. Her look was hard, but Mac could see a tear forming in her eye.

With the Cajun's fate decided, Mel took over the conversation. "Where is he going to be kept, and how do we keep in touch?"

"If I was you, I'd be getting a local attorney. They'll know what to do." The men effectively ended the conversation by walking Trufante away from the boat.

Mac saw Pamela tense and step onto the gunwale. Before he could reach her, Mel grabbed her arm. She turned around like she was ready to fight.

"You step foot on that dock and they'll quarantine you too."

Mac motioned for the fuel attendant and handed him several hundreds, rounding up to the next bill for a tip. He needed all the allies he could get here. The man thanked him and helped release the dock lines. Mac pulled forward and angled away from the long dock. With every foot of water between him and Bahamian soil, he was able to relax, and the boat was soon into the turning basin. Mac pointed the bow toward the inlet.

"We'll be back," Pamela said to no one.

He looked over at Mel to see if she could comfort Pamela, but she was already on the phone. Mac could only hear one side of the conversation, and it didn't sound good. She disconnected and called Pamela to the helm.

"This virus thing has the country in an uproar."

In the best of times, the Bahamian government was ineffective. Mac had seen the worst of times when he had come over to help his friend Pip after Hurricane Dorian had ravaged the Abacos. With the unknowns surrounding the pandemic, he expected about the same muddled reaction. Seeing the ineptness of his own government, especially at the local level, Mac was loathe to make comparisons. He did give some leeway to the Bahamians. It couldn't be easy to govern a country made up of seven hundred islands.

"There's not much we can do until they release him from quarantine," Mac said.

Pamela was about to say something, but Mel cut her off. "He's right. This could work to our advantage if they eliminate in-person hearings and go to teleconferences. That way, we can be there from anywhere."

"But I can help if I'm there in person," Pamela said.

Mac knew this was unrealistic, but let it go. "I'm going to lay in a course for Key West. It'd be good to check on Ned and we can use his help."

Pamela continued to pout and went below. Mac felt for her. They'd been through a lot together, including several other incidents where Trufante had faced jail. Every time, though, they had gotten him out. Her absence was appreciated, at least by Mel.

"Harry will take care of him," Mel said.

Mac had never met the lawyer, but knew of his reputation. "Sad thing is, this time he's actually innocent." It made Mac wonder if there was some kind of reverse karma going on.

Mel turned her focus back to her phone, leaving Mac to plot out their course. On the way over, they had used the power of the Gulf Stream to push them northward; now they faced the opposite. With Key West as their destination, the best way to counteract the current was to go straight across it.

Figuring a speed of eight knots, Mac estimated the width of the Stream at sixty miles. That meant it would take them around seven hours to cross. During that time, the current, which he rounded up to five knots, would pull them thirty-odd miles off course. Mac adjusted their heading to compensate for the force of the Stream and dialed in a course to the southwest, at the same time ensuring they would be well to the south of Bimini.

Time moved differently aboard a sailboat, and in Mac's opinion, usually for the better. Though their speed was slow compared to other forms of transportation, the boat seemed to eat up miles. In this case, though, Mac wished he were on something faster. Even *Ghost Runner*, not a "fast" boat by any stretch, would have cut the trip's time in half. When you were talking about a twenty-four-hour transit, that was a lot of time.

Once clear of Chub Cay, Mac deployed the sails. Using the cockpit controls, he was able to tweak them and soon found the point of sail that gave the best speed while still keeping close to their course. Aided by the twin engines, the boat sped up quickly and accelerated to almost ten knots. Mac worked another knot out of her then settled back in the captain's chair.

There was nothing much to do now besides keep watch until they were in sight of land again.

THE PREVAILING southeast wind had remained steady at twelve knots during the day and had increased to twenty overnight. Mac had divided the watches so he would be on deck most of the nighttime hours. With the wind classified as a "fresh breeze" on the Beaufort scale, Mac had enjoyed piloting *Sea Runner* through the night. When dawn broke, he had a better relationship with the boat, but he knew the night crossing wasn't the trial that Pamela had forecast.

Mel appeared just before daybreak and made coffee. She brought Mac a mug and leaned against him. "I know you're dying to check in. Go ahead. I've got this." Mel pecked him on the cheek.

"No service out here." She glanced at the chartplotter. "Making good time."

For most of the night, Mac had been able to maintain twelve knots. It wasn't all that much faster, but every little bit helped. He had been able to watch the chartplotter's ETA tick down by almost an hour over the course of the night. With the sun up, the gains seemed minimal. Their arrival was scheduled for three p.m., leaving the better part of the day to kill.

Though he'd been up all night, Mac now found himself wide awake with nothing to do. After reviewing their course with Mel one more time, he left the helm and moved inside. He sat at the table and pulled out his laptop to transfer the video he had made. Hooking Mel's phone to one USB port, he took another cable and ran it from the computer to the flat-screen TV mounted on the wall.

Pamela appeared from her cabin just as he had the image up on the screen.

"I'd like to dive sometime," she said, moving to the galley and pouring a cup of coffee. She lifted the pot towards Mac, asking if he wanted a refill. He shook his head, and she came to sit beside him.

Mac started the video, and they both sat quietly and watched.

"He's going to be okay, isn't he?" she asked.

Mac pressed the space bar and paused the video. "We'll get him out." He wished he could sound more confident. "As soon as we get close enough for a signal, Mel will call the lawyer again."

"We can't afford this," Pamela said.

"No worries. I'll make sure it's taken care of."

"He doesn't want charity."

Mac knew Trufante was proud. He might have been a train wreck, but he wasn't scared of work. "I owe him for coming over here and, seeing this happened while he was working, consider it part of his wages." Unless the plane was full of gold, the Cajun's wages wouldn't come close to the lawyer's cost, but it seemed to satisfy Pamela.

"You're a good man, Mac Travis."

Mac wanted to move on and started the video again. They watched the coral for anything that might identify the plane.

"I can barely see it," Pamela said.

"I'd guess it's been down there fifty or sixty years. There's a lot of coral on it."

"How would you ever uncover it?"

"I think the question is more what it has aboard. As a wreck, it's probably not worth salvaging, especially since that would destroy the reef."

"How would you know if something of value's aboard?"

Oftentimes, Pamela's questions irritated him, but she was actually helping him clarify things in his mind. "That's for Ned to tell us." Mac wished he had something besides the video,

Mel's sketch, and the discovery of the turret to help. A tail number would have been nice.

"He's pretty smart, but you're not giving him much to go on."

"The old man'll surprise you." Mac hoped so, anyway. Ned had been one of Wood's friends and helped them many times in identifying wrecks and salvaged goods. A retired underwater archeologist and professor at the University of Florida, he knew his stuff and wasn't bogged down with the preservation aspect, which had become fashionable in the government's latest attempt to control treasure hunters.

Treasure hunting had been a calling since the first ship had sunk back in antiquity. Recovery methods had remained unchanged for centuries, until scuba diving became accessible in the seventies. Once the equipment became commonplace, the salvage arena had become something of the Wild West, until the government stepped in and started to regulate it. Mac supposed there needed to be some form of control, but it had become a quagmire of bureaucratic requirements.

Surveys, reports, paperwork, and inspections now took more of the treasure hunter's time than actually searching for anything. This left working anything but a known wreck, with a documented inventory, out of reach for most. To complicate things even more, the countries that the wrecks were registered to when they sunk were now suing for their rights.

They watched the video several times, until Mac decided there was nothing more he could see that would reveal the origin of the plane. Hoping Ned would have better luck, he disconnected the cables and stowed his laptop.

Back on deck, he checked their progress. The ten miles they had covered looked like nothing in the scope of the trip. "Seventy miles." Mac didn't think he could bear another six hours of nothing. He thought about dropping back a fishing line, but his melancholy mood said no.

"Mind if I take over?" he asked Mel.

"Going crazy?"

"Yeah. At least it'll give me something to do."

"Okay. I'm going to see if I can get a signal."

"The service is turned off."

"Well, I'll just have to turn it back on." She saw the look on his face. "There's too much going on here. Between the virus, Trufante, and the plane, it'll be worth it."

Mac had no say in the matter and kept his opinion to himself that she was just having withdrawal from the news feeds she followed. The boat was equipped with satellite internet, but the plan had lapsed. It was simply too expensive to justify the monthly costs for something that he didn't need when they had a portable unit for emergencies. Mel did need it, though, and with the equipment in place had decided to contact the provider.

She went below, leaving Mac alone in the cockpit. The solitude allowed his mind to roam and, finding the path of least resistance, it moved directly to the plane. Despite the lack of evidence to identify it, there was something about it stuck in his mind. Every wreck had a story, and somehow he knew this one's was unique.

STEVEN BECKER

A MAC TRAVIS ADVENTURE

WOOD'S HOPE

Key West

PAMELA POINTED TO THE HORIZON. MAC STRUGGLED TO SEE anything and needed a glance at the chartplotter to tell him that it was the weather blimp flying over Cudjoe Key. Even knowing it was there, he could barely make out the white shape. It was the first visual sign that they were closing on Key West, though it meant little, as Mac knew exactly where they were. The excitement of past generations from spotting land and celebrating a safe passage had disappeared with the advent of chartplotters. For the past hour, Mac and Pamela had been watching the boat-shaped icon representing *Sea Runner* approach the coast.

Mel had acquired a signal about an hour ago and was deep in her computer. Mac heard several curses thrown out but knew she was better left alone. When she had something to report, she would.

The low line of the Keys was just visible and the water started to change color as they crossed from the indigo blue of the Gulf Stream to the lighter turquoise over the reef. He was careful as they made their way into the lighter green water of the shallows, before relaxing when they entered the deeper Hawk Channel. Mac had based his route on the conditions, allowing the current to dictate their course, rather than the rhumb line shown on the chartplotter. Because of this, they had crossed the reef to the east of Key West. Once he had established his westerly course, Mac hit the buttons that automatically furled the sails.

Under power, they continued along the oceanside coast of Key West. Mac could just make out the White Street Pier jutting over the shallow water on the side of the island. Past that, although not visible, was the painted concrete buoy that marked the southernmost point of the continental US. The iconic tourist spot, located on the corner of Whitehead and South, was located more for convenience than geographic accuracy. Ballast Key, a small, inaccessible island ten miles away, was the true point, though it was only reachable by boat and not technically connected to the mainland like Key West. Even then, five hundred feet further southwest lay the more accurate southernmost point on the island, but it was located on Navy property. Having the buoy right off Duval Street made for a better story—and countless photo ops. On many days there was a line to take a picture with the colorful buoy.

Turning into the main channel, they passed the cruise ship docks, which Mac noticed were empty for the first time he could remember.

"They're all offshore somewhere, if you're wondering," Mel said. "No one is willing to let them dock."

"Always thought they were floating petri dishes anyway." Mac had been aboard only one of the leviathans and then only for a short time. He and Trufante had used one of the ships to evade a crazed drug runner.

The smaller harbor was empty as well. They continued around the island, where another marina lay just past Sunset

Key. Housing mostly charter fishing boats, parasailers, and sunset-cruise ships, the docks were full. Without the larger cruise ships and tourists, the island was quiet.

Mac gave the Coast Guard base a wide berth and worked his way around Fleming Key. The Navy-owned island was quiet as well. Garrison Bight, the harbor and marina where he intended to put in, was just ahead when Mel stopped him.

"I don't think it's a good idea to go in."

"What's up?"

"The mayor's adding restrictions every five minutes. I'm afraid if we dock, they won't let us leave."

Mac let his comments on both the mayor and her policies go. "I can put you ashore at the pier, or I can go in?"

"Best if you did. I'll take the boat back out, and pick you up when you're ready."

Mac had no objections, and grabbed his phone and wallet. He found his flip-flops in the cabin and was on the bow as Mel idled slowly to the dock. Just before the bow pulpit touched, Mac readied himself. Sensing Mel shift into neutral, he jumped across the two-foot gap before she dropped into reverse and pulled the boat away.

Mac waved to her that he was okay and started walking down the pier. He noticed that every charter boat was in its slip, as were most of the private vessels. This time of day, the marina was usually quiet, as most boats were out. Today it was a ghost town, and they were all here. Truman Street, usually a busy thoroughfare, was deserted as well. Mac had planned on finding a cab, but the streets were deserted.

Somewhere around the cemetery, he found his land legs and increased his stride. The smell of asphalt permeated the air as he crossed Duval Street. The only vehicles in sight were the city trucks repaving the road. He continued past the closed Blue

Heaven restaurant and turned right onto a narrow street. Ned's house was just on the left.

His friend answered the door, but retreated into the house before greeting Mac, who entered and waited in the foyer. Ned wobbled down the hallway. Mac watched him carefully, making sure his bowlegged walk was not a sign of inebriation. Ned drank, as did everyone on the rock, but not to excess. But these were different times, and Mac was worried about him.

"Come on, then. I've dismissed the staff if you're waiting for someone to take your flip-flops."

Mac smiled, relieved that Ned was still Ned. He followed him into the study. As Ned approached the desk, he moved one of the chairs a few feet back and indicated to Mac that he should sit there.

"Gotta be careful these days. And I'm never sure who you've been around."

It took Mac a minute to understand his precautions. "Bad deal, I hear."

"Especially for old folks like me. Say we're in the high-risk group."

"You're healthy though?"

"If you don't take my pills away I am. Cholesterol, blood pressure, blah blah blah. . . . At least I stopped smoking back in the day, and the scotch keeps the diabetes at bay."

Mac didn't know if any of his complaints were bad enough to put him at risk. "How 'bout a little taste, then?"

"Little early for you, isn't it, unless you're subscribing to my theory?"

"Been up all night. Had to make a quick exit from the Bahamas." Mac went over to the sideboard and poured a hefty dose from a decanter into two glasses. He took them to the desk and slid one across the narrow gap between the books and papers to Ned, who eyed the glass warily. Mac felt his gaze turn to him.

"Been around Tru?"

Mac nodded. Ned picked up the glass and wiped it down with a disinfectant wipe from a nearby container.

"Got about enough patience for another few days of this. If it goes much longer, I'll take my chances." Ned took a long sip. "Don't suppose you came all this way to check on me?"

"Partly, yes." Mac took a sip and rolled the scotch around his mouth before swallowing. "Nice."

"Ought to be. At least they've got enough sense to call alcohol essential. While the rest of 'em were out after toilet paper, I took care of the more important things. Got a freezer full of steaks and a cupboard of this." Ned raised his glass and took another sip.

"Toilet paper?" Mac asked.

"Guess you have been away. Idiots. So, what else brings you this way?"

Mac told him about going after *Ghost Runner* and finding the plane. The story took them through their first drink and into their second. Mac noticed that this time Ned didn't wipe his glass down. Hygiene was a moving target.

"So, Trufante's gonna be over there for a bit. I'm guessing Mel's got a lawyer for the boy?"

"She does, but that leaves me with Pamela."

"Don't know what's worse. Anyway, this plane. What have you got for me?"

Mac propped his phone against the spine of a thick book on the desk and started the video. "I can put it up on the TV if you have the right cables."

He placed a pair of thick reading glasses on his nose. "No need."

"I've got dimensions and a few pictures of a turret by the tail section."

Ned looked up from the screen, his eyes magnified by the readers. "Was the turret in the tail or in front of it?"

"In front." Mac took the phone back and brought up the pictures of the turret.

Ned's interest overrode his caution again, and he picked up the phone. "Let's see those measurements."

While Mac found the picture he had taken of the dive slate, Ned got up and went to the opposite side of the room, where after a moment's search he found a book and brought it back. Mac was always amazed at Ned's ability to access any of the thousand books lining the walls. The library was probably one of the most complete collections of anything and everything lost to the sea.

Ned cleared a space on the desk and opened up the coffee-table-sized book.

"If it's anywhere, it'll be in Jane's."

Mac was familiar with the Jane's Guides, a collection of books documenting just about every vessel that ever sailed, but had never seen the *Fighting Aircraft of World War II*. He waited patiently while Ned thumbed through the pages.

"What'd you have for the length and wingspan?"

Mac had to pan and zoom the screen to see the handwritten dimensions. "Looks like sixty feet long with a seventy-five-foot wingspan."

"That'll be close enough. The turret's pretty much a give-away." Ned slid the open book across the desk.

"Martin B-26 Marauder?"

"Little doubt. Must have crashed, because the relief of the reef is too low, but it all fits."

"Any way to drill deeper?"

"Any kind of paint identifiers are long gone. Maybe a serial number off one of the key components?"

"Little late."

Ned sat back. "There's other ways, but it'll take some time. I'd have to trace the location and status of all the planes in this area."

"How bad could that be?"

"After the war, a lot of that equipment was auctioned off to Third World countries. I'm not guessing you'll get any help from Cuba or any of the South American countries that bought them."

"I remember one of Wood's stories about some lost B26s from Cuba."

"Old Wood had a lot of stories."

The both laughed.

"He never let that one go. Even worked the Gulf up towards Fort Myers for a while looking for Batista's lost plane."

Mac started to remember the story. "Something about looting the treasury?"

Ned got up and went to another bookcase, where he scanned the shelves. While he searched, Mac glanced outside. Bahamian shutters covered the windows to keep out the sun, but through the slats he could see it was getting dark. He had been here longer than he thought.

"I'm gonna have to get going soon. Don't want Mel out there in the dark." It was bad enough he'd have to run the boat up the Gulf side at night.

Ned found the book he was looking for. "Just a minute." He sat back down and laid the new book over the Jane's Guide, and after consulting the index, found the page he wanted.

"In 1952, Cuba signed a military pact with the USA, which involved an extensive program of American assistance to the Cuban military. Under US Mutual Defense Assistance Program

Grant Aid deliveries, the *Fuerza Aerea del Ejercito de Cuba* received sixteen transparent-nosed B-26Cs in 1956."

"Any way of tracking them down?"

"Take a day or so. Finding the serial number would help. Says here that they were serialized in the range between 901 to 935, with even numbers being skipped, perhaps to give people the impression that the FAEC had more planes than it really did."

"Crafty bastards," Mac said, and got up. "Can I get you anything?"

"Truth is, I'd like to get out of here. When things go bad, the people on this rock get pretty interesting. Not sure I want to stick around for that."

Mac paused, wondering how Mel would react. He could have called, but figured this might be one of those things it was better to apologize for later than ask permission for first. "You'd be safe as anywhere out on the island. Why not come back with us?"

"Damned if I wouldn't like that, but that'll slow down my research."

"Take the books with you."

"This ain't no lending library. The Florida climate's not very book friendly. Got a separate dehumidifier and air conditioner just for this room."

"We do have the internet."

"Shoot, why didn't you say so?"

STEVEN BECKER

A MAC TRAVIS ADVENTURE

WOOD'S
HOPE

Key West

NED DIDN'T WANT TO LEAVE HIS CAR IN THE MARINA LOT FOR AN extended time, but he was willing to leave his beater bikes there. While Mac had called Mel to arrange to be picked up, Ned had packed a backpack and duffle.

Mac grabbed the heavy duffle, slung it over his shoulders, and placed his arms through the two loop handles. "Traveling light?"

"Gotta be prepared. We're going to the Bahamas, I'm gonna need my cruise wear. And there're a few bottles of scotch in there too, so be careful."

Mac shouldered the load and climbed aboard the bike. It took a few minutes of swerving until he figured out how to balance the weight of the awkward load. With each near miss, Ned reminded him about the value of the cargo.

When they reached the marina, *Sea Runner's* navigation lights were visible from the street. Mac noticed several other masthead lights in the basin, marking cruisers that had anchored there. The Surfari appeared to be the only vessel underway. Mac and Ned dismounted and made their way to a stand with a dozen or so weather-beaten bikes, probably belonging to liveaboards. Bicycle maintenance in the tropics was almost impossible. Even garaged, the bikes were rust magnets. Ned slid a lock around both frames, while Mac called Mel to bring in the boat.

By the time they had reached the end of the dock, Mac could see the red and green bow lights of the Surfari coming toward them. He looked around, worried that Ned would be unable to make the jump aboard. With no one around, he motioned Mel to pull parallel to the dock. It seemed better to remove the risk for the old man—and the scotch.

Once Mac and Ned were aboard, Mel pulled away from the dock, and pointed the bow to the harbor entrance.

"Brought a guest?" Mel asked.

"Safer with us than here, and he's got some ideas about the wreck."

"You could have warned me."

Mac shrugged and moved to the other side of the wheel, where he could access the electronics. Backlit by their red night-time lights, Mac ignored the chartplotter. He knew this harbor and the trip back to Wood's Island by heart. It was the radar that drew his focus.

Only half the display was useful, since the other showed nothing but clutter from the landmass behind them. A handful of signatures was returned, which, after remaining stationary for several minutes, Mac guessed were anchored cruisers. There was one larger return that bothered him.

"What's the deal with the Coasties out there? I saw the cutter put out a bit after you left." Mel said.

"Not like them to have something that size patrolling so close in. Anything new with the shutdowns?"

"Gotten a little out of hand. Seems like every hour there's

another restriction put in place. They just shut down the bridges to fishing."

They shared a worried look. "What about boats?"

"Boat ramps, too. I haven't heard anything about those underway."

"Not worth the risk." After what had happened with Trufante, Mac preferred to slip past the cutter. He glanced at the chartplotter and saw right away that the draft of the Surfari limited his options. "We run dark and stay close to land, their radar won't do much good."

"If they see us, they're bound to be interested," Mel said.

"Yeah, but if they can't get to us . . ."

The northwest passage was the main route through the shallow flats surrounding the island to the Gulf. Mac knew two other routes to deep water. Bluefish Pass might have been an option during the day, but was badly marked, if at all, making a nighttime transit risky. Mac decided to hug the west side of Fleming Key and take the Calda Channel. The pass was plenty deep and well-marked, but too narrow for the Coast Guard boat to maneuver. There was always the chance the cutter would take an interest and pursue them in the open Gulf, but Mac could always duck into one of the numerous small channels and avoid them. It was a strategy proven by centuries of pirates and smugglers.

Heading into the channel, Mac had Pamela and Mel stationed with bright searchlights on either side of the bow. The chartplotter showed the markers, but even with the supposed thirty-foot accuracy of the GPS, the channel was too narrow to rely on electronics. The markers, invisible in the distance, were easily recognizable when the beam of light hit them. Mel called out the red triangles to port and Pamela the green squares to starboard. Ned watched the screen and told Mac which was next, allowing him to focus on the water ahead.

Even with the precautions, transiting these waters at night was risky.

A collective sigh of relief fell over the boat as they passed the last marker. Mac was the last to celebrate open water, though, until a glance at the radar screen told him the Coast Guard had shown no interest in them. He started to work out their route from here. The barrier islands on their starboard side ran in a straight line, with a slight tilt to the north. Had he been aboard *Ghost Runner*, he would have had access to all the tracks of past trips in the chartplotter's memory, but with *Sea Runner* being a virgin in these waters, he had to lay in a route. Once that was done, he engaged the autopilot and sat back.

Pamela had remained on the bow, and with Mel and Ned catching up by the stern, Mac was free to think. There were two things on his mind and both were in the Bahamas.

Wood's Island

Rudy was growing frustrated. He'd been waiting in a side channel behind the island for hours. He was also decidedly not comfortable. There had been little choice in choosing the flats boat over his go-fast boat. The shallow draft and jack plate, which raised the engine almost a foot when needed, allowed the boat to run in less than a foot of water. The flats boat allowed him access to areas even at low tide. Areas where other boats were unable to follow—and that was good for business.

Both boats lacked shade, but for different reasons. In order for the flats boat to run in skinny water, weight was an issue, as was its fishability. On the small boat, the supports of a T-top or even a Bimini would be in the way. Rudy's goal when designing the boat had been to maintain a low radar signature. To that end, any non-critical metal had been eliminated. There were many other small changes he had made, but the ones he was most proud of were the engine shields. The heavily insulated, over-sized cowlings contained a system of tubing running over the entire engine to keep it cool. As a result, the boat was virtually invisible on radar.

Finally, the sun set and another plague set in—the mosquitos found him.

Rudy had sat through the heat of the afternoon and now well into the night. The tide change had already spun the boat on the single Power-pole. As the hours ticked by, Rudy's already bad mood was not improving—he had expected Travis hours ago, and it wasn't the first time he had been stuck waiting today. But to him, time was an occupational hazard. Meetings were often delayed, and Rudy knew anything could have happened to the motorsailer and its crew, so he settled in and swatted mosquitos.

He had been lucky and gotten out of the Bahamas without incident. His mission might not have been a success, but in his line of work, there were always losses. During his run to reach the safety of international waters, Rudy had monitored his radar. Before he was out of range, he'd seen Travis heading in the direction of Chub Cay, and called his source there.

Sitting on the edge of the Gulf Stream twelve miles west of Bimini, he had waited for confirmation of Travis's plans. Several hours later, a call from a source on Chub Cay confirmed the Surfari had been there and left. Hearing about Trufante's plight amused him, but changed nothing. It was Travis he wanted. When he was sure Travis was returning to the US, he sped across the Gulf Stream, dropped Commander off, and swapped boats.

He knew he might have miscalculated the time the motorsailer needed to make the crossing, but not by this much. Rudy had already checked out the island and could do nothing but wait. He'd been here before and knew Travis wasn't concerned about protecting its western end. With a skinny flat extending a quarter of a mile at high tide, it was inaccessible to all but the shallowest draft boats.

Rudy finally saw the navigation lights of what appeared, from the height they were mounted, to be a sailboat cruising past the western tip of the island, but dismissed it. At first, he ignored the boat, but when it turned into the channel on the other side of the island, he realized his prey had arrived. Rudy jammed his Glock into his waistband and climbed over the gunwale. He had one foot in the water when he saw the light come to a stop, he entered the water and quickly waded to shore. It was a dance rather than a walk, as he tried to avoid being sucked into the muck. The quagmire didn't end at the water. For another hundred yards he braved the quicksand-like muck that had emerged when the tide changed. Squishing through the mud, he swatted at clouds of no-see-ums and mosquitos. Finally, the footing improved, but the bugs stayed with him as he worked his way through the next barrier, the mangroves.

The tree branches were tightly woven, causing Rudy to pry them apart as he forced his way through. Just when he thought he was in the clear, his foot snagged on an exposed root. He cursed under his breath as the bugs swarmed around his head, unable to swat at them because he needed his hands to move the branches out of the way. He was both physically and mentally exhausted when he finally saw a security light mounted on a shed in the clearing where the house was sited.

Backing away, he watched as four figures emerged from the trail on the other side of the clearing. Mac and Mel were easy to identify, as was Pamela, but the last figure eluded him. At first, he thought his information was wrong and it was Trufante, but this man was shorter and heavier than the Cajun.

As they passed through the light, he saw it was an older man who he didn't recognize. Thinking he was the reason for the delay, Rudy's interest peaked, and he changed his plan. He'd had the feeling that Travis was up to something besides salvaging his trawler and hoped the stranger held the clue to what it was.

The group climbed the stairs and entered the house. He ducked back as Mac came out a minute later to slide open several of the hurricane shutters. Mac went back inside, and as soon as the door closed, Rudy crept closer. He decided to take the chance that the bugs would keep them inside and started up the open staircase. The feel of the gun in his waistband reminded him that there was always his original plan if things went sideways. Just in case, as he reached the wraparound porch, he pulled out the pistol and grasped it in his right hand. Rudy crossed the decking and placed his back to the wall.

He waited there for several long minutes, until he was sure he hadn't been observed. Keeping his back against the exterior of the house, he slid to the nearest window. With no permanent power supply, the house didn't have an air conditioner, and the windows were open. Rudy heard talking and concentrated on who was speaking.

He knew Travis's voice, so the man speaking had to be the stranger. He sounded like some kind of academic giving a lecture on Cuban history. Having grown up here, Rudy knew a good deal about the Revolution and the circumstance which led to it. The talk was about that period, and when he heard Batista's name, Rudy's interest perked up. The previous dictator had been notorious for corruption and his ties to the mob. His wealth had never been retrieved.

Rudy cursed under his breath as Mel interrupted with another question. He sensed the lecture was coming to its conclusion—one that he was interested in. Finally, she was satisfied and allowed the speaker to continue. Rudy heard the man start to talk about a fleet of B-26 bombers that had carried off Cuba's looted treasury.

17

Wood's Island

WOOD'S ORIGINAL FLOOR PLAN, WHICH MAC HAD KEPT THROUGH the renovation, was designed for a hermit; not for a party. Most evenings the breeze, along with the elevation of the stilt house, kept the bugs at bay, but this night was still and humid. Tonight, clouds of insects made the extra space offered by the wrap-around porch off-limits. The signs all foretold a cold front was coming.

"It'd be just as easy to cut into the cargo compartment than to find the serial number." Mac paced the crowded floor.

"And you and Tru will be sharing a cell if they find you looting a wreck without permitting and documenting it first," Mel said.

"It'll take years to get the permits." Mac was frustrated. He wasn't a looter by any means, he just had a hard time dealing with the obstacles the bureaucracy placed in your way to salvage a wreck. From obtaining a contractor's license to passing the bar, many institutions made the process of acquiring a license harder than the actual work was. They did this to screen those they considered poor prospects out, but failed to realize that passing a test or completing a ream of paperwork didn't qualify anyone for the work—experience did. Left to their own devices, most who weren't qualified failed.

Mac hadn't initially been sure what his interest in the plane was besides curiosity. After hearing Ned's story, that had changed. Commas in bank account balances didn't really appeal to Mac. They had the opposite effect by making him worry more. He and Mel had been generous with their last finds, donating money and setting up trusts. Mac could live off the sea if need be. He was a dinosaur in a cashless economy. For him, more important was the thrill of the discovery—to be the first to find something.

He went for the front door. "I need some air."

"Want company?" Mel asked.

"No, just gotta think." Mac left the house and leaned against the railing. This side of the porch overlooked the interior of the island. Most builders would have sited the house to face the water. Wood had chosen differently. Men who made their living on the water generally grew tired of staring at it. Wood had built the house to benefit from the shade and the prevailing winds, not the view, which was best from the outside shower on the back of the house.

Mac sat on the top step and tried to think through what his motivations were and how he should proceed. It went against his grain to leave the wreck without at least uncovering the secrets it held. Though Mel had been in contact with their local attorney, she was already frustrated with how slow the wheels of justice turned in the Bahamas. Mac wasn't sure if he could wait for the Cajun's release before returning.

The separation was taking a toll on Pamela. First thing tomorrow, he intended to take her back to Marathon. Leaving the volatile woman to her own devices might be risky too, but she was spun out about Trufante being in jail. There was no chance she and Mel could survive each other under the same small roof.

A thought occurred to Mac that perhaps there was a deal to be made, but they would need to reach the right person—or the wrong person—in the Bahamian government to do it. Mac's friend Pip was well connected in the Abacos, but the archipelago covered a vast area. Still, it wouldn't be surprising if Pip knew someone helpful, and decided to give him a call. Commander had fallen out of favor with Pip but, like Mac, he had a soft spot for Trufante. He might be able to help on that front as well.

With at least his next few steps sorted out, he turned to go back into the house, but stopped when he heard a sound come from the bush. There were few large animals out here, at least of the land-based variety. American crocodiles ranged this far, but were very rare. There was always the chance of a Key deer making the swim from Big Pine Key. Irma had scattered part of the endangered population of "mini deer" throughout the surrounding islands, but they had mostly returned to their natural habitat.

The sound he heard was louder than the birds, iguanas, snakes, and rodents that were populous on the islands. It was because of Mel's war with those critters that a .410 shotgun lay inside by the door. The "snake charmer" was the closest weapon, but Mac didn't want to bother anyone inside. Remaining quiet, he waited.

Though they were eight miles from civilization, "silence" was relative. The wind, water, birds, and insects all contributed to the background noise. Once Mac filtered those sounds out, he was sure he heard something moving through the brush.

The breeze was just strong enough to disturb the smaller branches and helped disguise any but a major movement, and the dark night would aid an intruder. Over the years, the prevalent predator on the island had been human. If Mac wanted to know what or who it was, he would need to go after it. Moving back to the door, he opened it and reached inside for the shotgun. Grabbing the barrel, he picked up the weapon.

"Snake?" Mel asked.

Mac grunted in the affirmative and left the house. The last thing he needed was any other bodies roaming around in the dark. Staying to the edges of the stair treads to avoid any sound, he descended the staircase and quickly moved across the clearing. Using the shed for cover, he waited, tuning his hearing again to locate the intruder.

Mac heard a rustle in bushes coming from the far side of the clearing. With the intruder clearly moving toward that area, Mac could only expect that if it were a human, their intentions were not innocent. Occasionally people, especially lost kayakers, found the island and sought help. At most tides, the flats on the back side were too skinny for even a kayak, and the island was small enough that they invariably entered at the dock area.

With his senses on alert, Mac found the narrow path and started down it. He knew the way through the maze of mangroves and palmetto bushes as well as he did the water surrounding the island and was able to move quickly and quietly, without the need for any light. That gave him an advantage over the intruder, which became apparent as the sound became louder.

Mac didn't want a confrontation. He would be happy running whoever, or whatever, it was off the island. He was wary of tangling with anyone or anything in the brush and decided to push whatever it was onto the flats, where the intruder would be exposed. After the decision to spook, rather than confront, whatever was out there, he chambered a round and fired a shot over the mangroves. It was several long seconds before the sound died and his hearing rebounded. When he was finally able to distinguish sounds, he heard the bushes rustle nearby.

Mac was sure he hadn't misread the situation. There clearly had been only one intruder before. The source of this closer sound had to be Mel, Ned, and/or Pamela, who must have been drawn out by the shot he'd fired. With a new urgency, Mac started into the brush. He cradled the shotgun in both hands, using the barrel to move branches out of his way, but ready to fire at a second's notice, no longer worrying about making noise.

RUDY BARELY MADE it to the edge of the clearing when he turned back and saw a figure emerge from the house. He slid around the back of the shed, knowing how lucky he was that he had heard Travis state his intention of stepping outside a few seconds before actually doing so. He pulled his pistol from the waistband of his shorts and sighted it on Travis, realizing that if he hadn't overheard about the plane, his thirst for revenge could have ended immediately.

Lowering the weapon, he tried to figure out how to leverage Travis's discovery instead of killing him—that would come later. Smugglers came in several varieties. The one-timers, the part-timers, and the few who made a sustainable income from it. Rudy's career had spanned several decades and several itera-tions. His instincts of when to turn down jobs or not make a questionable run had kept him alive and in business. For now, retreat seemed the best option.

Though he was adept at moving goods under the radar, he relied on boats, planes, and technology. Fitness was not a neces-sity or priority. His sprint across the clearing had left him winded. If it came down to a race between him and Travis, he would lose, which made getting back to the boat a priority.

Stepping backwards into the brush, he turned and swung his

arms back and forth to clear the razor-sharp palmetto fronds out of his way. Inside his head, the noise seemed minimal compared to his heavy breathing. He ignored it and plowed forward. He was lucky that navigation wasn't an issue and he soon saw the tree line—the last barrier to the water—just ahead. A shot rang out, causing him to stumble on an exposed tree root. He got up and, moving with a sense of urgency, he crashed into the foliage.

Rudy reached the beach and stopped to catch his breath. Once the rasping had calmed enough that he could hear what was going on around him, he realized the situation had changed. The sounds of several people could be heard, and he realized this might be his chance. In the dim light, the low-profile boat would be indistinguishable unless you knew it was there, but reaching it would leave him exposed for too long. With the chance of Travis recognizing him, it wasn't worth the risk. Sliding back behind a large bush, Rudy waited.

He assumed Travis was the closest and the one he most wanted to avoid. The brush would conceal him if he remained silent, but sooner or later he would have to move. With what sounded like multiple people outside now, he decided to take the chance. The fury of the mosquitos around him contributed to his decision, and he rose from the brush. Rudy's plan was to stay near the shoreline and backtrack away from the search and toward the other end of the island. He figured Travis had heard him, rather than seen him. As long as he kept his cool, he could remain unseen until they gave up.

Every few feet he stopped, both to listen and catch his breath. There were voices now, revealing the speaker's identity. Travis seemed irate that the others had come out, and he heard Mel call that they had heard the shotgun fire and were concerned. When Rudy heard the older man who had sounded like he knew about the plane, he decided on a course of action that would allow him both to escape and find the treasure.

With his pistol in hand, he worked his way toward the sound of the man's voice. Reaching him was fairly easy—it was taking him hostage that concerned Rudy. Though he was much younger, Rudy doubted he was in condition to take down the man without a fight, and that would allow the others to reach him. Instead, he decided on a frontal assault. It was easy to track the man, and he soon found himself just a few feet away.

Rudy stepped in front of the man and raised the gun. The man was startled, but instead of calling for help, he merely looked defiantly at his captor. With the gun in hand, Rudy motioned the barrel in the direction of the flats. Unflinching, the man moved forward.

Rudy stayed alert, both for any action from the man in front of him or the searchers. A few minutes later, he heard them appear to regroup, calling out a name.

"Ned?"

"NED!"

The search had shifted from the unknown intruder to their friend.

They reached the shoreline without being discovered. "Into the water. I've got a boat a little way out."

Rudy had to nudge Ned into the water with the barrel of the gun. It was a slow few feet before they found their footing. There was no choice but to tramp through the muck, and Rudy at first worried they were moving too slowly, but then realized that Travis wouldn't shoot if Ned was beside him. His pursuers would face the same obstacle. With that realization, Rudy stopped for a breather. They were about a hundred feet out in no man's land when he turned back and saw three figures outlined by the moonlight.

"HE'S GOT A GUN!" Ned called back to the group on the narrow beach.

"WE'LL BE TALKING, TRAVIS!" the smuggler yelled.

18

Wood's Island

MAC FELT THE QUICKSAND-LIKE MUCK SUCK AT HIS FEET AS HE watched the two figures walk away. Even if he hadn't heard the man speak, he still would have recognized his blocky figure. There was no question it was Rudy. Mel and Pamela soon found Mac, and the three stood together as the pair of men disappeared into the dark night. A minute later, the sound of an outboard starting broke the silence and the luminescence of a boat wake appeared, then moved away.

"Why Ned?" Mel asked.

"You know Rudy. He doesn't care if it's an old man."

Pamela stood with her hands on her hips. "Poor guy. First he's in trouble with that flu thing; now he's been kidnapped."

"What are we going to do, Mac?" Mel asked.

Surrounded by the women, Mac was forced into a decision he wasn't ready to make right away. He knew Rudy better than he wanted to and had suspected he was connected to the mob. Though the big three, Dade, Broward, and Palm Beach counties, got most of the press for organized crime activity, the Keys were not immune. Far from it; they were the supply chain for the drugs and counterfeiting distributed on the mainland. Mac knew he was on dangerous ground.

Having lived in the Keys for almost thirty years, Mac knew his Cuban history as well. He'd even been there twice—both illegally. Batista had been a polarizing figure. Though the average Cuban probably lived better under his regime, it was every bit as corrupt as Castro's. The difference was political ideology: unbridled capitalism versus communism. The island had prospered during Batista's reign, but was far from ethically run. Rigging elections, mob involvement, and death squads to silence any objectors were all commonplace.

A corruptible dictator had made it easy for the mob to move in. When the unstable political atmosphere had the island nation primed for communism, the CIA became involved. The agency had hedged their bets in the power struggle for the country. Forced to protect American interests in Cuba from the threat of communism, they had backed Batista, but there was also an off-the-books program to provide some minimal financing to Castro, just in case he won. They had failed at both.

"I know where he lives, but don't expect that would do much good," Mac said.

"We're in the right here, Mac. There's nothing to hide. We can go to the authorities," Mel said.

She was right and wrong.

Pamela saved him. "Commander ran off at the mouth when he was drinking one night. He was going on about how big and powerful the syndicate was here. We go to the police, Ned gets killed."

Mac didn't doubt her. "He must know we're onto something." Rudy had already chased him to the Bahamas, though Mac suspected that was about revenge. Provided the gangster could escape back to US waters, killing Mac in foreign waters would have been an easy answer. But Pamela had delayed them, and the intervention by the RBDF had aborted Rudy's attempt. But when Rudy had his blood up, he was not that easily deterred. He had come here to finish the job, but must have been listening to their conversation.

"So, we wait?" Mel asked.

"We know what he wants, so we might as well make some plans. Before this happened, I had reached the conclusion that there's no need to find the serial number of the plane. There's no reason that we can't just break into the hold and see if anything's there. Now, claiming we need the serial number to confirm the wreck would be the perfect excuse to delay him until we can figure out how to get Ned back."

Mel slapped at a mosquito hovering around her head. "Can we take this inside?"

Mac led them back down the narrow trail to the clearing. The combination of body heat and perspiration brought a swarm of bugs that attacked them, and as they made their way to the house, their pace picked up from a fast walk to a run. Mel, who was probably in better condition than Mac or Pamela, and with her loathing for bugs, made it up the stairs first. Mac let Pamela go past him and followed the two women into the house. Mac set the shotgun in its place. After taking turns rinsing off in the outside shower, they regrouped around the table.

Mac explained his theory, then sat back and waited for Mel to poke holes in it. Instead of asking any questions, she turned to her computer. Mac waited patiently, but Pamela had been fidgety since seeing Ned taken. She excused herself and went outside, probably to smoke a joint.

"There's quite a bit on those B-26s, but I'm seeing more of a CIA involvement than the mob."

"From what I've heard, in the late fifties, they were in bed together."

Mel was quiet for another few minutes as she researched that angle. Mac became impatient and moved behind her. She read faster than he did and was quickly plowing through news clippings and forums. Mac knew her furious scrolling had caused him to miss some details, but he got the gist of it. With the help of the CIA and the mob, Batista had looted the Cuban treasury before Castro rolled into Havana.

"I don't see any names, at least on the CIA side. The mob guys, or at least the leaders, are all dead, and probably their CIA counterparts, too. I'll bet the CIA guys buried this deep."

"Tampa was where they were headed. What's this one doing in the Bahamas?"

"I think that plane was Batista's and heading to the Dominican Republic, where he was exiled. It's not too much of a stretch that they tried to fly around a storm and crashed in the Bahamas."

"Is there any record of what the planes that arrived in Tampa carried?"

She shook her head. "B-26s landing at MacDill Air Force Base might attract some attention, but the CIA could easily provide a cover story. Once in a hangar, they would be quickly unloaded and the loot would disappear into their coffers."

"Or someone's." Mac had been around the block with enough three-letter agencies to foster his distrust.

Mel continued to browse.

"It also could have been planned. At that point, you could do pretty much anything in the Bahamas. That was a different era. Cruise ships were few and cheap puddle-jumpers were rare. Nassau was just starting to modernize. With Batista on his way out of Cuba, it was pretty easy to see that the party was ending. The Bahamas were the perfect opportunity for the mob to recreate what they were about to lose in Cuba—a tropical Las Vegas."

Mac continued to read over her shoulder. "Looks like Meyer Lansky saw the writing on the wall and was in the process of moving them from Cuba to Grand Bahama and New Providence islands. Maybe the plane contained his cut."

"He was known as the accountant for the mob, not one of the bosses," Mel said.

"I've been around enough to know that whoever controls the money is in charge. Luciano and Capone had the notoriety, but I'm guessing that Lansky knew where the treasure went."

"We're into some serious speculation here, and the mob isn't an octopus with one main body and many arms. Most of those families hate each other," Mel said.

The door opened and Pamela entered. There was nothing to hide, and Mac and Mel continued with their research. A much calmer Pamela sat down next to Mel.

"When can we find out what Tru's deal is?" she asked.

Mel started to say something, but Mac cut her short. "I'm thinking we need to head back over there. Maybe drop you and Mel in Nassau, and I'll go check the wreck. Something I need off it."

Mel gave him a questioning look. "We need a faster mode of transport. Wasting twenty-four hours each way isn't going to help either Tru or Ned."

Mac knew she was right, but didn't have an answer.

"What about Pip?" Pamela asked.

Mac's old friend had gone back to Green Turtle Cay a few weeks after Hurricane Dorian ravaged the island. Neither Mac nor most of his friends were the kind of guys to keep in touch just for the sake of it. Facebook might have bridged that gap for some, but not Mac or Pip.

"Good idea. He's probably sick of rebuilding his house." Mac could only imagine how that was going. Pip was a retired contractor, which often made for a difficult customer. Mac picked up his phone, found the contact info, and pressed connect.

"Yo yo. Mac Travis calling me?"

"Hey, old man. How's it going?"

"This, that, and the other thing. Need me to put up a few refugees again?" Pip laughed.

He was referring to the past fall, when Mac had sent Trufante and Commander to put some time and distance between them and the local authorities, with the hope that a legal issue would resolve itself—or at least cool off. He looked around the table, thinking Pip would much prefer hosting Mel and Pamela.

"You know where we lost *Ghost Runner*?"

"Etched in my brain. You go over and have a look?"

"Yeah. Pretty much decided to give up on salvaging her, but found something else in the process."

"And this is a 'not on the phone kind of thing'?"

"You could say that. Did you replace your boat yet?"

"So, here's the thing. Downscaled the house and bought a Freeman. Nothing like an insurance payoff to change your priorities." Pip laughed again.

Mac wondered how he had done that, but knew the old man was crafty. He had to have dropped a couple hundred grand to buy the custom boat. A quick calculation told him that Pip might be living in a trailer. "You're not doing all the work on the house yourself?"

"I got some help."

Seeing what Pip had created without real tradesmen would be worth the trip—as would seeing the Freeman. There were two types of contractors: those who did the hands-on work themselves, and those who pointed. Pip was in the latter category. He was very good at it, though, and had done well for himself. "Airport over in Marsh running flights?"

"You got the internet. Lemme know when to pick you up."

Mac thanked Pip and disconnected. Pip lived on one of the barrier islands separating the Sea of Abaco, a shallow-water estuary, from the Atlantic Ocean. There might be a seaplane base or private strip on the island, but the closest commercial airport was across the water in Marsh Harbor.

"Can you see about getting a flight over to Marsh?" Mac asked Mel.

"You know it's going to cost you to have your attorney book your flights," she answered. She pulled up the Silver Airways website and started scanning. "They have a warning about closing down travel. If we're going, we better do it now."

Mac wasn't sure he was ready to pull the trigger yet. He expected to hear from Rudy before too long. He checked his watch. The gangster should have easily made it back to Marathon by now. But action was better than sitting here. If they didn't use the tickets, they would take a credit. "Okay. First flight out."

"Wait, I can't," Pamela said. "But I have to get over there."

Mac suspected that she didn't have much more than a driver's license—if she had that. He'd only gotten a passport himself after Mel insisted.

"You can take the Surfari back over," Mel said. "Might be useful and then we can figure out how to see Tru."

Mac wondered what had gotten into Mel. Pamela had come a long way with her boating skills, but a single-handed crossing was not a walk in the park. He quickly put things in perspective, and decided that while the boat meant nothing to him, her life did.

"I know you want to be there, but it would really help if you stayed here and coordinated things. I'll check the wreck and Mel will see what she can do about Tru."

"That'll work, Mac Travis."

"So, book 'em, Dano?" Mel asked.

"We're a go. I'll call Pip." Mac picked up his phone. Just as he was about to search his contacts, it rang.

"My old friend, Mac Travis. Here's the deal."

19

Wood's Island

THE ONLY THING MAC COULD THINK WHEN HE DISCONNECTED THE call was, *What if the gold isn't in the plane?* The other option was to rescue Ned outright, but he didn't have the firepower. There was no question that Rudy's threat was real, and the only way Mac could see to get Ned back lay inside the belly of a plane buried under sixty years of coral growth.

There was every chance—probably more than Mac wanted to admit—that the plane he had discovered had nothing to do with Batista or the mob. From what Ned said, there were only so many Marauders in this part of the world. Ned might have been able to figure out if the plane off Chub Cay was the real deal or not, but without the old man's expertise, it would take time and resources that Mac didn't have. There was also the possibility that he had discovered only a part of the plane. Many of the WWII-era wrecks had broken up on impact, with their parts strewn across acres of ocean floor.

Mac was thankful he had anticipated Rudy's demands. If he could stay a step ahead of him, they might stand a chance. At least making a show of retrieving whatever was inside the plane, would buy them some time. Mac doubted that Rudy had any idea what it took to salvage a wreck—in fact, Mac was counting on it. What he hadn't figured on was that he had involved Pip in something dangerous.

Mel had booked two seats on the first plane out, but the process of getting from the island to the airport in Miami took at least six times longer than the hourlong flight to the Bahamas. And that was if everything went right. Once they were packed, Mac brought the two carry-ons down to the dock and loaded them aboard the center console. Taking the motorsailer would have left Pamela with a more functional boat, but the two-hour trip to Marathon in *Sea Runner* would blow their timeline. As she saw them off, Mac reminded her that Jesse McDermitt was only a few miles away. He had an array of boats, and as Mac's closest neighbor, they were always willing to help each other. It had been Jesse who rescued them from the wreck last fall.

Pamela waved and tossed the dock lines to Mel. It was midnight when they pulled away from the dock.

With the next dozen hours of his life planned out, Mac relaxed as best he could—which was not at all. Though it was a beautiful night with the moonlight reflecting off the calm water, he found it hard to enjoy now that Ned was in jeopardy. Even with Mel by his side, ready to share another adventure, he was neither excited nor happy.

At least Rudy had been smart enough not to put a time limit on the recovery. Mac had been in several forty-eight-hours-or-they-die scenarios, and had spent more time worrying about the clock than about what he needed to be doing. The downside was, the leniency came more as a result of technology than trust. With the ability to track Mac through his phone, boat, or who-knew-what-else, Rudy could watch him in real time. If Mac strayed from his demands, Rudy would know instantly.

"He's going to be alright," Mel said, reading his mind. "Even Rudy won't harm an old man."

Mac doubted her, but kept it to himself. "I'm not so sure that Rudy is our only problem. He's not the top of the food chain. If the mob guys are involved, they could care less about body counts."

"I get that, but Rudy is holding him. At least that's something."

Mac shrugged. Mel knew the smuggler by reputation. He was sure that if she'd met him and seen the sadistic look in his eyes she would be more concerned. Maybe that was for the better, though. He didn't need her all stressed out—it was bad enough he was.

Mac steered by memory, only occasionally checking the chartplotter. Once the lights on the bridge were visible, he veered toward port and the mainland. A quarter mile off the coast, he cut the wheel to the avoid the shoal and headed east. Following the shoreline, he ran for a few miles, until he saw the old Faro Blanco lighthouse. Just ahead he could make out the two pilings marking the entrance to the 33rd Street Boat Ramp and the Yacht Club. Checking his watch as they passed the first set of markers, Mac saw that at least the first phase of the trip was on schedule. He pulled into an empty slip and secured the boat. They dragged their bags across the dock and parking lot to the grassy field where the old pickup lived. Mac unlocked the doors, tossed the bags in the back, and as he started the truck, said a prayer under his breath that the vehicle would make it to Miami.

Best case, they had a two-hour-plus drive ahead of them. With only two lanes servicing the seventy miles between Marathon and Florida City, the first town on the mainland, the worst case was not even worth thinking about. A single wreck could close the road in both directions and cause them an hours'-long delay.

Mac generally dreaded the drive, but at this time of night it was quiet, with most of the traffic made up of long-haul truckers trying to get in or out of the islands before the tourists hit the roads. Incoming traffic was especially light. The reason became evident when they reached the stretch of the highway just east of the Card Sound Road turnoff. A blockade was being placed along the incoming lanes.

"What's that about?" Mac asked.

"Got to show ID that you're a resident or own property here to get in."

"Can they do that?"

"I'm not really sure if they can do a lot of what they're doing now."

Mac hoped that their drivers' licenses would be enough to regain entry, though he knew if they came back by plane something had probably gone wrong. He had thought about asking Jesse to fly them over, but Mac hadn't yet returned the favor from the rescue last fall. He had decided to save any new favors from the former Marine for an emergency.

The officers manning the checkpoint at the county line didn't even glance over when they drove by. As they passed the barricades, Mac saw that their hands were full. Already cars were being turned away.

They continued through the main strip of Florida City and entered the turnpike. Besides the usual construction, it was a speed-limit ride to State Road 836, where Mac exited and headed east. Another few miles, and they had reached a very quiet Miami International Airport.

Leaving the truck in long-term parking would cost a fortune, but Mac was not going to search for an off-site lot and play the shuttle game. He parked, then they wheeled their bags for what felt like miles, even with the moving sidewalks to help. Finally they reached security, where a stern-faced woman stood in front of a podium and eyed them suspiciously.

Mel took over. She handed over their passports and showed her their boarding passes on her phone. The woman gave Mac a long look when comparing his likeness to the picture, but eventually accepted that it was him. Finally, she nodded and allowed them to the next step on the trail of degradation. At least, it was quick work for Mac to take off his flip-flops, and after placing them, his phone, and his keys in a tray, he hoisted their bags onto the conveyor belt and waited his turn to go through the metal detector.

The TSA agent nodded him through, and he waited while his bag went back and forth through the x-ray machine.

"What'd you pack?"

"Same as you. Change of clothes and dive stuff."

"Like a knife?"

The mention of the word turned heads, and Mac nodded as his bag was pulled onto the separate off-ramp, where another agent took it to a small table.

"Any sharp objects?" the agent asked, as he unzipped the bag.

"Dive knife. I haven't traveled in a while and forgot."

The man shook his head while he opened the bag. Riffling through it, he removed the blade. "You can check the bag if you want to keep it. Otherwise, I'll have to toss it."

Mac tried to restrain himself, but accepted that the knife was lost. Mel's travel policy was to never, ever, ever, check a bag. After what he thought was a useless exercise in re-running the bag back through the machine, it was returned to him. He retrieved his flip-flops and phone and scrambled to catch up with Mel.

"Forget it. Let's find the gate."

They had actually made record time, and with several hours

until the flight, the small-plane terminal was quiet. Mac tried to get comfortable in the rigid chairs, but found himself fidgeting. Mel didn't seem to notice. She was ensconced in her phone.

"Shit," she said.

"What?"

"They're not allowing any foreigners into the Bahamas."

20

A MAC TRAVIS ADVENTURE

WOOD'S HOPE

Miami International Airport

Before Mac could react, a uniformed woman stepped behind the desk, and the LED monitor behind her came to life.

Mac squinted. "Says it's on time?"

"Put on your glasses and give me your passport."

Mac handed her his paperwork and watched her walk to the stand. Mel spoke to the woman and handed her their passports. A minute later, the attendant returned the documents, and Mel walked back to where they were seated.

"Last flight. We got lucky, but it's overbooked. They'll bounce us in a hot second if there are residents returning home."

The lounge was filling up quickly now. Mac could guess by the way they were dressed, or their accents, that many of people were Bahamians, but others were too hard to identify. A thought interrupted his survey. He dug through his backpack and found an orange passport-sized booklet.

"Don't do anything stupid," Mel warned.

Mac glanced back. "It's not like that. I have an idea." He turned back to the line forming at the podium and took his place at the end. It appeared to be mostly people checking on the status of the flight, and Mac was quickly at the counter.

"I heard the flight was overbooked." He extended his USCG 100 Ton Master Captain's credential. "I've got a contract that is time dependent. They want a cruise ship moved out of port. You know, the virus thing and all."

The woman had probably heard all kinds of excuses, but she indulged Mac and took the credential. Comparing it to what appeared to be a passenger manifest, she checked off his name. "Are you traveling alone?"

"No, Melanie Woodson is with me."

The woman moved down the list to the last entry and placed a check mark there. "I'll see what I can do." She smiled and handed the Merchant Marine credential back to Mac.

He thanked her and returned to their seats. "See what happens."

"What'd you tell her?"

"Top secret." He put the credential back in his pack.

An announcement soon came over the speakers, asking for volunteers to take a gift certificate in lieu of the flight. No one answered the first call, but when she changed it to a cash offer and upped the ante, several people approached the desk. Mac breathed a sigh of relief and, a few minutes later, they found themselves ushered outside and down a yellow-lined path to the boarding ladder of the small plane.

Once they were airborne, Mac leaned forward and looked out the window. It was interesting to him to see the water from above. After takeoff, the plane made a sweeping turn as it ascended. Mac saw the beaches ahead. The tip of South Beach and Government Cut were just past them. Five minutes after takeoff, they had left land behind. The rising sun obscured the color changes that identified the reef systems off the coast, but he soon saw a current rip, which indicated the edge of the Gulf Stream.

Mac relaxed and closed his eyes. He jerked awake when an announcement came over the PA system.

"Good nap?"

Mac shook his head to get the cobwebs out. He felt more tired now than before. He turned and looked out the window. "Look, there's Marsh Harbor."

Mac watched as the plane went "feet dry" over the harbor, which was more an outpost than a city, and left the turquoise waters behind. Though this wasn't a cruise ship port, the water was quiet. As the plane descended and turned to land, Mac noticed how few cars were on the road. As the plane dropped to the runway, he studied the terrain.

"Can't wait to get out of here." Evidence of Dorian's destruction was still visible, especially from the air. Many of the buildings had been repaired, but a good number still had blue tarps covering their roof framing. The landscape was where the storm's wrath was most evident now. Mac knew the vegetation would take years to come back. Going on three years after Hurricane Irma, many of the outer islands in the Keys, including his own, still showed signs of the storm. His small island, like every other bit of land between Key West and Islamorada, had been submerged in the storm surge. Many of the leaves had grown back, and with every season, green growth replaced the brown and grays. The same would happen here.

Mac felt his stomach drop and gripped the armrest as the wheels skidded onto the pavement. The plane fishtailed and slowed down enough to turn and taxi to the terminal.

"Now, if we can just get past immigration."

Marathon

"I ain't in the mood to watch him sleep. You got me down here, now maybe you better explain why."

Rudy had given the boss man just enough information to ensure he would make the drive from Miami. He walked over to the recliner where Ned was sleeping and tapped him on the shoulder. Ned's head popped up from its place on his chest.

"Why you got an old man tied up?"

Rudy turned to the speaker. As the man paced back and forth across the tile floor, the tapping of the expensive leather shoes of Dominic Luciano was starting to annoy him.

"Ain't worth taking any chances. He may be old, but he's still feisty." Rudy looked down at the marks on his arm from where Ned had tried to escape his grasp.

"You really think his buddies found the plane?"

Ned appeared alert now. "Is that what this is about? Well, you've got the wrong guy. What's an old fart like me going to do for you?"

"I'm guessing Travis will do whatever it takes to see that you're safe."

Luciano stopped and turned to face both men. "Enough of the bickering. Tell me a story, old man."

"I got a lot of stories. Which one do you want to hear?"

"You're right, he is feisty," Luciano said. He turned to Ned. "Do you know who I am?"

"This is probably one of those situations where it's in my best interest not to."

Luciano laughed. "Don't worry. I don't have my grandfather's mean streak."

"Alright, then indulge me, and I'll tell you a story."

"Luciano, Dominic Luciano." He waited, like he'd done this before.

He must have seen the realization in Ned's eyes.

"That's right. Lucky Luciano was my grandfather."

"So, that's the connection. Meyer Lansky stole your grandfather's loot. I thought all you guys changed your names?" Ned asked.

"I took it back. Kind of a trend now. Lansky's grandson is cashing in on his family's name with some gangster museum in Vegas. Not real bright, that one. Who goes to museums in Vegas?"

"Anyway, with Castro and his army knocking on the door of Havana, Batista made a deal with the CIA. That plane your buddy found is loaded with gold—and it belongs to me."

"You think Lansky's family would cause you trouble if you tried to get a permit?" Ned said.

"Maybe not, but the agency would. As for Lansky's family, they're grandstanders. Think the law's on their side. You know they're trying to sue the Cuban government for reparations for the Riviera. Like those commie bastards even have enough to pay for it?"

Rudy watched the exchange between the two men. It was enlightening, to say the least. His lust for revenge had uncovered something much bigger. He'd done some contract work for Luciano. The association made it easy to add two and two together when he'd overheard the conversation about Lansky's treasure.

"I got the coordinates on my boat. What's stopping us from going ourselves?" Rudy was tiring of the conversation. He'd tracked Travis and knew he was in Marsh Harbor now.

"You know how to do this?" Luciano asked.

"Well, I know where it is."

"We've got the old man. Settle down and let your buddy do the work and take the chances."

Rudy nodded. There was no point in fighting about it. In

theory, Luciano was right. That didn't change his plans, though. He wanted to be there when the loot came up, and as soon as Travis had finished the task, Rudy would take care of him.

"If we're just going to sit here, I'm going to check on the boat."

Luciano nodded and sat on the couch. "Might want to make some breakfast first."

Rudy stomped into the kitchen. Despite his own hunger, he didn't like being bossed around. He thought about pouring some cold cereal into a bowl and handing it to the gangster, but knew Luciano well enough to be wary of getting his temper up. As he started to peel apart the bacon strips and place them in the skillet, Rudy realized he had overplayed his hand. All the gangster had to do was sit here, babysit the old man, and wait for Travis to call. He didn't really need Rudy or his boat.

The knowledge that he could be cut out of the deal changed his perspective. What he needed was an excuse to get out of here and pursue this on his own. The old man had said the treasure aboard the plane was worth billions. If he could snake it away from Travis before Luciano found out, he could disappear a wealthy man. If he failed, as long as he had Luciano's blessing for leaving, there was no loss.

"Turn on the fan before you set off all the damned smoke detectors," Luciano yelled across the room.

Rudy returned the demand with an annoyed look, which he was thankful didn't register with the mobster. Turning his attention back to breakfast, he flipped the bacon strips and started to break the eggs into a bowl while imagining they were, alternately, Luciano's and Travis's heads he was cracking. It was so enjoyable that he had cracked the entire dozen before he stopped and poured the mixture into a hot pan.

As he stirred the eggs, an idea came to him, but it would

have to wait until after breakfast. With the eggs at the proper consistency, he plated the food and brought it to the table.

Luciano sat down. "Full service, very nice." He took a bite of the eggs and grimaced. "What the fuck? There's pieces of shell in here." He spat it out.

Rudy smiled inside. "Sorry. I'm not much of a cook." He looked over at Ned, who was moving the eggs around his plate. Whether the old man ate was not a concern. He turned back to Luciano. "You're good if I go down and work on the boat?"

"What the fuck do I care? I'll order takeout for lunch."

Rudy finished his eggs, fighting past the broken shells just to make a point, and took his plate to the kitchen. He'd had his fun with the gangster, but didn't want to incur any further wrath, so he cleared the other men's plates and cleaned the kitchen before heading downstairs.

For whatever reason, the more custom the boat, the more maintenance it took, which had forced Rudy to become adept at most repairs. The annual service fees on four engines alone climbed into the thousands. He had learned to do most things himself, except for the computer circuitry that boats now relied on. The work was only an excuse to escape, though, but as the boat was visible from the living room of the house, he needed to make it look real.

After pulling the cowling from the starboard engine, he made a show of checking the fittings. In his line of work, he was vigilant with maintenance and serviced the engines every hundred hours, although it was less than fifty now. Happy to be away from Luciano, he played around with the first engine for a few more minutes before replacing the cowling and moving to the next engine. He figured he'd have to at least get to the third engine before he found the "problem" that would give him an excuse to leave.

STEVEN BECKER

A MAC TRAVIS ADVENTURE

WOOD'S
HOPE

Marsh Harbor

THE MARSH HARBOR AIRPORT WAS QUIET AND THE IMMIGRATION line short. That didn't help Mac's anxiety any. He always felt people tended to work to the level of the demand placed on them. If the line had been longer, he was sure the immigration officers would be less thorough inspecting documents. With only the two-dozen people from the small plane, and most of those being residents, he suspected the officials would take their time with each person. Government workers seemed to have a mindset that, as long as they looked busy, their jobs were safe. This was certainly the case here, as the line crept along.

It had been Mel's idea to travel "separately," instead of as a household. The designation was a gray area, with no real determination that people actually lived together. She had decided to use the loophole to their advantage. If one of them, most likely Mac, was detained, the other would be unencumbered and allowed through.

Mac was nervous. If the cursory inspection in Chub Cay had been logged, he would be listed as still in the country. It wouldn't look right for him to show up on an international flight when he was still supposed to be here. The anxiety increased as the woman in front of him was escorted to a small office by another officer.

The officer signaled for Mac to step forward. With his customs and immigration form inserted in front of the passport page with his picture, he placed them on the desk and stood back. The officer opened the small book and glanced up at him. Mac waited while he thumbed through the empty pages.

"First visit here?"

Mac wasn't sure what to say and decided on a prearranged lie. "It's been a while. Don't think I've been here since I renewed the passport."

The officer looked back at the page, probably looking for the date of issuance. Mac was lucky it was relatively new. Another glance at him, then back to the passport, and the officer stamped a fresh page.

"Enjoy your stay, sir."

Mac breathed deeply as he thanked the officer, retrieved his documents, and moved quickly to the exit. Mel was already there.

"Any trouble?"

"All good." Mac didn't want to recount the necessary lie. He scanned the arrival area for a taxi and found a small building across the road with several brightly colored cabs parked in front. Mel pulled her bag easily across the pavement, but Mac's wasn't liking the rough surface, and he picked it up and carried it across the road, where they approached a cab.

"Can you take us to the harbor?"

"Sure thing, mon. That all your luggage?"

"Yes." Mac helped him load the carry-ons into the trunk. They got in and the driver pulled away.

Marsh Harbor resembled the majority of Caribbean towns.

Nassau, the largest city in the Bahamas, was more modern, which was one reason he wanted to avoid it. With its cruise ship ports, tourist attractions, multi-story hotels, and fancy restaurants and shops, it was more like Miami than this small town.

As they cruised toward the water, Mac watched the scenery flow by. Square, concrete block houses, mostly single story with rebar sticking out of their flat roofs, were the norm. In order to make room for future generations, the houses were constructed so a second, or even third, story could be added. From what Mac saw, this rarely happened, making for an unfinished look. Many yards had boats on trailers that probably cost more than the home.

The landscape was monotonous and still brown from Dorian. As they approached the harbor, the area became more commercial. After a twenty-minute drive, they reached the harbor.

Mel paid the driver while Mac unloaded the bags from the trunk. Pip's old boat had been lost in the storm, and he scanned the harbor for the new one. The Moorings rental fleet, which usually occupied the majority of the slips, had been decimated by the storm. Instead of dozens of sailboats bobbing in their slips, most of the boats lay scattered, like a game of pick-up sticks, in a lot across the street.

When Mac saw a cloud of smoke and heard country music coming from a large center console, he knew it was Pip. He pulled their bags across the uneven asphalt, hoping that the small wheels survived the trip. After a few feet he gave up and carried them toward a wheelbarrow sitting at the entrance to the dock.

Pip was perched on one of the three seats built into the leaning post, smoking a cigar. His feet were propped up on the console.

"Hey, old man," Mel called from the dock.

Pip popped up and moved to the gunwale. Mac noticed he seemed more agile than the last time they had seen each other.

"Moving pretty well there."

"Miracle, is what it is. Gave me a shot of some plasma shit. Feel twenty years younger." Pip reached over the wide gunwale and slung the bags into the boat.

Mac and Mel dropped to the deck. "Nice ride."

"Don't tell the wife." Pip laughed. "Here's the thing. Rebuilt the house about half the size and doubled the size of the boat. Figured I only got one more boat in me. Might as well make it memorable."

"That it is. I'd like to see your place, but if we could head to the site, I'd like to try and pull the serial number off the wreck."

"No problem. Got her gassed up and ready to go." Pip fired up the quad 300HP engines. "Got about a hundred-mile run, so you might as well get comfortable."

The Bahamas were similar to the Keys, where it was rare that you could travel in a straight line to get anywhere, though this trip wasn't as bad as some. Pip idled out of the marina and followed the markers, which kept him in the dredged channel. When they cleared the point, he turned to starboard and accelerated.

Mac was sucked back into his seat as the boat rocketed forward. By the time he located their speed on the display, they were already going forty-five knots. The low whine of the engines hid the monstrous force that propelled the boat forward. He could sense the speed increase further after Pip adjusted the tilt and trim. Skimming on top of the waves, the boat sliced through the crests ahead like they were butter.

"Rides nice," Mac called over the engine noise. He was surprised he didn't have to yell.

"Shit, wait till we clear the corner." Pip clamped the cigar in his mouth and winked.

Pip held the speed steady until they were around the southern point of the island. Turning slightly to starboard, he adjusted the route to the coordinates where *Ghost Runner* had gone down. With a straight run, and only deep water ahead until they reached the reef, Pip accelerated again. Mac felt the g-force and relaxed back into the seat. A glance at the screen told him their speed was up to sixty knots. The ETA showed as eleven o'clock, only an hour and twenty minutes away.

While they sped toward the site, Mac's thoughts turned to boats. He didn't need anything this fast, though he'd decided that the Surfari was too slow. Cruising at ten knots might be relaxing, but it wasn't in Mac's DNA to do it for long. In many ways, *Ghost Runner* had been perfect, and he thought about how to improve on her design. That naturally brought his train of thought to what he was going to need the new boat to do.

He was pretty much over commercial fishing. Since he could remember, it had been a crapshoot. Either the fishing or the market was bad; it was a rare occurrence when they were aligned. The last few years, with the Chinese buying lobster at inflated rates, had been lucrative, but as with all bubbles, it had burst.

Salvage was still possible, but Mac loathed the regulations. The depressing realization of how both his livelihoods no longer suited him was barely overshadowed by the exhilaration of riding aboard Pip's boat. He glanced at the display to see that they were less than an hour away. Mac had always been able to compartmentalize his thoughts and worries, especially when it allowed him to procrastinate. He did this now and started to concentrate on the coming dive.

Marathon

Rudy figured he had spent enough time on the ruse. He placed the cowlings back on the engines, stepped onto the gunwale, and crossed to the dock. Rehearsing what he was going to say to Luciano, he climbed the stairs to the main floor of the house and entered through the sliding glass door.

"I got some trouble."

"Doesn't surprise me with a boat like that."

Rudy bit his tongue and tried to sound humble. "Sometimes I think you're right. Something with the circuit board on one of the engines."

"Better get it taken care of. If we don't need it for the job, I got some strippers lined up in Miami that would love a booze cruise."

Rudy gave him his best fake smile. "I'm gonna run it to the marina and see if the mechanic can have a quick look."

"Stay in touch. I'll keep an eye on old folks here."

Rudy glanced at Ned, who looked to be asleep again. He wished he could sleep like that. "Be back soon." Rudy grabbed two bottles of water from the refrigerator and headed back out. Getting Luciano's permission was a small step toward his plan. He wasn't going to get excited yet, but at least he had an excuse to leave.

Hopping aboard, he started the engines and released the dock lines. As he idled out of the canal, he fought the temptation to look back. If he were going to get this done, his focus would need to stay ahead of the game. It was no big deal at this point, but when he wasn't back by dinner, he would have some explaining to do—he needed a plan for that.

Fuel docks were an issue for someone in his line of work. The old timers used to stash caches of jerry cans on some of the remote keys to fuel the smugglers' boats. But his go-fast boat required hundreds of gallons, which meant using a fuel dock. As a result, he'd cultivated many friendships with the attendants over the years. On the surface, pumping fuel might seem like a low-level job, but to the smart attendants it was a career. Knowing how to shuffle boats in and out to maximize tips was lucrative. It often took hours to fill the larger sport fishers and yachts, making it a priority for the captains and owners to access the docks quickly. With a half-day often in the balance, time was money. So was being able to fuel the smugglers' fleet after hours.

Once into the harbor, he settled into a fast idle in the direction of Burdine's Fuel Dock. Of the three docks available here, he found the attendants at Burdine's most likely to move him to the front of the line. It would cost him a hundred but, if you looked at it from the perspective of a four-figure fuel bill, it was a reasonable tip. This time of day, there was seldom an empty spot, and when he arrived there were two sport fishers and a sailboat occupying the dock space. Rudy dropped to neutral and caught the eye of the attendant, who smiled, showing a row of ragged teeth, and raised a single finger.

With the threat of the boat ramps and marinas being shut down, it looked like everyone was trying to top off their tanks. Several sailboats, a center console, and a handful of jet skis were all waiting their turn. Rudy used the size and power of his boat to push the jet skis aside and slid into a position to scoot into the dock when the sailboat left. The sport fishers were already gassing up, but they had tanks larger than his. The attendant knew his business and was trying to move the sailboat out to get Rudy in.

There was a clear pecking order with boaters, which had sailboats and jet skis on the bottom. As such, it was no surprise when the attendant motioned for Rudy to dock before them. He greeted the rail-thin woman, whose skin resembled a sun-dried raisin with a smile, and reached for the nozzle.

The Wreck Site

MAC RECALLED THE SAYING *YOU NEVER STEP FOOT IN THE SAME RIVER twice*. The ocean was much the same. The wind had come up, and there were small whitecaps on the majority of the waves. Pip's Freeman handled them without a second thought, where many boats might not have. Even at anchor, the boat, with its vented hull, rocked far less than a standard V hull. The boat had ridden so well on the trip that Mac had barely noticed the building weather conditions until they stopped.

"Got four tanks; two in each side."

Mac hoped that would get the job done—he didn't have a plan B.

Pip clipped the end off his cigar into the water before lighting it. "Clear as it is, I can't believe no one found it yet."

Now that they knew what was below, the shape was obvious. But with thousands of square miles of dive-able water here, there was every chance that the reef had never had human eyes on it. "I'm gonna gear up and have a look. What do you have for tools? Security at the airport took my knife."

"You tried to bring a knife through security? So, here's the thing. There ain't much on this boat I can fix. Might have a screwdriver, though."

"I'll take whatever you have." Mac had seen the old-style lead weights Pip had stored below. They were every bit a tool—or weapon.

Mac pulled the dive gear from the hold and assembled it, making every effort not to mar the boat's finish. Tanks, especially, had a mind of their own at sea, and were capable of creating a ding or divot wherever they touched. The boat was a dream cruising and fishing platform, but a little too delicate for Mac. With a tendency to be hard on his boats and gear, he needed steel beneath his feet.

Diving a new boat for the first time called for several decisions, and the answer to the first one was to enter the water from the bow. The sets of twin engines were separated due to the catamaran hull design, allowing ample space between them for a pull-out ladder. There was enough room to board, but Mac didn't want to enter the water that close to the engines. He checked it out for re-entry, but was unsure of the footing. He decided on removing his BC and tank in the water and handing it up. In the rocking seas, it would be all too easy to slip off one of the narrow ladder rungs and smash a cowling.

Pip had supplied a screwdriver. Mac carried twelve pounds of weight in the integral sleeves built with a quick-release mechanism if he needed to dump the weights in an emergency. In addition, he had two extra four-pound weights in the outer pockets. He worked with Pip to anchor the boat with the stern directly above the sand, near where he guessed the cockpit area of the plane was, and as with his previous dive, he chose to go with only booties.

Mac placed the regulator in his mouth, and with one hand

covering the mouthpiece and mask and the other around the hoses and gauges, he dropped backwards over the side. The twenty pounds of weight took him directly to the bottom, making him thankful the bow was over sand and not coral. Once he gained his footing, he started walking toward the reef.

The seven-mil thick booties he had brought were more suited for cold-water diving, but he wanted the additional protection of the heavy neoprene. In addition, he wore the three-mil suit he had brought in his bag. Walking as carefully as he could, he took a few tentative steps toward the center of the reef, where he expected the cockpit laid. The layers of coral seemed to peel away and the plane came to life in his mind's eye. Two humps appeared in a line before him, probably what was left of the engines.

Mac stepped onto what he thought would be a wing of the plane and moved toward the cockpit, knowing there was every chance that the glass windshield had broken on impact. He'd spent time online and had found an old training video that he used to familiarize himself with the design of the plane. Mac noticed a downward slope in the coral and expected that was the windshield. On most planes, this would be the logical point of entry, but the Marauder had a transparent nose where a gunner was stationed. If he could reach that area, it would be a much larger opening than the cockpit glass.

The coral looked heavier around the nose than the cockpit, but Mac decided to try anyway. As he suspected, the nose must have broken on impact and the coral had invaded the gunner's compartment. He moved back to the windshield and tried to envision it in his mind.

Mel had scoured the internet looking for the location of the manufacturer's tag with the serial number, but had found nothing. A search had turned up a place called Fantasy of Flight between Tampa and Orlando that displayed one of the few surviving Widowmakers.

The name came not from combat operations, but training accidents. The plane performed well but had a reputation for being unforgiving. Mac suspected that might be the reason this one had crashed. If he were flying billions in gold and loot around, he would certainly do it "under the radar," and with the plane's reputation for performing poorly at low altitudes, any error might have put them into the sea.

The man that Mel had spoken to at Fantasy of Flight had checked their plane and told her the tag was located by the navigator's station. From Mac's research, that would require he penetrate the aircraft, making the job all the more difficult.

Knowing the coral would grow back was some consolation, as he removed the screwdriver and one of the extra weights from the BC. The viscosity of the water muted his attempts, but the weight was heavy enough to do its work, and pieces of coral began to fall away.

Between the primitive tools and the force of the water, the work was tedious. He continued, determined to gain access, or at least determine if access was possible, on this dive. Taking a break, he stepped back and thought he could see the shape of the windshield emerging. That was reassuring, but when he checked the air gauge and saw he had only 500 PSI remaining, he realized that the exertion had increased his air consumption beyond what he planned.

Still, he figured he had another fifteen minutes and went back to work. As each piece fell away, the shape became more distinct. Knowing he was so close made it more difficult. With his limited air supply and only a few more tanks aboard Pip's boat, he needed to go slowly and work with measured blows. Mac started using a breathing pattern to conserve what was left in his tank. Inhaling for four counts, he held his breath and hit the screwdriver. Then, after slowly releasing his breath for a count of eight, he held his breath for several heartbeats before starting the process over. The measured blows and conservation seemed to be working, and after a few minutes, he saw something manmade appear through the coral crust.

A few more strikes, this time at more of an angle, revealed the thick glass. Working the screwdriver as a chisel between the glass and the coral quickly exposed a section of the windshield. Without a light, Mac was unable to see the condition of the interior, but with the glass intact, he assumed it would be a better entry point than his original plan of coming in through the nose. He had no choice but to shatter the glass, and with several hard strikes at the same spot, it began to crumble.

With a gloved hand, Mac started to pull away the loose material. In order to do so, he needed to put his fingers in the cockpit, and it was a few long moments before he realized that they had met no resistance. This section of the interior had not been breached. With that realization, Mac set the screwdriver and weight against a small coral outcropping and stepped away from the plane.

His admired his work, much like a sculptor removing the rock that hid his creation. In both cases, destruction was needed to reveal what lie beneath, and with some satisfaction, Mac inflated his BC and floated toward the surface.

He had been right about the ladder and asked Pip to throw a line. Releasing some air from his BC, Mac unbuckled the straps and pulled away the Velcro cummerbund before rolling forward. The gear floated to the surface, and he swam it to the line, attached it to one of the D rings, and climbed out of the water.

"Any luck?" Mel asked.

"Down there long enough, I'm into my second cigar," Pip said.

"I reached the cockpit. Next tank, I should be able to get inside. It looks clear."

"You should take a break, Mac. There's plenty of daylight."

Mac felt the breeze against his skin and looked around. The Freeman had hidden the deteriorating sea conditions. "It's too shallow. I'm worried the visibility is gonna go to shit if it kicks up much more."

Pip looked over the side. "Boy's got a point."

Mac went forward and pulled a tank out of the hold. Out of habit, he checked the valve, only to find that it was open. "Hey. Dead soldier here."

Pip came forward and shook his head. "Ain't checked them since the storm, and it was Trufante and that other one who put them up." Pip kneeled on the deck and removed a tank from the adjacent hold. "Shit." Nothing came out when he cracked the valve.

Placing the blame did nothing to help Mac, who was down to one tank—if that wasn't in the same condition. Moving to the starboard side, he checked the hold and pulled out the lone tank. At least the valve was closed, but he wasn't going to pass judgment until he put a gauge on it. Pip had already pulled the BC off the old tank. He handed it to Mac, who slid the vest over the cylinder and fastened the buckle, then screwed the first stage onto the valve. Turning the valve slightly, he was reassured when he heard air rush into the hoses. He glanced at the gauge and saw the red needle just a hair over the 3,000 PSI mark.

"This one's got a good fill." Mac checked the hoses and lifted the tank so it sat on the coffin cooler forward of the console. Pip was right there and held the tank while Mac slipped into the vest. He glanced around the boat looking for Mel and saw her deep in her phone. The boat's Wi-Fi obviously worked here.

"There's a dive light in my bag."

"Hold this. There's barely room for my fat head in there." Pip handed Mac the cigar and opened the door. The boat had more than enough storage but, because of the catamaran design, the console was small.

His head disappeared, and after a few colorful curses, he pulled Mac's bag out. He opened it on the deck and found the light. "What else?"

Mac thought about what he needed to do. "Maybe the slate too." There was no way he was going to remember the serial number. Pip handed it to him. Mac attached the gear to his BC and spun one hundred eighty degrees to sit on the gunwale. Once he was situated, he rolled backward into the water.

With only one tank remaining, he wasted no time and went directly to the cockpit. The opening was large enough for his body, but not the gear. Mac was prepared for this, and with the regulator clamped in his mouth, he removed the BC. It was awkward dragging the tank in with him, and he was so focused on making sure it didn't snag, that the two skeletons clothed in the rags of their old uniforms startled him.

Aware that the plane had a five-man crew, he prepared himself to meet the other three and made his way back to the navigator's desk. He hoped, as the flight wasn't a combat mission, that the pilot and copilot were the only crew. Surely there was no need for gunners or a navigator on the short flight. The cockpit had been open to this point, but the force of the crash had pushed everything that was loose toward the navigator's station, where the plate was. Mac started moving the debris away from the opening to the compartment, only to find that a bulkhead had caved in. He could see the plate, but not get close enough to read the numbers unless he removed the mouthpiece.

Mac checked the air gauge, only to find that he had again expended more energy than he planned. It was into the red area.

He was determined, though, and after unclipping the slate and light, he took several deep breaths and released the mouthpiece. As it floated toward the ceiling, he worked his way toward the plate. It was a tight fit, but finally, he could read the numbers and wrote them down on the slate.

STEVEN BECKER

A MAC TRAVIS ADVENTURE

WOOD'S
HOPE

The Wreck Site

MAC EASED HIMSELF BACK TOWARD THE COCKPIT AND RETRIEVED
the regulator. He took a deep breath and started to slip through
the opening he had made. He worked until he was free of the
wreck and pulled the tank out behind him. There was no need
to check his air or waste the time and energy to put his gear back
on. With the boat directly above, Mac inflated the BC, held the
shoulder straps, and allowed the vest to float him to the surface.

Pip was there to take the gear, and Mel reached over to grab
the slate that was clutched in his hand. Mac climbed out of the
water and went directly to the helm, where Mel's laptop sat.
There was only a small chance the plane was Cuban, and a
match wouldn't confirm there was treasure aboard, but it would
make it worth the effort to look. If it wasn't the lost plane, they
had a bigger problem than the expenses they had incurred: Mac
had no doubt Rudy would hurt Ned.

Standing behind Mel, Mac shielded his eyes from the sun,
knowing his polarized sunglasses would make it harder to see

the screen. Without his now-mandatory readers, it didn't matter. The data was a blur.

"Here it is." Mel pointed at the screen. "Last three numbers are 927—it's a match."

Mac had noticed the odd number when he wrote them down. It was the first indication the plane might be legit, but still had to fall into the range between 901 and 935.

Mac's elation quickly turned to frustration. They were so close, but out of air. There were two choices and neither was appealing. Only one made sense. Running into Chub Cay to get the tanks filled was an option, but a bad one. They could be there in less than an hour, but with the shutdowns and stay-at-home orders, there was no guarantee that the dive shop at the marina would be open. Finding another would require a cab ride. The whole operation was too problematic to consider.

Freediving was an option, and Mac would have considered it if the preliminary work had been done and the loot was actually accessible. As of now, he didn't even know if anything was there. He would have to do a good deal of work to penetrate the plane, and make sure it was safe, to even find it. Mac was glad for the head start they had gotten. Their planning had put them in a position to allow a few hours to expire without risking Ned's life.

The logical thing to do would be to relax and try and get some sleep, but Mac wasn't wired like that. "I'm going back down."

Pip laughed. "I got a few cigars left. Happy to share if you want to make it even harder."

Mel chimed in. "Bad idea, Mac. You need to rest. There's nothing to be accomplished by looking at something you already know is there. And forget about penetrating the fuselage without a tank. If I have to go babysit you, I will."

Mel had won several spearfishing tournaments in high school. Mac knew that even if she hadn't been practicing breath holds, the process was ingrained in her and, more importantly, she wouldn't panic at the first convulsion.

"You win." He sat down with an attitude.

Pip reached into the cooler behind the leaning post and pulled out three Bud Lights. "If we ain't diving, I got some blue Gatorade to take the edge off."

"That's an even worse idea," Mel said.

"Shit, gotta stay hydrated," Pip said, swirling the ice in his Yeti cup. He took a long drink, removed the cover, and poured in a fresh beer.

"You been doing that all day?" Mel asked.

Pip shrugged and sucked on his cigar. The end glowed red, hiding his flushed face.

"He's fine. Remember, we wouldn't be here without him." Mac knew Pip could handle his beer. Hard alcohol was another matter, but he could drink beer all day without ill effects. "We don't have time to wait until tomorrow morning."

Mac opened the top of the cooler. Sorting through the beers to reach a bottle of water, he saw there was less than a six-pack left. "Or enough beer?" Mac wondered if there was any food aboard, and after a quick search, found only a few bags of chips and some jerky. It was at that point when his stomach started to grumble.

Pip pulled hard on his cigar. "Wasn't like you gave me time to provision."

"All right, you two. There's no point sitting out here bobbing around and starving. I say we go in to Chub. If we can fill the tanks, great. If not, we can at least get some food."

"Sounds good to me." Mac went forward while Pip idled over the anchor. Set in the sand outside of the reef, the windlass made short work of bringing the anchor aboard. Mac made sure it was secured and clipped on the safety cable. He returned to the helm and sat beside Pip and Mel. With a glance at his passengers, Pip clamped the butt of the cigar in his mouth and pressed down on the throttles.

Thirty minutes later they reached Chub, only to find the marina closed. Handwritten signs on the pumps and door said that by order of the local government they would be closed until further notice.

"I'm gonna check around back and see if anyone's here." Mac noticed the lines usually provided to tie off with had been removed. He found a line in one of the holds and took it with him onto the dock where he tied off the bow. When he was finished, Pip tossed him a line for the stern.

Mel followed him. "I'm going to see if there's a grocery store open."

"My ass'll be right here. Ain't trustin' my boat in an insurrection, this, that, or whatever this shit is." Pip fired up his cigar.

Mac began to wonder what was going on. He had to admit he was relying only on what Mel had told him, but something felt wrong. Looking around the marina, he noticed a few people sitting on the decks of their boats, enjoying cocktails in the waning sunlight. As far as they were concerned, it was still paradise.

Stepping up from the wooden dock boards to a small rise to the pavement, Mac walked to the building and, seeing no one there, went around to the street side. The dive shop was located in a small outbuilding on the same property. From where he stood, even without glasses, Mac could see the letter-sized sheet of paper posted to the door. He didn't need to read what it said.

There was still a chance, though it wasn't entirely legal. Many small shops had their fill area outside. The compressor, mixing apparatus, filters, and water trough would fill a store's interior, and the noise would be unbearable. Mac smiled when he saw the equipment and tank on the side of the building—until he realized it was locked inside a chain-link enclosure.

He continued toward the cage and lifted the lock to make sure the shackle was engaged. After a good shake, he determined it was, and slammed it against the cage in frustration. As rusted as it was, he half-expected it to release, but it held. Mac continued around the building, searching for any means of entry, until he saw the fill hoses hanging against the chain-link cage. The small fissures between the woven wire had hooks on them that held the coiled hoses.

Mac paused. If he could wiggle the fill valve through the links, he would be halfway towards filling the tanks. The other variable was being able to turn on the compressor. He scanned the equipment. The emergency shutoff was clearly marked, but not the on switch. It might not be needed, though. Compressors used pressure switches with a high and low limit to turn the motor on and off. There was a good chance the unit was on.

Turning his attention back to the hoses, Mac slid his fingers through one of the openings in the cage and reached for the first stage on the end of the line. He was close, but the fencing closed around his hand before he could reach it. After several more attempts he was discouraged, but knew what to do.

Mac headed back to the boat and hopped aboard. He fished the tanks out of the hold and set them on the dock.

"Got air?" Pip asked.

"Got a fair shot at it, but I need Mel."

"What's she gonna do that I can't?"

"Let me see your hands."

Pip hesitated. "Ain't had no time for a manicure." He laid his hands out.

The swollen knuckles and scars were the same as Mac's. "Her hands'll fit."

"What the hell you been drinking?"

"Never mind." Mac saw Mel walking down the dock. He went to help her with the four shopping bags she carried.

"Got there just as they were closing. Apparently they're all freaked about toilet paper here too."

"Anything'll work." Mac didn't care what she bought. Calories were all he needed in the short term.

She handed him two of the bags and glanced at the tanks sitting on the dock. "You found an air fill?"

"Kind of, but I'm gonna need your help."

They handed the bags over to Pip, who scoped out the contents as he brought them aboard.

"What, no beer?"

"'Essential' is the word of the day, and in my opinion, beer is not."

Mac expected a rebuttal, but Pip knew better than to fight with her. With a tank valve in each hand, he walked over to a wheelbarrow, where he set them down. He returned for the last two. Once Mel had handed them over the gunwale, she stepped onto the dock. With the four tanks in the wheelbarrow, they headed back to the fill cage.

Mel stopped at the door of the cage and lifted the lock. "And what is it you need me for?"

"My hands won't fit."

"Is this important enough to be stuck in a jail for two weeks while they quarantine you?"

"Got a couple of twenties?"

Mel eyed him suspiciously, but reached into her pocket and withdrew a roll of bills. She peeled two off the roll and handed them to him.

"Four fills at six bucks and a tip." Mac motioned toward a plastic jug with *Tips* scrawled on it with a Sharpie attached to the screen. He was able to fold the bills in half the long way and insert them through the fence into the container. "Okay?"

"Dammit, Mac. One of these days, this shit is going to backfire."

"One of these days? That would be my whole life."

Mel nodded and reached her hand easily through the cage and grabbed the fill valve. She worked the first stage through the wire, and with an upward jerk, unseated enough hose from the hook to reach the first tank.

Mac tightened the valve. "Moment of truth." He opened the valve and smiled when he heard a stream of air come out. A long second later, the compressor turned on. While Mel watched the pressure gauges mounted on the wall, Mac kept his hand on the tank. Without being able to use the water trough to cool the tanks, they would become dangerously hot before they filled. He decided that if he were able to get 2,500 PSI in each tank, he would be satisfied.

With the commercial equipment, the tank filled quickly, which was partly why it was important to monitor the temperature of the tank. Mac knew he had been lucky to this point, and wasn't about to endanger them with an explosion. As soon as the tank felt warmer than the ambient temperature, he shut off the valve and started on the next.

Within fifteen minutes they were headed back to the boat, only in time to see Pip pushing a wheel barrow loaded down with Bud Light toward the boat.

"I thought we were done with that?" Mel asked.

Pip lifted the single case of water from the top and handed it to Mac. "Gotta stay hydrated."

Mac shook his head and helped load the provisions, and without seeing another person, they were soon pulling away from the marina.

Marathon

RUDY KNEW HE HAD TO MAKE HIS TIME COUNT. HE WAS BALANCED on a knife's edge; one mistake would cut him deep. Dealing with Luciano, he knew the metaphor was more real than abstract.

The sound from the nozzle increased, and Rudy released the lever. He handed it up to the attendant along with a half-dozen hundred-dollar bills. With half of that being her tip, the woman smiled as she cast off the lines and waved the next boat in. Rudy pulled out and pointed the bow to the channel, then stopped. He had an idea, the only downside of which was that it involved Commander.

The bait king ran his business in the same manner as most organized crime ventures. Through intimidation, coercion, and violence, he controlled the fleet of boats that brought fresh bait into the Keys. Smuggling was above his pay grade, and Rudy and Commander's paths had rarely crossed. That was, until the Chinese had driven the price of lobster up to ridiculous levels. Neither man could resist the money. For Rudy, it had been the illegal and forged tags that caused his run-in with Travis. Commander had used the boom to set and harvest casitas.

These manmade features, placed on the sandy bottom of the Gulf, attracted lobster. Made from large-diameter pipes or concrete slabs, the structures resembled the protective habitat that crawfish sought out. Placed in out-of-the-way areas, the attractors were rarely found by the masses skimming behind their boats searching the bottom for the telltale ledges and potholes where lobster were often found. The casual hunters, prevalent during mini season in July and most of August, covered huge swaths of the sea bottom by trolling a pair of snorkelers behind their boats. But come September they were mostly gone, leaving the waters to the commercial fishermen—and the poachers.

Commander used divers to harvest the casitas, which was why Rudy needed him. He pulled up to his dock, careful to place fenders before touching. Once there, he found the bait man holding court around a wire spool in the backyard. Commander saw him approach and hopped out of his chair.

"I need a pair of divers to check out that site Travis was on. And now," Rudy said.

"Wow, slow down, bro. This ain't no temp service."

Rudy felt his anger grow, but knew he needed Commander. "I'll pay and cut you in."

Rudy could tell by the lack of a smart-ass answer that he had the bait king's attention. "Grab two of your buddies who don't talk and as many tanks as you can and meet me in thirty minutes. I'll be here."

He glanced down at the time to see when the deadline expired, but he needn't have worried. Within minutes Commander approached the dock with two men behind him. He waited while the divers carried six tanks and their bags of gear across to the boat.

The boat was equipped for more forgiving cargo. Without a rack, the heavy cylinders would need to go into the holds, where the tanks could easily crush the carbon-fiber panels placed inside to create false bottoms. There was no option but to remove them, and he quickly stashed them in the console before placing the tanks in the holds. Rudy stood up and noticed that even the small movement had caused the tanks to shift and rattle. The Gulf Stream would turn them into missiles. To mitigate the damage, he grabbed a handful of PFDs from the console and wedged them in between the tanks. By the time he was satisfied, Commander and the men had loaded their gear and were making themselves comfortable.

"This here's Troy and Dave."

Rudy nodded at them, not sure who was who, and not caring. "They're good?"

"The best."

Rudy eyed the men. He had no expertise in diving or salvage, but he did know the wreck was in shallow water. Skill would take a backseat to discretion. "They can keep quiet?" He checked out Troy and Dave's tattoos. Everything about them said they were barstool braggarts.

Commander must have read his mind. "Sober for three years —each of them."

Rudy nodded. "We're running across the Gulf Stream to have a look at a wreck. You guys good with that? You recover something, you get a share."

They both nodded.

"Toss them lines." Rudy waited while Commander and Troy released the dock lines. Rudy eased forward and, once clear of the dock, reversed the port-side pair of engines, allowing the boat to spin on its axis. He idled out of the canal and entered the harbor.

"Stay low through here. Always people looking." Rudy

pushed the throttles to a fast idle and continued toward the channel. Once clear of the last marina, he inched them forward again, and moments later the boat was on plane, running for the reef.

On most of his runs, Rudy could choose his weather window. Today he had no choice and gripped the wheel tightly as the four-foot seas knocked the lightweight boat around. He settled into a speed considerably slower than he was used to in order to ease the beating. It would take them another hour or two to reach the site, but he deemed it worthwhile. Troy and Dave appeared to be asleep on the pull-down bench by the transom. Commander had the seat next to his at the helm.

"You sure those guys can keep quiet?"

"Scout's honor, dude. What's the big deal anyway? It's just Travis."

"A little more complicated than that." Rudy thought about how much to tell Commander and decided a little of the truth might act as some insurance for his silence. "A couple of guys from Jersey are interested." Rudy eyed the bait man to make sure he understood the meaning. It was clear he did.

"What's so valuable on *Ghost Runner*? That Russian bitch leave something behind?"

"There's another wreck down there." Rudy figured that in a few hours he was going to know anyway. "An old plane."

"Hot damn. Travis steps in shit every time."

"With any luck, this is going to be the last time." Rudy turned his attention back to the electronics displays. They were almost across the Gulf Stream now, and he checked his radar. The site appeared to be empty, but he knew that the size of the waves they were in could block a significant portion of a small boat's signature. Still, it was encouraging.

Feeling the thrill of the hunt, he started to inch the throttles forward, only backing down when a random six-footer slammed the boat sideways. Dave and Troy were jostled awake, and he heard the sound of the tanks moving in the hold. Rudy was forced to slow down. There was no point getting there faster if they weren't in one piece.

It was noon when they arrived on site. Rudy switched the right-hand display to the depth-finder mode and stared blankly at the screen.

"Dude, you know how to use that?" Commander asked.

The last thing Rudy wanted to admit was that he didn't, but then he had little use for a bottom reader in his line of work. "You keep an eye on it, I'll run the boat."

Rudy was surprised Commander was at least smart enough to not rub his nose in it.

The bait man adjusted some settings. "You got to do a pattern." Commander pointed to the black and white line that showed their track from the earlier visit.

Rudy zoomed in on the furthest point in the small loop. Studying their previous course, he could imagine where the motorsailer had been anchored. He might not know how to work the depth finder, but he was an expert at navigation. In his line of work, that was what mattered.

"We was about fifty feet from Travis's boat when Trufante's bitch started shooting. So, it'd be about there. Creep up on it real slow."

Rudy moved off the track line into virgin territory. He crossed over where he expected the wreck to be.

"Got it." Commander pointed to a shape on the screen.

Rudy had one eye on the display and the other on the water. As he passed over *Ghost Runner's* resting place, he could barely see a few feet into the water. He would have to rely on Commander.

"He dove here, right? But you said they found a plane." Commander looked over the side. "Murky now." He remembered being able to see the reef from the boat yesterday. "Let's work in circles around here and see what we can see."

Rudy's patience was at its limit, both with the tedious search pattern and the man dictating it. The only surprise was that Commander appeared to know what he was doing.

"Here we go."

Rudy glanced at the screen and saw something: a heavy red line above the flat yellow he had been watching.

"Yellow's sand, and the red's the reef. See it rising up?"

"This ain't got x-ray vision. It won't show the plane, will it?"

"I could tinker with the gain and such, but it'd be just as well to throw those boys in the water."

"Go ahead."

"Where's the windlass on this thing?" Commander asked.

Rudy smiled. "Watch this." He flipped a switch and a hatch opened on the foredeck. What looked like a large version of an electric trolling motor rose from inside it and extended itself, then a small, plastic propeller mounted to a long shaft dropped into the water. "GPS."

"No shit. Heard about them anchor lock deals, but never seen one."

"Better than cutting the anchor line when the law shows. Now, get them two ready."

Commander left the helm and spoke to the two divers. A few minutes later, they started assembling their gear. While they worked, Commander approached the helm. "How much should I tell 'em?"

"Let's start with the plane. They find that, we'll take the next step." Rudy planned on dishing out the details in small doses. There was no point in the men knowing what might lie aboard the wreck if they couldn't find it.

A few minutes later, two splashes told Rudy the divers were in the water.

Commander had the sense to distance himself. He stood at the transom staring into the murky water, leaving Rudy alone at the helm, where he glanced at his watch and then his phone. There was nothing from Luciano, though he didn't expect any problems yet—he knew the man was volatile and anything could happen.

"How long they gonna be down there?"

Commander turned away from the water. "Hour probably. Unless they find something first. How far you expecting to go with this operation? We got no real salvage gear."

Rudy wasn't sure what that entailed. "We'll see."

Just as he said it, something broke the surface of the water. Rudy crossed to the starboard gunwale and stood beside Commander. One of the divers had returned.

"Any luck?"

"Sure as shit. Someone's been here already, though."

Rudy smiled at the man's naiveté. Even he couldn't imagine pulling up on a blank piece of water and finding a wreck.

"We're gonna go in and have a look. What is it we're after?"

It was time for Rudy to give them a few more scraps. "About three billion in gold. Shouldn't be hard to find."

STEVEN BECKER

A MAC TRAVIS ADVENTURE

WOOD'S HOPE

The Wreck Site

RUDY SPOTTED A BOAT APPROACHING THE WRECK SITE ON HIS radar. He checked and saw no AIS tag associated with it, but its course was clear. Few would tempt their fate with the shallow-water reefs in this area if it wasn't their destination.

He could tell by the fast speed that is was not a "ship," but a fast boat like his, If the boat maintained its current rate of speed, it would be in sight within twenty minutes. Plenty of time for him to move off. In designing his boat, Rudy had chosen performance over utility. As a result, the boat was lighter and sleeker than a normal vessel. In this case, it would buy him precious minutes.

"You gotta get those boys up."

"Diving ain't my gig," Commander said.

"It sure as fuck is now if you don't want to spend the next few years in a Bahamian jail." Rudy doubted his years of running drugs and guns through the islands had gone unnoticed. Whatever version of the FBI's most-wanted list they had here, he expected he was on it—if he wasn't, he would actually be disappointed.

Commander waited a few seconds, then finally opened one of the hatches and dug out a mask and fins. On the way over, the bait man had bragged about his exploits during Dorian, and Rudy suspected the Commander was in a worse legal position than he was. Placing one long leg over the gunwale, he spat in the mask, reached over the side and rinsed it out, then placed it over his face. A second later, he slid into the water.

Rudy shifted his focus between the radar screen, the horizon where he expected the boat to appear at any second, and Commander swimming toward the reef. He watched as the bait king stopped and slipped underwater. Figuring they had five minutes to move out, he brought in the GPS trolling motor and dropped into neutral. Drifting with the current, he searched the water for the telltale bubbles from the divers.

A few seconds later, Commander's head popped through the surface, and Rudy laughed as the bait man gasped for air. Right behind him, the divers were now visible. Rudy carefully backed up to them, and with an eye on the horizon, waited for them to board. As Commander climbed the ladder, Rudy saw the T-top of a boat approaching.

"Hurry up," Rudy called back to the men, who dropped their tanks on the deck. The second they were all aboard, Rudy called for them to secure the gear. He didn't wait. The damage caused by a rouge tank was nothing if the other option was jail.

As Rudy turned toward the west, he couldn't see anything below the gunwales of the approaching boat. The T-top and outriggers trailing behind the boat were visible, and he realized right away that it wasn't the authorities. Rudy focused his attention on the boat, knowing that if he all he could see was their superstructure, that his boat would be even less visible. He didn't want to be identified, though, and before the approaching boat could close the gap, he took off, applying full pressure to the throttles. With a slight course correction, Rudy aligained his boat to run parallel to the waves. In the troughs, they would be invisible.

"Boys did good." Commander and the men had stowed the gear and were huddled behind the wind screen.

Rudy finally relaxed, as a glance at the radar showed the approaching boat had stopped over the reef. Glancing back, he searched the horizon. Judging that if the other boat was far enough away to be invisible to him, his boat was invisible to them. He slowed to a stop.

"What'd you guys find?" Rudy had noticed they hadn't brought anything aboard they hadn't left with.

"Someone uncovered the windshield. Took some work to get into the cargo area. By the time it was clear, Commander signaled us up."

"So, you don't know." The statement came out harsher than he meant it. Rudy couldn't imagine what it would be like inside the sixty-year-old plane.

"Another dive and we'll know."

"We'll have to sit and wait out whoever's there." Rudy turned his attention back to the radar screen. The first boat was still there, but another was also approaching. The new arrival was tagged as a RBDF cutter. Dodging the smaller boat was no big deal—he had an armory for that. Staying clear of the Defense Force would be much more difficult. Besides having advanced equipment, the RBDF had the ability to call in air support if they suspected anything. That was what Rudy feared most. His boat was designed to be invisible to land-based radar and other vessels. He had no doubt that, despite the boat's graphite finish, a trained observer could see him from the air. At this point, darkness was his friend, but there was still two hours until sunset.

"Everything stowed? We're gonna run back behind Chub."

While Rudy laid in a course, the men finished securing the gear and checked the hatches. Commander stood beside him, and the divers moved to the seat by the transom. With a quick glance around, Rudy pushed down on the throttles and headed toward Chub Cay.

Marathon

Luciano's phone rang, and he glanced at the display. He hesitated before answering, something he noticed Ned picked up on. The old man had turned out to be an interesting hostage. He was certainly no physical threat to someone steeped in violence, though Luciano knew well enough that anyone with the right weapon was dangerous.

The phone rang again. Knowing better than to let it go to voicemail, he pressed the green button and took the call. The voice on the other end was quiet and subdued. That didn't fool him. He knew well enough that the quiet ones were often the most dangerous. When you were confident in your power, you didn't need to yell.

"So, you found something and don't care to share with your old buddy?"

Luciano paused. It was who he had suspected when he saw *Unknown Caller* come up on the screen, but he had no idea how Taggart had found him. The mystery would likely never be solved. With the power of the CIA behind him, Gary Taggart had eyes and ears where no one expected them. Like Luciano, Taggart had familial ties to Cuba. His grandfather had been the CIA chief when the Revolution rolled through town. He had remained unscathed through that episode, but the Bay of Pigs ended his career.

"Just some rumors. Nothing credible."

"Well, it appears whoever found that plane is smarter than you. I was able to flag an internet search for the serial numbers of the B-26s. How many searches a month—no, a year, or even a freakin' decade—do you think someone asks Google that question?"

Luciano held the phone away from his head as the normally calm voice rose in frustration. He glanced over at Ned, who was listening intently.

He knew Ned was unable to hear Taggart, but even the one-sided conversation was enough for the old guy to surmise the purpose of the call. Glancing at his captive, Luciano opened the sliding glass door and stepped outside. Closing the door behind him, he tried to regroup.

"Do I have to remind you of the deal we made?"

Luciano cringed. The relationship between the two men's grandfathers, one a mob man, the other a CIA station chief, had been interesting. As it turned out, the two organizations were more alike than not. Secrecy, a taste for personal enrichment, and no qualms about using violence to attain those goals were just a few of the similarities. At that time, CIA-sanctioned assassinations were commonplace. When someone got in the way of either the agency or the mob, they were removed from the picture.

A deal had been made when the last B-26 took off. As was common with both institutions, it was based on threats if the other party failed to keep up their end. Aside from tarnishing their family names, neither member of the newer generation had any fear from those original reprisals, but the backbone of the deal was powerful enough to tie them together. Both men knew that Taggart held the upper hand. With the reach of the CIA behind him, he could make a lot of trouble for the mobster. Both men also knew it was a symbiotic relationship. The chances of one or the other finding the wreck and having the ability to salvage it were miniscule. Luciano had found it, but somehow word had leaked to Taggart.

"I got my eye on the guy that found it. He's not making a move without me knowing about it."

"You think so?"

Luciano could tell from the CIA man's tone that he knew something. Rather than being argumentative, Luciano stayed quiet.

"Got a satellite shot with two boats on it within an hour's time. The Bahamas Defense Force chased them off, but one of them is familiar to us."

"You gonna give me a clue or what?" Luciano was running out of patience.

Chub Cay

"This virus is some spooky shit. Freakin' ghost town." Pip steered through the winding channel that led to open water. "I'm guessing you're gonna want to get wet again?"

"I'm worried about visibility. It's bad enough hammering on the coral. I don't need any assistance from nature."

"Might be worth some of the inconvenience. Those RBDF dudes won't be as likely to take a pleasure cruise in this crap."

They were just entering the last bend when Mac spotted the small lumps on the horizon. Just as he started to measure them in his mind, the first gust of wind hit his face. It took a trained eye to estimate the height of the waves when they were this far off. From their position, the waves were just dimples on the surface, small enough that a casual observer wouldn't even notice them. But Mac knew from experience that if they were visible from a mile out, they were big. Mac figured the landmass was acting as a wind block for that first mile. The elephants walking on the horizon were too far away to notice any whitecaps, but Mac could tell from their profiles they were at least four feet.

"*The sea is angry, my friends,*" Pip grinned.

"*Like an old man trying to send back soup in a deli.*" Mac finished the bit. The first line was all Melville—the second, George Costanza. Mel gave them a curious look that only made them laugh harder. Having been buried in legal briefs, she had missed the mandatory Thursday-night sitcom craze of the nineties.

Pip passed a sign that marked the end of the restricted speed zone and opened up the throttles. Mac was used to his diesels and was surprised when the outboards started to whine as the RPMs increased. He remembered the days of the old two-cycle engines when it was almost impossible to talk over a single one-fifty. With eight times the power, they easily could hold a conversation.

As Mac expected, once they cleared the shadow of the island, the swells immediately increased. The Freeman handled them well, its twin hulls cutting through all but the largest. In most other boats, Mac would expect to get soaked, but there were no huge sheets of water landing on the deck.

Pip found the sweet spot between comfort and speed. Mac settled in for the ride. Mel appeared to be the only one not happy, as it was too bumpy to read her phone. She stashed it in the compartment below the helm and sat back in the bucket seat. Cruising into the head seas, it took about thirty minutes longer to reach the site than it had in the opposite direction.

Mac felt the boat slow and went forward to release the safety line. He stayed on the bow and waited while Pip released the anchor from the cockpit.

"I'm going with you this time," Mel said.

Mac had already thought about asking her. If he were going to penetrate inside the plane, it would be good to have someone standing by in case he got into trouble. Something as simple as becoming entangled in a loose wiring harness could be a death sentence.

"Good idea. You going to get lonely up here by yourself?"

Pip opened the compartment below the wheel and pulled out a weatherproof cigar case. "Me and my buddy Arturo Fuente'll be fine." He removed a cigar from the case and returned it to the compartment.

While Pip ducked into the shelter of the windscreen to light up, Mac and Mel started to assemble their gear. Mac noticed the mood in the boat was better than it should have been, and that included himself. He tried not to let the anticipation of what might lie below overshadow the fact that Ned's life was on the line, Trufante was in jail, and the weather continued to deteriorate. Mac knew he should be more focused on anticipating what was likely to go wrong.

After a quick buddy check, Mac took the port side and Mel the starboard. After exchanging glances, they simultaneously rolled backwards into the water. Mac immediately noticed the decrease in visibility. Compared to the top-to-bottom conditions earlier, he could barely see the reef from the surface. He knew where he was going, so it wasn't an issue, but once inside the wreck any disturbance would decrease the visibility dramatically.

He checked behind him to make sure Mel was there, and they exchanged okay signs. Mac knew the reef well enough that as soon as his feet hit the coral, he was able to make his way to the shattered cockpit window. His weight and screwdriver were still there, but not where he left them. A large chunk of the windshield was also missing.

"Shit!" Mac yelled in his mouthpiece. The word was indistinguishable, but the action released a flurry of bubbles from his regulator. Someone had been here in his absence.

Mel saw the look on his face. She raised her hands in a questioning gesture.

Mac opened his arms wide, but realized what made sense to him would mean nothing to her. Instead of wasting any more time and air explaining, he turned on his light and entered the cockpit. At least now the opening was wide enough to fit with a tank on. Before moving any further into the interior of the fuselage, he turned back and gave Mel the okay sign, then held up ten fingers to let her know how long he planned to be inside. She would wait outside to provide support.

Mac checked his watch and set the bezel on the minute hand, then moved back toward the navigator's station. The second sign of whoever had been here became visible when he was able to reach the cockpit door without taking off his tank. The caved-in bulkhead had been pushed aside, allowing him to move easily past it.

The light's piercing beam showed the surprisingly good condition of the interior. As far as he could tell, there were no large breaches that allowed the ocean to invade it. Only a light coating of algae covered everything. Mac fanned his hand and waved with the current, but the green film remained in place. He tried to brush it off and found it took a good effort to displace. He checked his watch and saw that five minutes had passed. The sightseeing portion of the tour was over. It was time to get to work.

Mac panned the light back and forth in the open area behind the navigator's station. He wasn't sure what three billion dollars in gold looked like, but he was sure he was not looking at it. The good news was that, judging by the algae growth, the cargo area appeared to be untouched. If anything had been removed, it would have been apparent. The beam from the light revealed no such disturbance.

He moved toward the tail, where he had uncovered the

turret, finding nothing of interest. A glance at his watch told him it was time to return, and discouraged, but not defeated, he retraced his steps toward the cockpit.

When he had to duck to clear the bulkhead by the cockpit, he realized something was strange. To step up on his way toward the cargo area had meant nothing to him, but on return, it struck him that the decks of the adjacent compartments all should be at the same level.

His brain was spinning trying to solve the problem, but he was out of time. Putting Mel into alarm mode would do nothing except hurt his investigation. One last glance behind him showed his footprints. The other divers, if they had made it this far, must have had fins. He directed the beam of light at the nearest print and noticed the surface underneath it appeared different than the surrounding flooring. The plane was largely made of aluminum, which was all in some state of degradation; this floor looked untouched by the elements. It could have been that the algae had protected it, but Mac suspected otherwise.

Mac turned away and stepped past the navigator's desk and into the pilot area, where he climbed out through the windshield. Mel was waiting, but she was not happy. With a mask covering much of his face and the breathing apparatus in his mouth, his eyes were the only thing left for Mel to judge his mood by. She must have seen that he had found something, because when he held up five fingers, she nodded. Mac took his mouthpiece out and smiled.

Placing it back in his mouth, Mac turned to re-enter the wreck. He saw the lead weight and screwdriver he had left previously and picked them up. There was something different about the floor in the cargo area, and he meant to find out what it was.

His body had become accustomed to the contortions required to enter the plane, and each time it was easier. Mac was soon through the cockpit and navigator's station. He stood, hunched over, in the opening in the bulkhead. He knelt down and rubbed his hand across the floor. The stubborn algae resisted his attempt to dislodge it. Taking the screwdriver, he lay the tip almost flat with the deck and pushed it forward. Acting like a chisel, the flat tip cleared a path as it moved.

Mac was expecting a diamond plate or other nonslip pattern to appear, but the tip of the screwdriver met little resistance. It was smoother than Mac expected. As he continued, a heavy material started to come away with the tip. It appeared a tarp had been placed over the deck. He was starting to get excited and began to clear off a larger area trying to find a seam, when the sound of a boat approaching caught his attention. He heard a knocking sound, which he attributed to Mel warning him that they had visitors.

Mac knew Pip was vulnerable by himself, and he needed to see if the approaching boat was a threat or not, but he was too close to solving the riddle. He had to know. Ignoring Mel's attempt to attract his attention, he ran the screwdriver across the deck, this time trying to cut through the material. As he did, he cursed the TSA for taking his knife, which would have made short work of the tarp. Unable to cut it, he finally found a seam and pealed it back.

Mac was out of time. He had expected the gold to be in the form of bullion, in which case there would be seams between the ingots, so he worked the tip of the screwdriver across the deck until he found a recess. It was quite shallow. He moved the tool to his left hand and reached for the lead weight. He hit the handle with an easy blow and waited. Mac had expected the bullion to shift, but the effort had no effect on the material.

If it were gold, a stronger blow wouldn't hurt it; if it wasn't, it didn't matter. Mac angled the tip a bit more and struck the handle harder this time. The outline of a brick-sized object appeared, but before he could leverage it out, something tugged him backwards.

Without thinking, Mac swung the screwdriver in an arc, barely missing Mel. She gave a slashing signal across her throat and pointed to the surface. Mac had been so involved in his discovery he hadn't paid attention to the sound of the engine. It was considerably louder now. Close enough to vibrate the algae off the ceiling. Mac pushed Mel forward and followed her out of the fuselage.

Once they were clear, he looked up and saw a long steel hull above him. It certainly wasn't a pleasure boat, which left one option: the Royal Bahamas Defense Force had returned. Mel started for the surface, but Mac tugged on her fin and stopped her. The last time the RBDF had appeared, Mac and company had been in the wrong. This time, they would find Pip aboard his Bahamas-registered boat. He had to assume the old man had his paperwork in order. Even though they had legally entered the country, there was no harm in waiting.

With his hand level and palm down, Mac made a horizontal movement meant to tell Mel to settle at their present depth. She questioned him with her eyes, but there was no real way to communicate. She would have to trust him. He checked his air and saw almost 1,000 PSI left. Mel indicated she had the same, which would give them at least thirty minutes for the RBDF to do its business and (hopefully) leave.

It took less than five minutes before the propeller started to churn up the water, and the boat moved away.

Mac waited another few minutes to be safe and indicated to Mel that they should ascend. Together, they made for the surface.

STEVEN BECKER

A MAC TRAVIS ADVENTURE

WOOD'S HOPE

The Wreck Site

MAC SURFACED IN THE SPACE BETWEEN THE OUTBOARDS JUST IN case he had misread the situation. Slowly, he popped his head above the surface and scanned the water. The hull blocked half his view, but it was clear behind him. He dipped down and signaled to Mel that it was safe to surface. If anyone was there, the boat would conceal them.

Mac was surprised Pip was not waiting for them, but when a cloud of smoke blew past, he knew his friend was alright. Taking his fins off, he tossed them onto the deck and watched Pip jump up in surprise.

"Scared the crap out of me. Wasn't enough I had to deal with the RBDF myself?"

Mac grabbed the ladder and started climbing aboard. Pip reached over and grabbed the tank valve to help him. Mac climbed into the cockpit and slipped off his gear. He looked back, but Pip was already helping Mel.

"What are you doing fishing when we're down there?" Fishing poles sat in the rod holders on either side of the boat.

Mac didn't care for people to fish while he was diving. The line, made to be invisible to fish, was also hard to see by divers in all but the clearest of waters, making it easy to become entangled. The bait also tended to bring in predators.

"I'm sitting here in four-foot seas eating my lunch? What the hell was I going to tell them?"

"Apparently they left you alone."

Before Pip could respond, one of the rods jerked, and Pip stepped up to it. Somehow a fish on the end of a line seemed to quell any discontent. As he and Mel stripped down the gear, Mac kept one eye on Pip. There were two schools of thought when bringing a fish in, especially one with some size. Judging by the bend in the heavy rod, Mac suspected this was a big snapper or grouper. Most of the work was pulling the fish free of the bottom and away from any structure it might bolt for. Once that was done, some anglers chose to horse the fish to the boat, while others enjoyed playing it. Pip was the latter. By the time he called for help to gaff the fish, Mac had already swapped tanks.

Reaching under the gunwale, Mac pulled out the smaller of the two gaffs and moved next to Pip. The leader was just breaking the surface when he set the pointed hook in the water. Mac and Pip had done this often enough they didn't need to communicate. Just before the leader reached the rod tip, Pip lifted the rod and walked backwards. Mac reached for the thick monofilament and carefully wrapped it around his hand, making sure the two loops were free of each other in case the fish ran. More than one mate they knew had lost a finger to such a mistake. He eased the line out of the water, and just as the fish turned its side to him, slid the gaff behind the head and in one smooth motion lifted it into the boat.

"Damn." Mac placed the thirty-inch mutton snapper in the cooler and reached into the top drawer of the tackle storage. He removed an ice pick and quickly dispatched the fish. With a pair of pliers, he dislodged the hook. Then with a knife, he cut the artery below the gills. Fish blood ran into the clean ice, but the meat would be better for it.

"Looks like I'm the winner, unless you got something to raise me with?" Pip said.

"We might have." Mac told them what he had found.

"You got a plan? If we're gonna sit out here all night—this, that, and the other thing—I need to start rationing my cigars."

Mac didn't really have a plan, but at least he had options. The best one was to raise the treasure tonight. The only problem with that was air—or rather, lack of it. He and Mel had burned through two of their four tanks. If they were looking around or doing light work, Mac could expect an hour from each fill. But he knew the exertion of bringing the treasure up would burn through their second tanks considerably faster. Time was of the essence, though. Once they exposed more of the treasure, it would be visible for anyone to see. If whoever had been in the wreck returned in their absence, they would know where the treasure was.

Even with the proper boat and a trained crew, Mac expected the recovery effort would take at least half a day. They had neither. Mac decided the treasure would be better left in place until he could line up the resources he needed to extract it quickly. Besides the mysterious divers, there was also the RBDF to worry about. Having already visited the site twice, they were obviously keeping an eye on it. Without a permit, which he didn't even know how to start the process of applying for, it was a fool's errand to bring up the gold in daylight.

That meant waiting until tomorrow night.

"We're gonna leave it down there and pull off until we can organize a proper effort."

"Damned shame to leave it."

Mac thought about that for a minute and realized he had

exposed one of the bricks. "I'm going down again to do a little camo work." He noticed Mel looking at him. "Don't worry, it'll be quick."

"What can I do, then?" Mel asked.

For all the trouble his deckhand caused, Trufante was the man he needed to bring the gold up quickly.

"You hear anything about Trufante?"

"I can have a look and call the lawyer."

Mac nodded and slipped into the BC. He readied his dive light, snugged his mask over his face, then dropped into the water. Though the sun hadn't quite set, its low position didn't provide enough of an angle to penetrate the water. Mac flicked on his dive light and got his bearings.

He had no fear of being in the water at night, but it was different than during the day. Once you got over the unknown of what lurked behind the veil of darkness, navigation and buoyancy were usually the issues. Mac was without fins and over-weighted, so it was only navigation that he needed to worry about. As soon as his feet hit the bottom, he pulled on the retractable lanyard and held his compass in front of him. A blue glow penetrated from above. The Freeman, lit by blue LED lights, glowed in the water, so it was only a matter of locating the plane.

Fish of all sizes and colors darted in and out of the light, and his hunter's eye was drawn to the larger predators lurking behind the coral heads and under the ledges. The few lobster he had seen earlier had seemed to multiply, but he knew that wasn't the case. The crawfish were nocturnal and hunted at night.

Mac reached the cockpit in minutes and slid inside. With the fuselage blocking any ambient light, it was pitch dark inside, causing the silt he disturbed on entering to be more of a problem than in the daylight. Waiting patiently for the water to clear, he looked around. Even though he knew the skeletons were there, they still gave him a start when the light flashed on them.

The water cleared and Mac moved further back into the wreck. When he reached the navigator's station, he grabbed the damaged bulkhead, hoping it was free. It moved easily, and he dragged it behind him. When he reached the cargo area, he dropped to his knees and crawled to the area he had exposed earlier. From several angles, he surveyed the gold floor. His footsteps were explainable and lent to the ruse. It was the disturbed area that would jump out under even a casual glance.

Mac crawled to the spot he had started to chisel out and shone the light on it. There was no replacing the years of algae growth. Instead, he pulled the tarp back, then dragged the panel and set it over the area. Adjusting it so there was no need for it to be moved to access the rest of the cargo area, he stepped back. It wasn't natural, but there was no reason for whoever had been here earlier to suspect it had been moved for any other reason than to get it out of the way.

Mac retraced his steps and was quickly through the broken windshield. He turned in the direction of Pip's glowing hull and made his way back to the boat. Pip helped him aboard, and he slipped off the gear.

"What'd be the plan?" Pip asked.

"Let's get somewhere out of the wind, but close enough we can keep an eye on the radar to see if we have any visitors."

"Might as well use the harbor. We're legal," Mel said.

Mac laughed. This was a first. His last few trips here had been under the radar.

Marathon

"Bad news?"

Luciano had just stepped back into the house, and now the old man was pestering him. "Looks like your deal's about to change."

Taggart had sent him the satellite photo of the boat on the reef. It was plain to see that Rudy had double-crossed him. Trying to remain calm, he went to the refrigerator and took out a beer. "Want one?"

"Don't mind if I do. Could use some food too."

Luciano took stock of the old man—Ned, if he remembered correctly—and it was from overhearing his theory that Rudy had gotten the information about the wrecked plane. He wondered if Ned was more valuable than simply as a hostage. He brought two beers back to the couch, and held one out to Ned.

Ned raised his hands, showing Luciano the bonds.

"I cut you loose, you gonna cause any trouble? Just so ya know, the guy on the phone was CIA. They got a line on your buddy, so would be in your best interest to cooperate with me."

"I'm a retired college professor. What am I going to do to you?"

Luciano was wary, but if the idea developing in his head was going to work, he needed to befriend his hostage. Pulling a folding knife from his pocket, he leaned over and cut the ties. Ned flexed his hands and took the beer.

"Why don't you tell me what you know about that plane?"

Ned began with the history of the B-26 fleet during World War II.

"Never cared for school. I'll trust you on the details. What I want to know is where it's at."

"I know it's a shallow reef near Chub Cay."

"All I want is the cargo. I got nothing to do with Rudy's gripe with your buddy. That's between them, but if you help me out here, I'll make sure he lays off. I ain't cuttin' you in, but you'll live."

Ned sat and quietly drank his beer. "Got it marked on a chart back at the house."

It was only a first step, but it was a good one. Once he obtained the coordinates, he could pit Rudy and Taggart against each other, then walk away with his grandfather's legacy. "They brought you up from Key West?"

"Yeah, but all the material I have is out on Wood's Island."

Luciano knew Key Largo, Islamorada, Marathon, and Key West. He'd never heard of the island. "Thought they called them all keys here."

"Probably could, but we just call it Wood's place. Lies about eight miles into the Gulf."

Luciano was a car guy. He knew little about boats or the water. It was even more important to get the old man on his side now. "You suppose you could get us out there?"

"Ain't no trouble, but we'll need a boat."

"I'll see what I can do there. Why don't you see what old Rudy's got for food."

Ned got up and went to the kitchen. He opened the refrigerator, then the freezer, and finally the pantry. When he was satisfied with his inventory, he started pulling things out and putting them on the counter. "Got some steaks, potatoes, and some salad stuff."

"Go ahead, and grab me another beer while you're at it." Luciano realized he was ordering Ned around. "One for you too."

He took the beer outside and stared out at the water. Rudy had taken the go-fast boat, but there was another smaller center console at the dock. He walked downstairs to take a look at it.

Compared to the custom smuggling boat, it was pretty vanilla, but maybe that was the point. Rudy kept the black graphite craft in an enclosed boathouse. This was his day boat. The best way for him to seem innocuous was to be seen in a run-of-the-mill boat.

Luciano headed back upstairs and found Ned plating up steaks and potatoes. He grabbed another beer from the refrigerator and took the offered food. They both sat at the table and ate in silence.

When he was finished, Luciano set his plate on the counter. "Don't bother cleaning up. I got a boat." He'd seen a set of keys, with the telltale foam float attached, lying on a small table that also housed a humidor, which he raided when he grabbed the keys.

Ned followed him out of the house and down the stairs. Before they reached the boat, Luciano handed him the keys. "Be easier if you drove, since you know where you're going."

"Just hope the electronics are good. Running the back-country in the dark ain't for the feint of heart. Been a while for me."

Luciano started to worry, but time was of the essence. He needed the chart tonight. Once he had it, he planned to let Taggart know that Rudy was the one trying to take the treasure. He would have liked to watch the CIA man take down the smuggler, but he had more important things to worry about—the gold.

Ned had the engines running and was fiddling with the touch screens. Luciano wanted to push him, but knew better. Finally, Ned asked him to release the lines, and they pulled away from the dock.

Weaving their way through the well-lit harbor was no problem. Luciano was wondering what the big deal was when they entered the channel and darkness surrounded them. Ned seemed to be steering more by looking at the screen than by what was in front of him, which only made sense, because the much younger Luciano was having trouble making sense of the markers. Ned asked him to call off the numbers as they passed, which he was barely able to do.

The lights of the bridge were reassuring, but after they had cleared it, there was nothing but water and sky.

28

Little Whale Cay

EVEN WITH NO OTHER BOATS IN SIGHT, MAC HAD THE FEELING they were being watched. Sitting on the northeast side of Little Whale Cay they were alone, but Mac, feeling anxious, could sense the radar beacons searching for them. The twin hulls of the Freeman mitigated the choppy waters to some degree, but it was still uncomfortable. Though the southwest side in the lee of the island would have been better protected, the exposed shore of the remote private island had several advantages. The RBDF was located in Chub Cay, and with several islands between them, their radar would be unable to locate them. There was also the unknown boat. Mac expected it was either Rudy or an associate of his. The landmass of the island would serve to conceal them from prying radar, and the exposure allowed their radar a clear view of the wreck site.

They were two very different threats—both dangerous in different ways. The RBDF could imprison them, an unsavory option for an American in a foreign country. Rudy would kill them.

"Might as well eat, then." Pip moved toward the bow and slowly bent over one of the storage holds built into the pontoon. He removed a stainless steel grill and took it toward the stern, where he placed the cylindrical base into one of the rod holders.

Mac watched him fuss with the position of the grill. Using the smoke from his cigar as a telltale, Pip decided to move the contraption to the opposite side. Pip removed his cigar lighter, and after turning on the valve by the small propane tank attached to the unit, he lit the burner.

Mel had already removed the snapper from the box and had one side filleted by the time the grill heated up. Pip took the fillet, seasoned it, and within a few minutes it was on the grill. The smell distracted Mac from the radar screen he had been staring at for the past hour. Sometimes looking away allowed you to see a thing more clearly, and whether it was a coincidence or not, when Mac glanced back at the screen, he noticed a very small signature he hadn't noticed before.

It was mixed with the radar clutter and was small enough to be a frigate bird, but what he noticed was the course, not the size. A bird riding the thermals would appear static, whereas a bird in flight generally swerved and dove in their search for food. The small object was moving at a consistent speed on what appeared to be a straight course. Fine-tuning the gain did little to define the object, but Mac was now sure it was a boat heading from Chub Cay to the wreck site.

Mac glanced back. Pip was just turning the fish. "Wrap that up. We gotta go."

Setting the lid back on the grill, Pip moved to the helm, where Mac showed him the small signature.

"Good catch. Get the anchor. I'll finish the dinner."

Mel was standing beside them. Mac turned the wheel over to her and moved to the bow. He gave Mel a thumbs-up and waited while the windlass brought the rode aboard. With a clenched fist, he signaled for her to stop the motor while he shook the chain to release the mud and seagrass. Once clear, he brought the remaining rode aboard by hand and secured the anchor in the chock. With the safety cable attached, he returned to the helm.

Mac patiently waited for Pip to scoop the fish from the grill, and Mel took the plate from him. Mac waited a minute for them to square away the boat. With the hot grill still in the rod holder, and Pip and Mel on either side of him, Mac spun the wheel toward the wreck and pushed down on the throttles.

Used to heavier monohulls, Mac was surprised by how quickly the boat planed out, and in seconds the twin hulls were slicing through the chop. Even with the exposed anchorage, the shallow water had held the waves down. As they crossed to deeper water the two-foot chop became four-foot waves. Mac trimmed the engines and dropped speed slightly. He was in no rush, and in fact thought about stopping in order to utilize the landmass behind them for concealment. If he were to determine what boat the other divers were from, he needed to be patient and let them get situated first.

"You got a scooter onboard?" Mac called over to Pip. Having Pip drop him a ways off, and then approaching underwater, would allow him to see who it was and remain unobserved.

Pip picked up on his train of thought. "Five hundred feet of anchor line, couple of fishing rods." He paused and pulled hard on his cigar. "Got an electric reel."

The twelve-volt reels were used for deep-dropping. Fishing in hundreds of feet of water was a laborious task with a hand-crank reel. The electric reels held thousands of feet of line and were powerful enough to haul a hundred-pound fish from the depths to the surface.

"Got about six-hundred yards of hundred-pound braid."

Mac thought about the logistics of using the line for his

purposes. It would have to be laid out in a straight line, restricting his ability to change course more than a few yards in either direction.

Pip was on the same page and Mac decided to talk it through out loud. "You drop me a quarter mile off, and put the reel in free-spool."

"Then I'll run a half-circle and come back to a straight-line heading."

"Right. Then engage the reel and pull me to the wreck site."

Mel moved her glance from man to man, and shook her head. "Y'all are crazy."

Pip laughed. "Hey, got nothing to lose. If it don't work, he bails. Worst case, I lose a bunch of line."

"Worth a shot." Mac turned the wheel over to Pip, who shut off the navigation lights, throwing them into the dark. With only the red night-light of the chartplotter for illumination, Mac went forward to gear up. He knew Mel was right. If things went sideways, he could always release the line, but it wasn't that easy. The narrow-gauge braid pulled by the motorized reel was strong and thin enough to act like a garrote. If he did avoid becoming entangled in the line, he would be adrift at sea—at night.

A light and whistle would mitigate the latter, and a knife the former. Checking that the safety items were firmly attached and accessible, he shot a squirt of air into the BC and, using it for a cushion, placed it on the deck to cushion the tank.

Mac waited for his eyes to acclimate to the dim screen. The red light's purpose was to allow the user to use the electronics without a loss of night vision. The downside was the soundings were harder to read. Mac adjusted the zoom to center on the wreck with a half mile on either side.

"Drop the speed. We're going to have to figure the current."

Pip nodded and slowed the boat. They were about a mile away. They would have been seen in daylight, maybe not in detail, but on the empty ocean they would stand out. At night they were invisible. Pip zoomed in further and watched the dotted black-and-white track as the current and wind had its way with the boat.

"Pretty much due west," Pip said. "Into it?"

Mac thought about the implications of using the current to his advantage, finally deciding to use the current as a brake instead of a motor. "Pull me into it."

"Roger."

As he waited for Pip to move into position, Mac rethought the whole idea. It was a complicated and risky scenario, but if he wanted to avoid a confrontation, at least at this point, he needed to be able to observe without being seen. He could find a place to conceal himself on the reef, then after a set period of time Pip would reel him in.

The radar screen showed the unknown boat holding its course. "Ten minutes?"

"About. Probably ought to drop you now. With their direction of travel and the current, they'll probably blow right over you." Pip pushed down on the throttles.

While Pip navigated toward the drop spot, Mac geared up and sat on the forward bench. Scanning the horizon ahead, he searched for the approaching boat. Assuming it was running dark as well, they both would be invisible, except to the radar each boat had. Hopefully, the other captain would see Pip moving off and disregard the threat.

"Ready," Pip called from the helm.

The boat slowed just enough for Mac to move to the gunwale, where he inched to the edge, ensuring the tank was over the side. Mel brought him the dive weight they had fastened to the end of the fishing line.

"Go — go — go — go — go," Pip called.

With both hands on the line to avoid it entangling him on

entry, Mac rolled over the side. He knew this was the riskiest part of the operation. The line could wrap around one of his appendages or his equipment, and if Mel failed to set the reel to free-spool, he could be dead in an instant.

Mac felt the line come taunt just as he righted himself and braced for the inevitable pull. With the other boat approaching, Pip had no choice but to move off at a speed that if he wasn't ready, would be fast enough to tear the mask and regulator from his face and drown him.

Mac felt the expected tug, but as he sank to the bottom, it released. He drew a long breath, then fell into the breathing pattern he used to conserve air. The adrenaline started to fade as his breath and heart rate slowed to normal. Once he acclimated to the situation, he settled down to wait.

A few minutes later, he heard the engine of the other boat. It was approaching quickly, and before he knew it, the bioluminescent wake passed over his head. Enough time had passed for Pip to move to the end range of the line, and he would see the other boat stop on the radar. Mac heard the engine die and the water was suddenly quiet. Glancing at his watch, he set the arrow of the bezel to the minute hand and prepared to wait the twenty minutes he and Pip had agreed on. That was more than enough time for the boat above to get its divers in the water.

The reef was a hundred yards off and invisible in the darkness. Mac sat in the sand, hoping to see some sign of the divers entering the water. As the time passed he started to wonder, but there was nothing to be done about it. With two minutes to go, he fixed his grip on the weighted line and readied himself.

The initial tug felt just like it would have on the other end when a fish hit, but slowly the line came taunt, and he started to move along the bottom. They had decided on a two-minute interval, allowing Mac the ability to pull on the line to signal what was happening below. The first came when he was still over sand, and he pulled twice on the line. A second later, he started moving again. By the time the second two-minute period had expired, he was over the reef. The pressure on the line dropped, and he tugged five times.

That gave Mac five minutes to evaluate what was happening ahead. He set the bezel on his watch again and moved toward the wavering lights ahead.

29

STEVEN BECKER

A MAC TRAVIS ADVENTURE

WOOD'S
HOPE

Wood's Island

PAMELA WAS GOING STIR CRAZY. SHE'D BEEN THROUGH HER YOGA routine twice and still wasn't feeling the release it usually brought her. Without an opportunity to replace her weed supply, she badly needed something to take the edge off.

Two long days had passed since Mac and Mel left. Though she trusted them more than most people, getting Tru out of a Bahamian jail wasn't an easy task. Dealing with the law was one of the few things that Mac didn't do well, and though Mel was an attorney, dealing with foreign countries required a degree of expertise that she didn't have. Pamela was thankful that they had retained a local lawyer to represent him, but the process was slow, and the virus was only making it worse.

With the walls closing in on her, she grabbed the last bottle of wine from Mel's stores, left the house, and walked down to the small beach. The Surfari sat alone at the dock. She could pilot it, and wondered if she should make the trip into Marathon, at least to replenish her supplies. Though she was confident about running the boat between the island and the mainland, the setting sun dissuaded her. She decided to wait until morning to see if there was any progress on the legal front; if there was no word, she would head to town. The Keys had its share of sleazy lawyers, and many specialized in immigration. She could easily enlist one to help. In addition, she needed to replace the wine she had drunk.

Stepping aboard *Sea Runner*, she removed the key from the battery compartment, switched on the power, and started the engines. The last few years had taught her quite a bit about boats, and she knew well that they only ran when they were run. Sitting was as bad for engines as for people. Leaving the engine idling, she reached into the console and removed a Phillips screwdriver. Lining the head up with the center of the cork, she slammed it through the neck of the wine bottle with her palm.

The cork dislodged, dropping into the bottle. Pamela replaced the makeshift opener, and brought the bottle to her lips. She smiled, thinking that Trufante would have been proud, as she used her teeth to filter out a few pieces of cork. She guzzled the expensive Zin from the bottle, repeating the process with each sip.

Three-quarters of the bottle was gone, and she remained in her funk. Pamela could feel herself creeping toward the edge of depression, and she wondered how she was going to make it through the night. She was usually able to cope with her anxieties during the daytime, but at night they often haunted her. As a last resort, there was still some of Mac's rum in the house, but hard liquor didn't suit her. She finished the bottle of wine and set it beside her.

Pamela was just about to get up when she heard the sound of a boat. Focusing her attention on the noise, she realized it was approaching. That ruled out a tourist. This time of day, they normally would be heading in the other direction—towards the mainland. There was a chance it was a local running out to one of the wrecks in the deeper Gulf water, but a glance at the sliver of a crescent moon hanging in the sky told her otherwise. Full moons meant better fishing.

There was nothing to do except wait. Surrounded for miles by only low islands, which were little more than humps rising above the water, sound carried forever. She shut down the engine to hear better.

Pamela didn't need her finely tuned sixth sense to know the sound was getting louder. As it approached, the odds increased it was heading for the island. There was always the chance the boat was running the deepwater channel just off the island into the open Gulf, but just in case, she walked quickly to the house. Mac had enemies, and though most were all talk—fueled by drugs and alcohol—the night brought out the worst in them.

The boat was close enough that she clearly heard it from the front porch. After the encounter with Rudy and Commander, she expected the worst. Grabbing the shotgun, Pamela ran down the stairs and back toward the beach. She was not one to hide.

The Surfari was her destination, and she reached it just as the boat slowed outside the dredged channel. Pamela didn't wait to see if they would dodge the rock standing guard at the channel opening as she dove into the cockpit of the motorsailer. She eased herself into a sitting position, using the high freeboard to conceal herself. Once she was situated, she checked the weapon, and peered over the gunwale.

The half-expected sound of the propeller hitting the rock never came. Whoever it was knew how to enter the channel. A few seconds later, a boat idled past. Her first thought was Commander, but when the boat stopped, she was surprised to hear Ned's voice. The sound of another, unfamiliar voice had her drop to the deck.

"So, where is it? I don't see nothing out here but brush and bugs."

"The house is up that trail."

"Alright, let's get on with it."

Pamela watched the two men walk down the dock and disappear into the interior of the island. She relaxed slightly but stayed where she was, wondering what they were doing here. This had all started when Rudy had overheard Ned speaking about the wreck. Now, she suspected their purpose was to retrieve Ned's papers. With Mac and Mel gone, Ned was her only connection to Trufante. She had to save him.

She knew that getting trapped aboard the Surfari was a bad idea if she wanted to rescue Ned. Moving into a crouch, Pamela held her breath and listened. They'd been gone for a few minutes, but the house was only a hundred yards away, and if it was Ned's papers they were after, they could be on their way back by now. Filtering out the sounds of the waves slapping against the hull, the trees rustling in the breeze, and the incessant insects, she listened for any sign of the two men. After a long minute she heard nothing, and made her move.

Her long legs got her over the gunwale and down the dock in a dozen strides. Pausing to listen again, she stepped off the pier and onto the beach.

"You see that?"

She heard the voice and knew she had waited too long. Ducking deeper into the brush, she stumbled. Biting pain shot through her leg. It didn't matter if it was the flora or fauna—she had to move. Pamela tried to regain her balance, but found herself embedded in a palmetto bush. She started to extricate herself, but even the slightest movement brought shooting pain from the razor-sharp leaves.

Up or down, it didn't make any difference. Staying still was not an option, either, so with a deep breath, Pamela rolled backward, hoping she would land on the trail. The pain stopped, but the noise attracted the men's attention. She heard footsteps coming toward her.

In the close quarters of the trail, the shotgun was useless as a weapon. The chance of hitting Ned was too great; a mistaken shot could kill or injure him. Though she wasn't willing to fire blindly, the other man didn't know that, so the .410 might still be useful. With the stock held firmly against her shoulder, Pamela raised the barrel and pointed it in the direction of the light.

She took the only course open to her. The man knew where she was. If she ran, she fully expected him to shoot. Her best chance was to confront him and hope the shotgun was enough to keep her, and Ned, alive.

Stepping out onto the trail, she waited. Around a slight bend she could see the light waver. The path was clear but not smooth, forcing the man to focus the beam down to avoid the roots and uneven terrain. Every few seconds he raised the light to check the path ahead. His movements told her he was either sloppy or didn't care. In either case, she suspected he wasn't a soldier. That was both good and bad. Men trained for combat were generally more cautious than the random thug who would shoot first and ask questions later. Pamela wondered if she should announce her presence. With the man's head down like a bloodhound, there was a distinct possibility of a collision.

"Right here." Pamela stood tall and pointed the shotgun at the man.

The light fell a few feet in front of her. Slowly it found her legs, then her torso, and finally settled on her face. Pamela fought the urge to shield her eyes with one hand and held the weapon firmly. The man was no fool. He kept the beam on her eyes, knowing it would blind her.

"Who the hell are you?"

Pamela breathed out. Whoever this was appeared not to

know her. "This is a private island. You're trespassing." She squeezed her eyelids together, hoping that by squinting her vision would acclimate to the unwavering light.

"Shit, I got a guide. Knows the owner. We was just about to leave when I heard you prowling around."

Pamela was barely able to discern the outline of the man. In one hand he held the light; in the other there was the distinct outline of a pistol. They were at a standoff. She took a chance and lowered the barrel of the shotgun, hoping he would do the same. It took a second, but he followed suit.

The adrenaline had sobered her, and her mind was clear. That allowed her to evaluate her options. There appeared to be only two.

"You can leave the old man with me."

"I don't think so. He's still got some value left."

That settled it for her. There was no way she could let the man take Ned. If the reason for the trip here had been to retrieve Ned's papers, that likely meant they would be heading to the Bahamas. If she let them go, in a few hours they could be hundreds of miles away and protected by a foreign government. With only the motorsailer available, she had no chance of pursuing them.

Pamela wished the chamber was empty. There was nothing like the sound of a round being chambered in a shotgun to let an adversary know you meant business—except for a shot over their heads. Faster than the man could react, she raised the barrel and squeezed the trigger, then quickly chambered another round and leveled the barrel at his chest. The action had the desired effect. He flinched just long enough for Pamela to cover the distance between them. As she did, she placed both hands on the barrel, brought the stock back like a club, and swung for the fences.

If she had paid a little more attention to her middle school softball coach, she might have struck him, but as with hitting a ball, it was the connection, not the power, that mattered. Her swing went wild.

The momentum took her off balance and likely saved her life as a bullet whizzed past her head. She continued to roll, ignoring the painful scrape from the bush she landed against. This time, there was no need for subterfuge and she let out a primal scream, both from the shooting pain and the expected bullet. As she rolled back onto the trail, she watched the man drop to the ground.

The light, which was apparently from his phone, flew into the bushes, leaving them in darkness. As her vision acclimated to the dark night, she saw Ned holding a stick and standing over the downed man.

Pamela sprung up like a gazelle and covered the ten feet between them in a few seconds.

"It's me, Ned," he said, bending down to recover the man's pistol.

His voice sounded shaky, and she realized she had instinctively raised the shotgun. She quickly lowered it. "Don't I know it." She wanted to hug him, but they had the man on the ground to deal with first. "There's got to be some rope in the shed." She started toward the clearing.

"Probably locked. Dock line'll do just fine." Ned held the barrel a few feet from the man's head.

Pamela reversed course and ran past him. She reached the Surfari and grabbed an extra line from the hold by the transom. A few seconds later she was back.

Ned handed her the pistol and bent down. With the handgun in her left hand and the shotgun in her right, she watched as he ran the bitter end through the eye and looped it around the man's wrists. Taking a few wraps around, he tied off a knot and stood. With a jerk, he rolled the man over, allowing Pamela to see his face.

The man spat dirt from his mouth. "That's gonna cost you, sweetie."

30

The Wreck Site

MAC WAS CLOSE ENOUGH TO SEE THE TWO DIVERS ENTER THE fuselage. It would have been easier to approach without the fishing line, but in the dark there was little chance of finding it if he abandoned it. With the weight in his hand, he finned toward the wreck. As he did, the problems with his plan became evident —mainly, that he didn't have one.

In order to identify one or both of the divers, he would have to subdue them, remove their masks, and shine a light at their faces. That was improbable, and they were probably merely hired help, anyway. It was the boat and its driver that would provide him the information he needed. Mac glanced up at the surface. He would be invisible to anyone looking in the water. Conversely, even with only a sliver of a moon, the stars were bright enough to light the surface. That neutralized any threat from above.

Checking to make sure both divers were still inside the wreck, Mac turned to the plane. The lights were moving but dim, meaning the men were deep inside the fuselage, probably inspecting the cargo hold. He could only hope that the darkness hid any sign of the gold. Mac turned his attention back to the surface.

The watch on his wrist was synchronized with the clock in his head, and both told him he had little time before Pip engaged the electric reel. With the shallow water mitigating the risk of an embolism, he finned quickly to the surface, slowing only as he was about to break through into the night.

Figuring he would look like one of the divers returning early, Mac popped his head out of the water and spun in a quick circle until he located the boat. It only took him a second to see the blocky figure, which told him it was Rudy. A voice called out, confirming the man's identity, but Mac didn't respond. There was no reason for him to reveal himself. He was about to duck back underwater when the realization that Ned might be aboard made him pause. He wavered a second too long, and a shot fired in his direction.

There was nothing he could do for Ned now, and he dropped back under. Several other shots passed close enough to his body to feel the vibration through the water as they passed. With time running out, Mac glanced back at the boat and saw the propellers bobbing in the water. An idea came to him. He knew he could disable one, or maybe two, of the motors.

Counter-rotating propellers had been around since the first twin outboards were mounted. They allowed the boat to run straight with little effort from the helm. Mac guessed that the two port engines would spin clockwise and the starboard pair counterclockwise.

He would take out a set of motors.

Dropping far enough below the surface to become invisible from above, Mac swam under the boat. He took the weighted line and wrapped it around the right-hand outboard, then around the one just inboard of it. A few more wraps and he was satisfied.

Abandoning his lifeline wasn't the smartest decision he'd ever made, but given the chance to disable Rudy's boat, he had to take it. As long as he was able to track the fishing line, it would lead him back to Pip. There was every chance his plan would go awry, so he used his compass to determine the direction of the line leading to the Freeman, then dropped it.

Just as he did, the line snapped taunt. He could almost sense the tension the braid was under and hoped the line would hold. Aboard the Freeman, it would look like Pip had hooked his biggest fish ever. Mac could only imagine the expression on his friend's face when he saw the rod doubled over and the drag screaming as it tried to reel in the smuggler's boat.

On the other end, Mac suspected Rudy was utilizing his GPS trolling motor to hold his position, rather than a conventional anchor. It would be a good test to see how the small motor handled the strain of the electric reel. Mac was counting on it having enough of an effect to force Rudy to start his engines to reset his position. Then all hell would break loose as the propellers sucked up the fishing line.

Before that happened he needed to be back aboard Pip's boat. Kicking hard, he followed the line. There was no way to tell how Rudy would react, or if he would even notice he was being pulled from his position. Thinking he would be watching for the divers and not the electronics, Mac continued to kick hard toward the Freeman. His measured breathing strategy long forgotten, he soon felt the familiar resistance from the near-empty tank. Mac took one last inhalation and spit out the regulator. With no choice but to surface, he pressed the button on his BC, hoping there was enough air left for the low-pressure hose to inflate the vest. Otherwise, he would have to stop and fill it manually.

A shot of air squirted into the air bladder, but Mac didn't ascend as he expected. The extra weight in his vest pockets was counteracting the added buoyancy. Reluctantly, he pulled the quick release and dropped the weights to the bottom. Free of constraints, the BC brought him quickly to the surface.

The line was lost now, but Mac still had the use of his compass. He spun in the direction he expected to find Pip, rolled onto his back and started kicking along the course. With no ambient light pollution, the night sky was brilliant. The Milky Way was clearly evident and the stars so bright that Mac had some trouble before he found a few familiar constellations. Once he did, he aligned himself with several key stars and continued kicking.

Every hundred or so kicks, Mac turned to check the horizon, and after the fifth stop, he saw the outline of the Freeman. The boat itself was not visible, but the shape was identifiable by the stars blocked out by its mass. Mac relaxed once he had a visual. He started kicking and counting again. His course remained true, and he could see a tiny red light from the end of Pip's cigar. He almost laughed as he resumed kicking.

The next time he turned, everything had changed. Rolling onto his stomach, he looked up expecting the boat to be even closer, but it was gone. Mac quickly checked his compass and confirmed that something was amiss. Moving his head from side to side, he scanned the water and finally found the boat almost behind him.

"Pip! Mel!" Mac screamed at the boat, now clearly moving away from him. He wasted no time in changing course and following. Mac soon found his rhythm again and started to focus on the task. It was then he realized that there was no engine noise, only the scream of the electric reel. Voices were audible, and though he couldn't make out what they were saying, it was clearly Pip and Mel. It took Mac a moment to figure out what was happening: Rudy had started his engines and the pull against Pip's electric reel as the line wrapped around his propellers was drawing the Freeman toward the smuggler's boat.

Mac thought he could catch them and kicked harder. On his next stop, he was able to see the boat clearly again.

"This, that, and the other thing! What the hell?" Pip's voice carried over the engine noise.

Mac turned toward the Freeman and watched as the rod snapped in two. In the distance he could hear Rudy's outboards strain as the propellers continued to eat the fishing line. Hoping Pip would have enough sense to put the reel into free-spool, Mac started kicking again, but the boat had moved further away. There was nothing to be done except continue after it and hope the line would break. Once again Mac settled into a rhythm, though this time it was more frantic.

His legs were starting to tire and he had just felt the first tinge of a cramp in his quad when his next breath brought water, not air, into his lungs. Knowing he needed to relax, he tilted his head back and started to breathe deeply. The angle of his head helped, but he felt himself slipping under the surface. As he breathed, he realized that the BC had deflated. He knew his air supply was dead, but instead of jettisoning the tank and BC, Mac reached for the fill valve and brought it to his mouth. Taking a deep breath, he pressed the inflator button and exhaled into the tube. A rush of air went into the bladder, but it wasn't enough, and he felt water fill his ears. Mac knew being adrift without the makeshift PFD was a death sentence. With his head dropping under the water, he kicked hard with his fins, ignoring the painful cramp now encompassing his right quad. It took several attempts until, exhausted, he bobbed freely on the surface.

The only problem was neither boat was visible.

Nassau

Trufante had been moved three times over the past few days, and each time the accommodations had improved. They had tested him for the virus, but the results hadn't come back. He was sure he was clean, though, and his self-diagnosis revealed that the only symptoms he felt were probably caused by his body being deprived of beer and weed.

He had been moved from the jail where he had been tested to a clinic that wasn't really sure what to do with him. From there he was taken to a hotel, where he was told he would ride out the quarantine period. It wasn't a bad deal until they removed the mini bar from the room. As he answered a knock on the door for his room service dinner, he thought that if this was the new normal of Bahamian justice, he was all aboard, at least until he could figure out how to get out of there.

It was day three of the fourteen days they told him he'd be in quarantine. A scan of the cable networks on TV provided a picture of what was happening in the outside world. Lockdowns were everywhere, which was both good and bad for his chances of escape. The first thing he needed to do was to scope out the hotel's security. He'd tried the door once and found he could open it, but he immediately garnered the attention of a uniformed officer sitting by the elevators.

A glance out his window told him he was too high up to jump. The only way out was through the building. Besides the safety edicts and regulations being placed on different areas, what his perusal of the cable networks told him was that the playing field was changing quickly. The way things were going, he could be moved back to the jail at any time. He had to escape now.

The Cajun was better at action than planning, but he knew he needed to wait for an opportunity. He was also aware that should he be able to break out, he would need help to get out of the country. Eyeing the phone on the nightstand, he decided to see if they had placed any restrictions on it.

A dial tone blared into his ear when he picked up the receiver. That gave him hope, and he dialed "O." The operator came on a second later, and rather than telling him that she would be unable to help, she politely asked what she could do for him.

"Yes, ma'am." He used his most cordial southern drawl. "I'd like to make an international call."

There was a pause for a few seconds. "Looks like your service is restricted."

Trufante was prepared for this. Remembering the days of calling cards, he asked, "What about a credit card call?"

There was no delay this time. "I can connect you to an outside operator."

Trufante's Cadillac-grill grin broke through. He had beaten the first line of security. When the operator came on the line, he gave her Mel's cell number. He had debated who to call. Pamela should have been his first choice, but she didn't always answer. Mac was worse. Mel was glued to her phone at all times. He might not get the same warm reception as from Pamela, but that wasn't what he was looking for.

The operator took the number and asked for a credit card. Trufante smiled again and rattled off the memorized digits of Pamela's card. He only hoped it wouldn't be declined. A few long seconds later, the operator thanked him and said she was connecting the call.

A frustrating minute of clicks and static took over the line, followed by an electronic ringing sound. It sounded four times, and Trufante was preparing a voice mail message in his head when Mel's voice came on the line.

"Hello? Melanie Woodson here."

"Yo, Mel. Trufante."

"How . . . ?"

Not sure how long the call would last, he interrupted her. "They got me in a hotel now—something about this virus and all. I'm gonna do a jail break later. Where y'all at?"

"That would be stupid. We're building a case against the prosecution. There's a very good chance that you could walk."

"I'd rather run, and I'm in a hurry."

The line went silent for a minute. Trufante was anxious but held back. He knew Mel, and she needed to process everything.

"Your only hope is to get out of the country and fast."

"Roger that."

"They could try to extradite you, but I don't think you're worth it."

He laughed, allowing another delay for her to figure out what to do with him. He knew once she made up her mind to help, she would move heaven and earth. "We're sitting out by *Ghost Runner*."

He liked the fact that she didn't identify the reef. Trufante felt his luck running strong. "I'll be there. Hang out on channel sixty-eight in case I can reach out." He hung up before she could change her mind.

A knock on the door interrupted his thoughts.

"Room service."

Trufante moved from the bed to the door and opened it. The same man who had brought his dinner earlier stood outside waiting to take the cart. The Cajun smiled again. The man was sullen, obviously knowing he wasn't getting a tip from the incarcerated COVID patients.

"Y'all want to get high?"

The man looked both ways and ducked into the room.

31

Wood's Island

WITH THE SHOTGUN HELD AT THE LOW READY POSITION, PAMELA stayed a few steps behind as Ned pulled the man by his bound hands toward the clearing. When Ned stopped near the steps to the house, she saw both fatigue and uncertainty on his face.

"You okay?" she asked.

"Been better, but yeah, I'm good."

"What's his deal?"

"Believe it or not, we've got a minor celebrity here." He went on to tell her about Luciano and his family's connection to the lost plane.

For the first time in several days she was able to focus on something besides Trufante. She smiled at the sky, trying to send some good vibes his way, and turned to Ned. "We need to find Mac."

"At least to let him know I don't need savin'. That's a fool's errand he's on, trying to bring that gold up. The government finds out, they won't let him keep enough to cover his expenses."

"You know that's where they went, right?" Pamela said.

"And they've got company. Our friend here has a buddy in the CIA who sent a satellite shot of Rudy's boat sitting on the wreck. He took off yesterday. Figured that was where he was going."

"So, what do you need your papers for? Can't the CIA just tell you the coordinates?"

"Greed. They all want it for themselves."

Luciano lifted his head. "That gold belongs to my family. We made it legally."

"Legal is a little ambiguous when you're talking about Cuba in the fifties."

"What the hell do you know?" Luciano spat.

"And he's in bed with the CIA?" Pamela asked.

"Things were different back in the day. Vegas was on the rise, but it was Cuba that was on fire. Everyone wanted a piece of the action." Ned stopped and looked at her.

Pamela nodded, telling him she was interested.

"Batista was as crooked as they came, and the mob's involvement was out in the open. As long as the money stayed there, the United States couldn't do anything but watch—and insert the CIA to keep an eye on things. Turns out they did more than that. They were so involved that when it became certain that Castro was going to seize power, the CIA actually gave his forces money to try and keep the countries allied after the Revolution."

"That didn't work out too well for them." Living in South Florida or the Keys, you had to have your head under a rock not to know the history, as well as the current events, in Cuba. Though the countries had maintained no diplomatic ties until a few years ago when Obama tried to normalize relations with Raul Castro, policy on the island affected much of Florida. Only ninety miles from Key West, the peninsula was close enough to be a receptor of both wanted and unwanted refugees. The rules about granting political asylum changed with each administration, but the people came regardless.

"You guys want it too, or at least your buddy does," Luciano said.

All this information confused Pamela, and she tried to concentrate on the parts that might help Trufante. Even if there was only a fraction of the three billion dollars rumored to be aboard the plane, she figured someone in the Bahamian government would be sketchy enough to accept a "payment" for his release.

Mac and Mel were incorruptible. Mac would try a jailbreak before he bribed an official, and Mel did everything through legal channels. That left the man tied up in front of her and his connection to the CIA as her best bet for freeing Tru. It was time for Luciano to face the facts.

"You can't do this without the CIA." She spoke directly to Luciano, ignoring the confused expression on Ned's face.

"Hold on, missy." Ned's face was turning red, and he motioned for her to move out of earshot.

He secured the line to the stair railing and followed her to the side of the shed. Luciano was in plain sight, but they were far enough away he couldn't hear the conversation. Pamela kept the pistol pointed at the gangster.

"What are you playin' at? Mac's over there. This half-baked connection of our gangster here and the CIA could get him killed—and Mel too."

"I'll admit it's about three-quarters baked, but it's the only way I can figure to get Trufante out."

"Oh, the bad-boy boyfriend."

She ignored him and thought about how to work this to her advantage. "The government there. They're not going to let Mac just poach their treasure, right? You said so yourself." Pamela had been around Mac long enough to know how hard it was to get a salvage permit in the US. She had to assume it was worse in the Bahamas.

Ned crossed his arms. "You're right about that."

They were distracted by Luciano waving his bound hands in front of his face. It appeared as if he was striking himself, until Pamela realized he was batting at swarming mosquitos. "So?"

Ned was quiet for a minute. "It ain't my fight. The gold don't interest me either, but the plane does. Maybe having the government involved isn't such a bad idea."

Pamela started for the stairs to the house, ready to implement her plan, but Ned grabbed her arm.

"Listen now. That's a dangerous man, and if the CIA guy's playing nice with him, that means he's working off the books." He looked her in the eyes. "Just be careful."

Pamela leaned over and kissed him on the forehead, then marched towards Luciano. She pulled her phone from her back pocket and handed it to him. "Call the CIA dude."

Luciano looked up defiantly.

"Got a few deputies at the sheriff's station that are friends. Trespassing out here'll land you in jail."

LUCIANO SMELLED A DEAL. How good it was didn't matter if it got him a shot at the plane. If there's one thing he'd learned from being a third-generation gangster, it was that deals could be changed.

"What do you have in mind?"

The woman stood with her hands on her hips. Luciano knew that look. She hadn't thought things through and was scared to dictate terms—another advantage for him.

"You want a piece of the cake?"

"It's for my boyfriend." She paused. "And Mac needs a new boat."

This was going better than expected. Luciano saw her glance at Ned, who was standing beside her.

"And Ned wants the plane preserved or something."

"I don't see a problem with any of that. You will leave me free to deal with the government aspects?" He knew Taggart would cooperate. He would have liked to cut him out, but he had no government connections to get her boyfriend out of jail or legally recover the wreck. At this point, Luciano needed the CIA guy. Later on, he would figure out how to nullify whatever deals he cut.

"His number's in my phone." Luciano held up his bound hands and shrugged.

"No tricks, now." Pamela raised the pistol.

"I appear to be outgunned."

Pamela whispered something to Ned. The old man stepped close enough to untie the line while still being able to evade Luciano if he tried anything. Once his hands were free, he rubbed them together to get the circulation back.

"It's out there somewhere."

With the barrel of the shotgun trained on him, Luciano crawled through the brush, trying to find the phone that had flown from his hands. Fortunately, the phone's flashlight revealed its location, but reaching it meant a battle with the brush. Swatting the bugs from his face as he made his way in the dim light, he swore the woman would pay for this. At first, he had taken her at face value, but he'd seen enough people with a finger on a trigger to know when someone actually would pull one. He had no doubt she would shoot. A few minutes later, he grasped for the phone and retreated toward the trail.

He would have liked to make the call in private, but that wasn't going to happen with Annie Oakley pointing a shotgun at him. Scrolling through his recent calls, he found Taggart's number and pressed the "connect" icon. While he waited for the call to go through, he looked up and studied the woman.

He was generally good at evaluating people—especially threatening ones. She surprisingly fell into that category. Her dress and grooming pointed toward the free-spirited side of the spectrum, but she could clearly handle the weapons she carried. He'd sensed she was a little flighty, but there was clearly intelligence in her eyes, though they were clouded by a fog created by too much booze or weed.

A voice on the phone turned his focus away from her. "Taggart," he muttered.

"Luciano. I thought you were going cowboy on me."

"Just a little investigative work. I got a deal for you."

"The CIA doesn't make deals with the likes of you. I know where the wreck is."

"If you could get it done by yourself, you would. We both know you need help. I got a Ph.D. guy here and a salvage guy there. I need you to do the paperwork." Luciano paused, wondering if he should address the woman's boyfriend now or let it slide. Her muscles had tensed and he watched her finger, resting just outside the trigger guard, twitch. "And I need someone sprung from one of their jails."

"Anything else? Maybe your own island or something?"

"I know you got the connections to do this, and we'll split the proceeds." The line fell silent.

Finally, Taggart replied. "Alright. I've got the coordinates. Maybe best if you headed over there. I'll be on site and have some answers in the morning."

"We'll be needing for you to handle the transportation." One of the conditions for Luciano to remain at large during one of the many ongoing investigations he was involved in had required him to turn in his passport.

"This is gonna cost you."

"Whatever. You gonna help me out here or what?" Luciano was losing patience.

"Marathon airport. Eight tomorrow morning. I'll have a company plane waiting for you." The line disconnected, and Luciano turned to Pamela.

"Agreed. We need to get over there to meet him in the morning."

"He'll get my boyfriend out of jail?"

"It's the CIA, sweetheart."

She frowned, and he started to wonder how high maintenance she was going to be. It was a trait in women he had little tolerance for.

"I don't have a passport," she said.

He laughed. "Like I do? We'll be traveling courtesy of the CIA."

"I'm going up." Ned started to climb the stairs.

Luciano paused and wondered if he should try to talk them both into coming. He was their captive, but with a little luck and some help from the CIA, that would change in the morning. Having two hostages was trouble, and the old man had already provided him with what he needed. The last thing he was worried about was the archeological significance of the find. In fact, it would probably delay the recovery of the gold to have the old guy along.

"Go ahead, with my compliments."

"Hmmph." Ned leaned heavily on the rail as he made his way upstairs.

"I should check on him," the woman said.

"You got a name, honey?"

"Pamela." She started to follow the old man.

"Good. Pam. You make sure he's set."

She turned back. "Pamela."

Luciano looked up at her. There was a fire in her eyes that he hadn't seen before, and he felt himself becoming aroused. "Right, Pamela."

He watched her ascend the stairs, staring at her butt until she disappeared into the house.

STEVEN BECKER

A MAC TRAVIS ADVENTURE

WOOD'S
HOPE

Nassau

TRUFANTE STEPPED BACK AND WAITED UNTIL THE MAN CROSSED the threshold. The Cajun had placed the cart well inside the room, which allowed him to get behind the man. Once the guy was inside, Trufante shut the door and slammed the lamp into the man's head. It wasn't meant to be a deadly blow—even the worst-case punishment for the charges he was being held on was better than that for murder. There was still a moment of worry when the man crumpled to the ground. A glance at the lamp showed that there was no blood. That was a good sign.

Trufante put the lamp back on the nightstand. and knelt down over the man. Before he could check for a pulse, he heard a moan, and the man moved. Relieved that the guy was alive, Trufante pulled the man's clothes off. He grabbed the bedsheet that he had already prepared by tearing strips and rolling them up, and bound the guy's hands and feet.

The man was still unconscious when Trufante left the room. He'd studied the evacuation map posted on the back of the door and chosen to exit using a secondary route, indicated by a staircase and freight elevator, on the opposite end of the floor from where the guard was sitting. He had no way of knowing if there was another guard posted there, but he had to take the chance.

Feeling like an uptight hipster, Trufante pushed the cart in front of him and walked as casually as his borrowed pants would allow. The clothes were sized for a man a few inches shorter, causing the inseam to pull at his crotch. He looked down at the gap between the cuff and his flip-flops—clearly the weakness in the disguise. There was nothing to do about it. For the slim Cajun, while the pants were a squeeze, the shoes were just too small. He felt odd to be out of his standard cargo shorts and T-shirt. His adolescent growth spurts had made him the butt of many jokes, and as a result, he couldn't remember the last time he'd worn long pants.

Trufante used the tablecloth draped over the service cart to help hide his feet, and he expected with his thousand-dollar grin he could talk his way past all but the most observant guards. Turning the last corner, he breathed a sigh of relief when he saw the exit sign and the unguarded freight elevator. The stairs were preferable, but he needed the cart to perpetuate his disguise. As he approached the elevator, he had a moment of panic when he couldn't find any buttons. Searching the trim around the door, he noticed a card reader similar to the one on the doors.

That wouldn't have been a problem if he were a guest or employee of the hotel, rather than of the state. But something had been rubbing near his groin, which he thought was due to the poor fit of the pants. Now he realized what it was. It took an effort to get his hand into the pocket, but it came out with a key card. Stepping to the reader, he inserted it into the slot and heard a chime. A display above the door illuminated, showing the elevator was several floors above him.

Trufante kept one eye on the display and the other on the

open end of the hallway. He knew at any second someone could come around the corner. Finally, the chime sounded again, and the doors opened. A woman in a maid's uniform looked up at him, and he could see from her expression that she expected someone else.

"Sorry to disappoint, ma'am." Trufante used his best Southern drawl, dripping with courtesy. He probably could have subdued her as well, but leaving a trail of bodies behind was not his style. He had better luck with honey. "Room seven-fifteen. You'll find him a little groggy."

Her face wrinkled and he felt for a second that she was getting ready to scream. Stepping toward her he smiled, trying to dissuade her. "Please. He's okay."

"If youse says so." She pushed the cart past him and disappeared around the corner.

Her reaction, or lack of one, was a gift, but he knew he was out of time. The elevator could hold the cart, but otherwise was an unknown. There was a very good chance it would stop again before reaching the ground floor. Instead of chancing another encounter that he might be unable to control, he opted for the stairs. Grabbing a plate with a silver dome on it from the cart, he slid the key card into the reader beside the door jamb, pushed open the door, and started down the stairs.

His long legs made short work of the descent, and he quickly found himself at the ground floor. He had no idea where the steel door in front of him would open, but suspected it was at the back of the house—the kitchen or laundry areas. Taking a deep breath, he opened it and found himself in a hallway. The kitchens were off to the left and what looked like the laundry to the right. Following a sign that indicated there was an exit ahead, he moved down the hallway, passing several offices and storerooms on the way.

Something felt wrong, though. Trufante trusted his instincts.

His gut had saved him more times than he could count. It took him a minute to realize what it was. The place was near deserted. The virus must have shut most of the hotel down. The revelation changed his plan slightly, and backtracking, he found an unoccupied office and stepped inside. Removing the dome from the plate, he recovered his clothes from their hiding place and quickly changed. Feeling more like himself, his unease disappeared as he approached the exit door and pushed through into the parking lot.

Thankful that it was nighttime, Trufante ran toward the street. His plan was simple from here. Find the first boat he could steal and head out to meet Mac. In doing so, he knew he was adding theft to the other charges on his resume, but it was too late to go back now. Freedom was worth the risk.

Trufante could smell the saltwater from a mile away and headed down a slight incline to the harbor ahead. As he approached, he noticed the lack of activity on the water. With the usual array of boats coming and going, it would have been easy to blend in and escape, but with the harbor a ghost town, he would surely be noticed. There was nothing to do about that now. His goal was the reef that held *Ghost Runner*. Once he got there he hoped things would become simpler.

Slowing to a fast walk, Trufante reached the dock and found a finger pier with several rental boats tied off. He checked the first and saw there was no key, then looked around for the office. A sign across the way caught his attention, and he changed direction and crossed the street. Standing in front of the plate glass window, he watched the reflection for anyone approaching. Finding the street and marina deserted, he slid over to the door and checked the handle. It was locked, as he expected, but the old wooden jamb and antiquated lockset would be child's play to dislodge. A closer inspection revealed several grooves dug in the wood, as if someone had already tried to break in. From the looks of it, they had probably succeeded. A screwdriver or knife was all he needed.

Moving around the back of the building, he found himself in an alley. The stores were a mixed bag of bars and restaurants, tourist shops, and boating supplies. There was nothing to be found on the first block, but ahead he could see a boat repair yard.

Trufante approached the fence and scanned the alley. There was no one in sight, but a recollection of a similar incident came to him. He shook the fence, making more noise than any burglar would, and waited. The yard remained quiet, and he quickly scaled the chain-link fence. Landing lithely on the other side, he waited to make sure there were no dogs, then walked toward a small shed. The door stood open, allowing him a selection of tools. He grabbed a screwdriver and flat-tipped pry bar.

A few minutes later, he was back in front of the old door. Leaning over the flat bar, he wedged it into the gap between the door and jamb. A glance around told him he was unobserved, and he levered the bar, prying the door and jamb apart just enough for the latch to slip out of the receiver. Pulling the door open, he checked the street once more and entered the shop.

Having spotted the key rack from the large window, he was in and out in seconds. With a half-dozen key chains in hand, he crossed the street to the finger pier where the rental boats were docked. It took only seconds to match the numbers scrawled on one of the little buoys attached to the key chain to one of the boats. It was a small outboard suitable for fishing the shallow reefs offshore, not for a longer, open-water trip. Continuing to work his way through the keys, he finally found one to a midsize center console. Hopping in, he inserted the small plastic ring into the receiver of the kill switch, stuck the key into the ignition, and turned it clockwise. The engine roared to life, and after checking that the gas tank was full, he freed the lines and tossed them onto the dock.

Minutes later, he was exiting the harbor. He found the boat sluggish and underpowered, but the complaints ended after he found the previous renters had left a six-pack in the cooler. After his jail break, the warm beer tasted like champagne, and he quickly emptied several cans. The Cadillac grill was back, and his mood soared as the boat left the harbor and entered open water.

The Wreck Site

Mac found himself between the two boats. Instead of frantically kicking toward Pip and Mel, which would have attracted the attention of Rudy, he moved slowly through the water. Kicking on his back, he was able to see Rudy's boat and watched as the smuggler and his divers worked on the two fouled engines. The engines were angled out of the water with their lower units and propellers exposed.

In the great fishing debate between monofilament and braided line, Mac had leaned toward the mono side. He liked to feel the line stretch when a big fish was on the end. Braid's thinner diameter and superior strength made it a natural for deep-dropping and casting, but for trolling Mac had preferred mono—until now. There was no doubt the shafts were wrapped tightly with the thinner material. The divers were working from the water while Rudy was above, all three trying to hack away the fishing line that had crippled them.

Once he had moved out of sight, he started to kick harder, but the tank valve kept banging into his head. He had been too panicked to realize or do anything about it before. Now, he flipped the gear over his head, unscrewed the first stage, released the low-pressure hose from the inflator, and freed the strap. The tank dropped to the bottom, leaving him holding the inflated BC. Unencumbered by the weight and bulk of the tank, he moved forward.

When he was about a hundred yards away from Pip's boat, he started to call out, but his voice was lost in the sound of the outboards. His sense of urgency increased and he called out louder. This time his voice was lost to the wind as the twin engines kicked up a rooster tail of white spray and moved away. Seconds later, the boat was lost to the night.

33

The Wreck Site

DRIFTING TEN MILES FROM LAND WITH ONLY HIS BC HOLDING HIM above the water, Mac tried to focus on the positives. This wasn't the first time he had been in this situation, but he knew unless he was rescued, the probability of reaching land was near zero. In the waters off the Keys, the hundred-mile-long chain of hundreds of islands was fairly easy to locate; out here, he was looking for small isolated islands that were like drops of oil in a very large pool of water.

The water was warm, and Mac was afloat. That was the good news. Pip had to realize he was missing, and Mac knew neither he nor Mel would give up the search. He questioned why they had moved off, though. Without knowing his position, they very easily could have gone back to the drop point to start a search pattern. Mac thought that made sense, but with only his head and shoulders out of the water, he could barely see over the waves. There was little chance he would see the all-around light on Pip's T-top.

Just after Pip disappeared, Rudy, too, had limped off on his two functional engines. Having him out of the picture was a relief. Mac figured it would take the crippled boat several hours to cover the ten miles to Chub Cay. It would then have to be put onto the hard to have the propellers pulled. Removing the line was a simple matter after that, but there was a good likelihood the lower units were damaged.

Rather than wear himself out kicking toward an unknown goal, Mac decided to conserve his energy. He bobbed on the waves, hoping to sight the Freeman each time he was lifted by a crest. Several times he saw a light in the distance, but it quickly disappeared the next time he was able to look. That didn't mean it wasn't still there. At the mercy of the seas, he had little control over where the crests would place him. One wave he would be facing east; the next, north.

Still, he had faith, and he had accomplished his goal. He now knew that Rudy had recruited the mystery divers who had been down to the wreck. He had also crippled the smuggler's boat. If he could get back to Pip, there was a real chance they could bring up enough gold to keep Rudy at arm's length. Even without the government's interference, the salvage operation would be risky. Mac hoped the smuggler would be happy for his cut—in exchange for Ned.

Mac noticed over the last few minutes that he had been sinking slowly into the water. Where once his shoulders and chest had been supported by the buoyancy of the BC, now his neck was barely above water. He'd had to manually inflate the BC several times already, and he reached for the inflator valve. It filled with three breaths, reassuring him that there perhaps was only a small leak, but Mac knew that could change.

As Mac dropped the hose, his hand brushed against something. Reaching down for the tube, his fingers found the signal whistle attached to the hose. Bringing it to his mouth, he blew three long blasts. Mac had learned from past experience the value of a quality signal device. The whistle's shrill sound pierced the night air. He didn't expect an immediate response, but if Pip and Mel were still out there, they would eventually hear it. Knowing that consistency was important, he counted ten breaths then repeated the pattern. He would continue to do this until he was rescued.

Without his watch, Mac would have had no idea how long he had been alone. When he looked down to check, he saw it had only been twenty minutes since the boats had moved off. He wasn't sure how that aligned with his perception, and it didn't matter. It was getting to be too long. If Pip was searching for him, Mac would have at least heard his outboards in the distance.

Mac started to worry.

The warm water and flotation device that had comforted him earlier were at some point going to be his demise. It took a long time, but it was possible to become hypothermic in eighty-degree water. The leaking air bladder in the BC also worried him. Drifting along, he was not uncomfortable. The rising and falling of the waves was almost hypnotic and was one of the reasons he had lost track of time. As his body temperature slowly decreased, he would become sleepy. If he dropped off and the bladder lost enough air, he might drown.

Mac put those thoughts aside. He had to have confidence in Mel and Pip. That hope faded after the first hour, and he started to wonder what had happened to them. Pip had the smarts and the boat to avoid Rudy, so Mac doubted they'd had a confrontation. His best guess was that they had seen the smuggler's boat remain stationary and moved out of sight.

Well into the second hour, both his energy and faith were waning. By the third hour he was starting to get tired, and had already nodded off once. His head bobbed and hit the water, waking him up. Mac had no idea how long he had been out, but it was long enough for the bladder to have deflated. At least that was his first thought. As he became more alert, he heard the sound of an outboard in the distance.

This time of night there was no reason for anyone to be cruising these dangerous waters. Several miles in any direction were deepwater channels that bypassed the reefs. As the sound increased, Mac suspected it had to be someone coming to the wreck site. That left either Pip and Mel; Rudy and crew; or the RBDF. Evaluating his condition and chances for survival, he decided that even the latter two were better than being lost at sea.

Mac started blowing the whistle again, repeating the three-blast sequence. For a while, he thought it had gone unnoticed, but he knew persistence was often the attribute which separated winners from losers, or in this case, the living from the dead. There was a point where the sound of the boat faded away, but it soon returned.

Mac focused on the whine of the motor between bursts on the whistle. He wasn't sure if his faculties were diminished, but it started to sound as if the boat was moving in a circle around him—like a search pattern. His hope soared and he blew with renewed vigor. Finally, the boat was noticeably closer. Most people could tell the difference between a multi-engine outboard and an inboard diesel. Mac's experience boosted his ability to define boats by their sound to a point where he knew right away that it was neither Pip's nor Rudy's boat. It wasn't the Royal Bahamas Defense Force, either. It sounded like a single-engine outboard.

The white all-around light became visible a few minutes later, and he knew the whistle had been heard. The question now was who was onboard. Mac had reached the point where he didn't care. As the boat approached, he saw the outline of the driver, and he smiled.

"Mac freakin' Travis."

Trufante's thousand-dollar grin brightened the scene. "Never mind that, get me onboard."

Trufante put the boat in neutral and moved to the stern. He picked up a dock line and tossed it back to Mac. The first attempt missed, and he had to reposition the boat. The second throw landed right in front of Mac. He grabbed the line and allowed Trufante to pull him in.

"Hot damn, Mac. What are you doing floating out here? And where's Mel? Talked to her a couple hours ago."

"You talked to Mel?"

"Hotel telephone. Can you believe they put me in a hotel room?"

There wasn't much Mac didn't believe when it came to the Cajun. "That story's gonna have to wait." Mac climbed the small ladder mounted to the stern and slid over the transom. He started shivering as soon as the night air touched his skin—it had been warmer in the water. Trufante must have noticed and stripped his shirt off and handed it to Mac. He took it and resisted the urge to smell it before he put it on. Once he did, he was glad for the warmth.

"The questions can wait. We need to find Pip and Mel. Where were you supposed to meet them?"

"On the wreck site. Knew generally where it was, but Mel gave me the numbers."

Mac glanced at the display. The coordinates were in degrees, minutes, and seconds. He, like most fishermen, used degrees and decimal minutes. The difference would get you in the ballpark, but not on the same base. Mac spared his deckhand the explanation. He knew the coordinates by heart. In the settings menu of the GPS unit, he changed the format, and then re-entered the coordinates. The waypoint was about a half-mile away.

Mac knew this wasn't Trufante's boat, but the Cajun had

claimed temporary ownership and stayed at the wheel. Mac hit the "GOTO" button and leaned against the seat as Trufante accelerated toward the correct spot. As they approached, Mac could see a boat on site. It took another few minutes to identify the owner.

Mac expected Pip was armed and called over while they were still well away from the boat.

"Son of a bitch." Pip sounded relieved.

Mac heard the response clearly enough to allow Trufante to approach the boat.

"Hurricane did the old man good," Trufante said, as they pulled alongside.

The difference between the freeboards of the two boats made tying up alongside almost impossible. Mac settled on a single line down-current that kept the boats close enough to talk, and far enough away to prevent damage to the Freeman. After discovering that the boat Trufante had used to rescue him was a "liberated" rental, Mac decided it was disposable.

Mac sent Trufante over first, noticing the warm embrace from Pip, and the more distant greeting from Mel. She had to be wondering how he was here. Trufante turned, ready to help Mac aboard, but Mac held up his hand and let the rental boat drift back on the line. Even with the lockdown, he figured the missing boat would be discovered in the morning. It wasn't worth looking to see if it had a GPS tracker, which he assumed it did. The best thing would be if it were found far away from the wreck site.

Boats this size had kill switches, small pieces of plastic that fit into a slot on the dashboard. In theory, the driver would be wearing an expandable cord looped around their wrist. If they were thrown overboard, the plastic disk would be pulled free of the slot and the motor would shut off. In practice, the only time this was done was with jet skis. This boat would run as long as the spacer was in the ignition.

Mac released the line and brought it back aboard. He noticed the questioning looks from Mel, Pip, and Trufante, but ignored them as he idled around the larger boat and set a course for the west. The only thing lying between the boat and Miami was Bimini, and that was almost a hundred miles away.

Once he was sure of the course, he tied the wheel off and pressed the throttles. The boat started to take off. Once it had planed out, Mac pulled the throttle back until the boat was running smoothly, then ran toward the stern and launched himself into the water.

34

STEVEN BECKER

A MAC TRAVIS ADVENTURE

WOOD'S HOPE

The Wreck Site

MEL REACHED DOWN AND HELPED MAC ABOARD THE FREEMAN. Showing some pent-up emotion, she embraced him. "If you're done with all this drama, maybe we can figure out what our next step should be."

Mac took her hand, climbed aboard, and returned the pressure of her hug. Letting her go, he turned in the direction of the rental boat to make sure his latest attempt at being lost at sea had been worth it. The only thing visible of the boat was a small streak of white from its wake.

"Good idea, but you could have told us first. Getting tired of fishing you out of the drink."

Mac knew that recovering him from the dark sea had been difficult. Man overboard drills were hard enough in the daytime, where protocol was for one person to point continuously to the person in the water. But the result was what Mac was interested in: Trufante was here, and the boat would be many miles off, if and when it was recovered.

He moved his thinking to the present. Mac had plenty of

time to think when he was in the water, and aside from his safety and bringing Ned back, his overriding concern was if Rudy's divers had discovered the gold. The algae-covered tarp concealing the bullion was a delicate ruse. The saving grace was that divers prided themselves on their technical skills and banging against the bottom was a sign of a novice diver. They would do their best to remain neutrally buoyant—even though it would unknowingly cost them the treasure.

"We need leverage," Mac said. "That was Rudy's boat that we buggered up with the line. He limped away on two engines, but he's got to be around here watching his radar screen. I need to see if his divers found anything, and if they didn't, bring a bar or two back up to show him." Mac figured that if Rudy's divers had failed, then producing a sample of the treasure would buy them time—and hopefully the freedom to recover the gold without any interference.

"If you think you're going back in the water for a third time tonight, you've got another thing coming," Mel said. "I'll go."

Mac had known Mel since she was a teenager. They had been close then, but their romantic involvement hadn't started until almost a decade later, when she returned to the Keys. Her expression told him this was not a battle he was going to win, and in the scope of the war, it was a minor one. He nodded his head in defeat. In truth, he had no gear after ditching his earlier, and getting back in the water was the last thing he wanted.

"Okay, you win."

Mel gave him a wary look, like he had surrendered too easily, but Mac ignored her and moved forward to help assemble her gear. The boat was quiet while she kitted up, and a few minutes later, she dropped backwards from the port-side gunwale and entered the water.

Pip relit the cigar butt. "Think that's a good idea?"

"I don't know, but you got any of them blue Gatorades?"

Trufante asked.

Pip nodded to a cooler behind the leaning post. "Been a while, eh?"

"Shit, they took out the minibar."

Mac let the two men ramble while he leaned over the side and watched the beam of Mel's light sweep back and forth. The wind had dropped over the last few hours, and the seas had quieted enough that he could make out features of the reef below as she panned the beam back and forth. He followed her until the light stopped, then watched it disappear when she entered the plane.

Mac checked his watch, trying to determine when he should start to worry. In truth, he had to admit he was already anxious. Glancing at Pip and Trufante talking quietly by the helm, he assessed the readiness and ability of the crew if there were a problem. Trufante, though a natural fishermen and good help on a boat, was a train wreck in the water. It was actually pretty common with men who made their living from the sea. Pip, though he bragged about his freediving exploits as a younger man, might be able to pull off a rescue with tanks, but Mel had the only gear.

If there was any trouble, that left Mac. He would go if needed, but he knew after this evening's exploits he was in no condition. His anxiety eased as the beam became visible again, and a few minutes later, Mac stood by the dive ladder to help her aboard.

Mel reached for the ladder and removed her fins. She handed them to Mac and took a step up, then removed her mask and spit out her regulator. Mac knew right away from her smile that she had been successful.

"Two bars enough? Suckers are heavier than I thought."

Mac extended his hand and helped her aboard. She released the Velcro band and buckles of her BC and turned her back to

Mac, who took the gear as she shrugged out of it. He immediately noticed it was heavier than it should have been. With her body fat measuring in the low teens, Mel dove with only a few pounds of weight. The gear seemed about ten pounds too heavy.

Mac set the gear down on the deck with the BC protecting the fiberglass from the tank and reached into one of the vest's pockets. His fingers touched metal and he pulled a bar free. They had kept the boat dark, using only the red screen of the chartplotter and the moon for light, but the gold still shone brightly.

"So, that's what this is all about?" Trufante said. "How much more's down there?"

Mac saw greed in his deckhand's eyes, but knew he was better than that. Mac realized unless Pip had told him that Tru didn't know about Ned being taken hostage. "Rudy's got Ned. Unfortunately, we gotta make a deal with him."

"But how much?"

"A lot."

Mac knew that the Cajun was just dreaming, and in a few minutes he would realize the gravity of the situation. The beer needed to stop, though.

"Now that we got something, what do you want to do?"

Mac moved to the electronics box over the helm and removed his phone. "Call Rudy."

"And your plan is?" Mel asked.

"See what he says. The cargo bay was undisturbed, right?"

"No sign they found anything."

"That's the third time he's had divers in the wreck, and they haven't found it," Mac said.

"Granted. He's got to be getting pretty frustrated, but we can use that to our advantage."

Mac looked at her. "How?"

"Okay, so he knows we're out here, and from what you said,

his boat's going to have to be pulled to clear the line in his shafts."

"A diver could maybe get it off, but yeah, he's out of action until at least noon tomorrow."

"We have to assume that Ned's okay. That's the only leap of faith here, okay?"

Mac nodded. He wasn't happy about putting his friend's life in danger, but he knew Mel was being pragmatic. That's what she did. The least he could do was to hear her out, not that he had any choice in it.

"Unless Ned's given him a history lesson, he probably doesn't suspect there's as much gold aboard as the rumors suggest."

"And they're just rumors," Mac said. He had been around the salvage game long enough to know that what was supposed to be there often wasn't. It went two ways, though. In the days of the Spanish Main, governors and some of the wealthier nobles often smuggled goods back to the continent without including them on a ship's manifest. It was fairly common practice, but it was more often the case that things disappeared. Taken by the sea or pilfered, there was often less bounty found than was rumored to be aboard the wrecks.

"For the sake of argument, let's pick a number that's going to satisfy him. Say two million." She paused and started punching numbers into her phone. "That's a little over a thousand pounds." She continued to work the calculator on her phone. "Or two hundred bars."

"We can bring that up on this rig," Trufante said.

Mac knew he was right. Adding that much weight, as long as it was split equally between the port and starboard fish boxes, wouldn't even lower the waterline of the Freeman. It was doable. The trick would be to recover it before mid-morning, while Rudy was immobile. They would, of course, take something for themselves to cover expenses and some profit, but it could be done. After the initial salvage operation was complete, the best thing to do was to leave the plane sit until everyone forgot it was there.

Mac thought the plan had a good chance for success, but he needed to play devil's advocate and see what its weaknesses were. The first point was obvious.

"We've got one more tank and only one set of gear. We need equipment and air. What's the harbor looking like?" Mac asked Trufante.

"Dead, man. Like a ghost town."

"It'll be even quieter now. I say we go back and raid the dive shop. We can pay for whatever we take later." He knew Mel wouldn't like it and was surprised when she offered no objections.

"Wear masks. I've been reading that's the latest. Two weeks ago if you walked into a bank with a face covering it was a felony. Now if you don't it's a misdemeanor."

"I got some fishing buffs from a tournament." Pip moved toward one of the forward holds and removed a swag bag.

Trufante sensed one of the key tenants of his existence—free shit. He leered over Pip's shoulder as he opened the bag and started rummaging through it. He came out with a handful of lightweight cotton buffs. Trufante continued to look over his shoulder, forcing Pip to hand him a shirt. He quickly slipped it over his lean frame. Mac suspected that Mel, at least, was thankful.

"What about Rudy?" Mel asked. "Isn't there a good chance he'll be there waiting for the marina to open?"

"Shit, I bet he's backed up on some deserted beach with his motors in the air making the divers cut the line from those props," Trufante said.

There were a few things that Mac never doubted about Trufante, and one was knowing how the criminal mind worked.

He did wonder, if the Cajun was so astute, how he found himself in so much trouble. Tru's idea did fit, but it also meant that if he was correct, their time window had shrunk.

"He's probably right," Mac said.

"All the same, I'm gonna sneak on into Chub. This boat cost me half a house, and I ain't in the mood to have it confiscated."

"You don't trust my Cajun *juju*?"

Pip turned back to the helm and pushed down the throttles. Mac heard him mutter something under his breath, but didn't catch it. Trufante was reaching into the cooler for another beer and missed the comment entirely. Mac decided to leave it alone. He wasn't in the mood for entertainment.

The trip back to Chub was faster and easier than the way out. The two-foot seas were indiscernible in the Freeman and within a half hour, Pip made a sweeping turn and entered the channel. Mac glanced at his watch. It was four a.m., the time of night when no one doing anything productive would be around. Their time window was small, though. Within the hour he expected fishermen to be arriving at the docks. When they reached the marina, Mac pulled up the buff to cover his mouth and nose and waited for Trufante to do the same.

Pip eased the Freeman up to the dock and the two men jumped off. Mac, knowing his way around, grabbed one of the wheelbarrows sitting near the end of the pier and moved quickly in the direction of the dive shop. Using bolt cutters would have been fast and silent, but Mac had to settle for the screwdriver and lead weight that Pip had aboard. There was no time for a trip to the hardware store.

They reached the fenced area housing the tank fill and rental equipment for the dive shop. After two loud smacks, the lock fell away easily, and they entered the cage. The wheelbarrow was quickly filled with gear for Mac and four tanks. Within fifteen minutes they were back at the dock.

The Wreck Site

MAC ALTERNATED HIS ATTENTION BETWEEN THE RADAR DISPLAY and the dark horizon. He only needed a quick glimpse at the screen to see the radar was clear. Knowing Rudy's boat had a minimal radar signature, Pip had turned the gain on the unit up enough to see a bird flying five miles away. It took longer for him to evaluate the horizon, but with patience, Mac determined that it was clear as well. It was a good sign, but he knew the clock was ticking on Rudy's return.

Tired, he clung to the insulated tumbler filled with coffee that Mel had brewed. Though Pip might look rough around the edges, he was a stickler for several things: fishing rods, guns, boats, cigars, and good coffee. After a second's reflection, he added dessert to the list. Though Mac had finally warmed up, he was still bone-weary and hoped he could accomplish his goal before dawn.

If he'd had *Ghost Runner*, bringing up the entire load of the five-pound ingots would be a matter of loading a basket and using the winch aboard the ship to do the work. Pip's electric reel might have helped, but it had been trashed by the pull from Rudy's props.

Mac settled on using a standard dock line—several lengths of it. Taking the lines Pip had aboard, he looped the eyes through each other, making two twenty-foot lines. Using a sheet-bend knot, he tied the lines together. Figuring on ten loads of twenty pounds each, Trufante should easily be able to handle the work—especially knowing what was on the other end.

Mac looked around the boat for something they could load the ingots in. He settled on a plastic basket now filled with gear and stashed in the console. Used to transport ice and fish, it was about the size of a round laundry basket, but of heavier construction. Mac dumped the contents on the deck and brought the basket to the transom, where he rigged a bridle from one end of the line and attached it to the basket.

Satisfied, he looked up and was surprised to see Chub was a dot on the horizon. Glancing at the chartplotter, the icon representing their boat was only a couple miles from the site.

"Better gear up. Don't want to waste any time." Mac moved toward the pile of gear they had "borrowed" from the dive shop. Mel was already sliding her BC onto a fresh tank.

"Five minutes," Pip called from the helm.

Mac glanced over the gunwale and watched the hull cut through the water. The boat was deceptively fast. They were still running around forty knots, and it felt like half that. After a few missteps with the unfamiliar gear, Mac turned on the air and was relieved when the needle came to a stop just north of the 3,000 PSI mark.

The boat slowed and Trufante moved forward to free the safety line clipped to the anchor. He released the tension on the windlass, and the anchor splashed quietly, followed by the jangling sound of the chain rode as it ran out. He waited until Pip called out to tie off the line. A minute later, Mac felt the boat swing. During the process, he and Mel had geared up and were sitting on opposite sides of the bow, ready to dive.

"Go," Pip called.

Mac pushed himself backwards over the side of the boat. Once in the water, he flipped over and searched for Mel. He sensed a disturbance in the dark water and was relieved when her light flashed on. Mac was surprised at how well Pip had anchored. With no marker buoy or fuss, he had the stern of the boat directly over the plane. Just as they reached the bottom, the basket, illuminated by a glow stick and weighted with a six-pound dive weight, dropped to the bottom.

They reached the broken windshield together. Mac paused and gave Mel the okay signal. She returned it, and he removed his fins and handed them to her, then entered the fuselage. Since there was only room for one diver to move through the cockpit and navigator's station, they had planned for Mel to remain outside the plane to shuttle the bars Mac brought forward to the basket for Trufante to bring to the surface.

Mac adjusted his buoyancy to allow his feet to contact the bottom. Once they did, he purged enough air that he was able to walk lightly, and more importantly, use his legs to balance himself. It was not quite like being in zero gravity, but close. Mac passed the navigator's station and entered the cargo hold. Flashing his light across the deck, he saw no sign the tarp had been disturbed.

Mac moved to the corner where he had seen the first ingot and pulled the tarp back. He found the spot where Mel had taken the two bricks, and within a few minutes he had a stack on the deck. They had decided on five bars per load, and Mac shuttled the first group to the cabin, where he handed them to Mel.

Mac paused, knowing he was wasting valuable time, but he had to see if the retrieval method was going to work. Mel quickly had the basket loaded and pulled twice on the line. A second later, the basket jerked and moved toward the surface. It was a little wobbly going up, but it appeared that Trufante had no trouble with the load. A minute later, the empty basked dropped to the bottom.

Marathon

"You good to run this back to Marathon?" Luciano asked.

Pamela blinked, tired from a sleepless night, and studied the mobster's figure, which was slightly blurry in the predawn light. They had reached a truce of sorts, or at least an agreement, that they needed each other. Though Pamela didn't trust him, it did take some of the tension from the situation, though she would have to be blind to have missed Luciano's lecherous looks. As a result, she had remained awake last night.

She rubbed her eyes. "Not a problem."

Ned stayed on the dock and released the lines as Pamela backed away. She made the sharp turn to avoid the rock at the end of the channel and spun the bow toward Marathon. Pamela knew men were attracted to her and had learned several defense mechanisms. One was to create personal space. Without even thinking about it, she positioned her body in the center of the leaning post. The news was saying that to remain out of harm's way, six feet was safe for social distancing, but Pamela already knew that was the magic number. The seat was built for two, but with the way she centered herself, there was no space for Luciano.

Clear of the rock, Pamela pushed down on the throttles, and the engines revved as the boat came up on plane. She heard Luciano say something, but his words were lost in the engine noise. She smiled as he gave up and moved to the drop-down seat against the transom. Free of Luciano, at least for now, she savored her victory as she drove into the rising sun.

As the last hint of night fell away, something lightened in her as well. Although Ned was safe, Trufante was still incarcerated —or at least he was supposed to be. But as the sun broke the horizon, her sixth sense told her he was somehow free. Despite how she felt, she realized she was dealing with a dangerous man and placed the pistol on the dash in front of her. Their arrangement was tenuous, but as long as things were moving in the right direction, she had to resist her natural urge to push them.

Pamela was as much an enigma to herself as she was to other people. She liked, and even nurtured, the shroud of mystery that surrounded her. It was no secret that she received a stipend of some kind on the first of every month. Her spending patterns were transparent, mostly because she didn't care. Anyone knowing her or Trufante was aware that they blew through money like a house on fire into third week of the month. Money was scarce after that, until the cycle repeated itself.

She also knew that like others, Mel had tried to pierce her veil of secrecy, and it was rewarding that the safeguards she had set in place had not been thwarted. Pamela also suspected, even though she rarely showed any sign of it, that Mel thought her somehow inferior.

Mac was the only one who had figured out there was more to her than met the eye. He'd seen her in too many situations where the real Pamela had been exposed. To most everyone else, she was the cute, hippy-dippy chick hanging around Trufante. Her choice of boyfriend was not intended to help her ruse; she really did love him.

It was her lack of motivation, or as her father had said, her inability to make good decisions, that had built a wall between them. As it turned out, her father had been right. Pamela was happy to take each day as it came, one of the reasons she had drifted to the Keys, where that was the overriding lifestyle. To have carried on unnoticed for the last five years was a testament to her past—one that no one had a clue about.

With the last out island behind her, Pamela shifted her course directly to the eastern edge of the Seven Mile Bridge. She'd have to watch for Knight Key Shoal, but she figured her angle of approach would avoid it. Closing on her destination, she shifted her mind into tactical mode, one she was trained for but rarely used. It might be a little rusty, but it was still there.

Most people guessed that she was a trust fund baby from a wealthy family. The first part was false—the second true. As with many people, the conditions of her upbringing forged her path in life, though it was far from what her father had planned. By high school, Pamela had grown bored and liked the escape that pot gave her. With money and designer drugs readily available, her appetite had increased. She'd gotten out of high school without incident—and without attending much school, and didn't have the grades or drive for college. That was where she and her father had parted ways—and to her rebellious mind, the army appealed to her. Most of her friends had been shocked to hear she had enlisted, but there was one thing they didn't know about her: Shooting guns, the one passion she shared with her father, was as much fun as getting stoned.

With her tall, lithe physique, which hid her surprising strength, she flew through basic training. Her high PT scores and aptitude for shooting and weapons placed her in the sights of a special forces colonel. He took her under his wing and quickly became her father figure—until he decided he wanted more than a patriarchal role. That decision had cost him and the army a rather large monthly disability payment.

Pamela let her training remain dormant, but she could channel it when she needed to, and as she steered into Boot Key channel, she felt the old confidence course through her veins.

Reaching the first green marker, she slowed to a fast idle,

which allowed Luciano to approach her. Needing direction from here, she had no choice and gritted her teeth, knowing for the next few hours they would be closer than she preferred, but erecting barriers in her head was easy, and she quickly built a strong one.

After passing the gas docks, Luciano directed her to turn into one of the side canals and then to an empty space at a dock. She eased the boat alongside, and observing the gangster's boating ineptness, directed him to tie off the stern. He fumbled with the line but got it done, and she eased the bow to the dock.

It was a nice house on a nice block, but they didn't spend enough time there for her to see more than the exterior. Luciano led her around the side of the house to a car parked in the driveway. Motioning for her to take the passenger seat, she got in the car and settled back for the short ride to the airport, where Luciano turned left onto an access road. He pulled directly onto the tarmac and stopped beside a private jet.

STEVEN BECKER

A MAC TRAVIS ADVENTURE

WOOD'S HOPE

Marathon

PAMELA KNEW SHE HAD MADE A MISTAKE. THE GANGSTER WAS EASY enough to handle, but she had underestimated the CIA agent. Just because he appeared to be corrupt didn't mean he was incompetent.

As she boarded the plane, Pamela was having flashbacks to her spec ops days. The door closed and they were quickly in the air. When Taggart asked if she'd like a cup of coffee, she said yes, but it did nothing to calm her nerves. Her always extra-sensitive perceptions told her she had made a bad decision to get on the plane. A few minutes later, Pamela began to feel lightheaded, and her limbs felt like lead. She couldn't move. The coffee had been spiked with some kind of paralytic agent. Within minutes, she was unable to move.

"So, let's have a chat, shall we?" the CIA agent said.

Pamela could only watch as the man glanced down at his phone.

"Pamela Rydell." He looked down again.

Pamela guessed he was reading her dossier. No one else

knew her by that name. Her alias in the Keys was Schwartz. She made an effort to respond, but her mouth was frozen. The discovery caused her a moment of panic until she discovered that she could easily breath through her nose. Her head was immobile, but she had enough control over her eyes to scan the cabin. Luciano appeared to be in a similar state.

"I don't expect answers, but I will lay out the groundwork for what is about to happen." The man smiled.

Pamela remembered him being introduced as Taggart. She thought back to the incidents leading to this moment in an attempt to see if her thinking had been affected by the drug as well. She could recall everything from when Luciano had appeared on the island. She remembered that Ned was safe, or at least she thought so, which gave her some comfort.

Despite the drug, her mind was sharp, and she felt the professional edge that she'd tried to suppress through alcohol and drugs return. Many "retired" operatives still craved the adrenaline rush of their past assignments and sought it out through other areas. She'd been in trouble several times since coming to the Keys and often wondered if part of her attraction to Trufante was his tendency to land on the wrong side of events. As a result, her skills were still sharp, though only used intermittently.

Facing the CIA man, she thought this might be the test.

"Batista's gold. Lost to the world, until your friend"—He glanced at his phone again—"Mac Travis found it." He paused. "We never looked in the Bahamas. The other planes were bound for Tampa, and this one for the Dominican Republic, where the deposed dictator and his family were exiled.

"How it got there is anyone's guess, but now that it's been found, I want my piece of it."

The Wreck Site

Things so often went wrong that as Mac watched the last bar go up, he was surprised. There was other good news as well. The ingots they had removed had barely made a dent in the gold-lined deck of the plane. The rumors may have been right.

Mac followed Mel to the surface and waited for Trufante to manhandle the last basket over the gunwale. When Mac climbed aboard, Pip was on his hands and knees placing the last brick into the starboard fish box. He pulled the zipper shut on the large insulated bag he used for his tournament catches and closed the hatch. Grabbing hold of one of the tubes used to brace the T-top, he smoothly pulled himself up.

Mac was surprised to see a smile on his friend's face, creeping up around the cigar butt.

"What's up with you? Seeing that gold take twenty years off your life?" Trufante asked.

"So, here's the thing. They took some blood out of me, spun it up, and this, that, and the other thing, put it back in my knee. Damned thing's like new again. Almost worth it, except for all them needles."

"Shit legal?" Trufante asked.

Mac knew how his friend hated shots. "Whatever they did, I'm glad for you."

"And what's up with you? From that shit-eating grin on your face, I'm guessing there's more gold down there," Pip said.

"Enough for you to dump this and upgrade to a forty-four."

"Damn. We still got trouble, though. Saw a boat on the radar running this way a few minutes ago."

They gathered around the console and watched the boat creep toward them on the radar screen. With the zoom set to twenty miles, any visible movement meant the boat was moving fast. The recovery had gone well, but had taken longer than Mac expected. They'd used two tanks each, and the sun was now working toward its zenith. "Well, we know it's either Rudy or the RBDF. It's about time to deal with the smuggler, but I don't want to be here if it's the locals." If the liberation of the dive gear had been discovered and reported, Mac suspected there were enough cameras around the marina and stores to identify Pip's boat. He was counting on the lockdown to buy them some time. If the theft was discovered, the RBDF would laugh at his claim that he meant to either return or pay for the stuff. The only positive was that he and Mel were in the country legally, but especially after the jail break, Trufante's presence could land them all in jail.

"The sooner we're out of here the better. My vote's for international waters," Mac said.

"Makes sense. There's a good chance that Rudy stashed Ned in the Keys. There'd be no reason to bring him here," Mel said.

"Probably right. You good with taking a ride?" Mac asked.

"Brought my US passport. I'm ready for anything. What about the Cajun?" Pip asked.

"It'd be a lot easier to handle on US soil," Mel said, reading from her phone. "Pleasure boats are only required to call in on entry. If ICE wants a face-to-face, the agent will let you know where to report. Might not even be a problem."

Mac knew that with Trufante, everything was a problem. "With this virus, I'd bet they waive any contact." Mac turned to Pip. "It's your boat, though, so your call."

"So, here's the thing. What about all that gold down there?" Pip asked.

"It'll keep, at least until we get Ned back," Mac said.

"And get a permit," Mel said.

"Before we hightail it out of here, I'd be curious to see who that is." Mac turned to the radar screen.

The depth-charge ringtone on Mac's phone sounded, interrupting the conversation. He reached into the electronics box and pulled it out. "Pamela?"

"This Travis?" The voice definitely was not Pamela's.

Mac placed the call on speaker. "Yeah. What can I do for you?" Trufante was in his face. He pushed the Cajun away and tried not to let the emotion he was feeling into his voice.

"I'm assuming you saw whose phone the call came from?"

"I did. Put her on. It's pretty clear you want something from me, so let's cut the BS," Mac said.

"Mac?" Her voice sounded like someone coming from a dental procedure.

"You okay?"

"This guy says he's CIA, and he's involved with some other guy that sounds like . . ." Her voice sounded anxious, but not distressed.

"Where are you?"

The male voice interrupted. "Enough, Travis. I'm sure you've seen the boat coming toward you. Sit tight and we can do this face-to-face."

Mac regretted putting the call on speaker phone. About most things, Trufante was cool as a cat, but when Pamela was involved, his emotions took over. "She sounded okay, right?" He watched the others' faces for confirmation. Mel and Pip nodded. Trufante just glared at the spot on the horizon where he expected the boat to appear.

"Sitting out here in the open is not going to get her or Ned back," Mel said, which was what Mac had been thinking. They were in an indefensible position with a boat approaching that clearly did not have good intentions.

"I still say we make a run for it. At least get out of the Bahamas," Mac said.

"It's a two-hour run if we want to get to international waters," Mel said.

Mac shook his head. There was a lot of ocean between them and Bimini. The governments of the US and Bahamas had been in negotiations since the late seventies about where the boundaries fell. Mac knew they would only be safe if they were a dozen miles west of Bimini—and that was a hundred miles from where they sat now. The Berry Islands fell roughly in the center of the archipelagic waters of the Bahamas. There was no easy exit.

With every minute of indecision, the blip on the radar screen came closer. "We at least need to get off the wreck site. No point giving that away."

"Sorry to burst your bubble. They have radar, this, that, and the other thing, they know where we are," Pip said.

"Crap."

"Say that again," Trufante said.

Wood's Island

Ned had spent most of the night on Mac's computer. Fortunately, it had no security measures or passwords. He had just opened it and it worked. Fishermen were typically only concerned about their waypoints and logbooks, and those links Ned left unopened. What he needed was information.

The discovery that both the CIA and the mob had their hands in the Batista regime's pockets was common knowledge. The history of cooperation and possibly an unknown partnership was what surprised him. Ned didn't have access to any secret websites, but he knew his way around the internet.

He missed being in the middle of things. In his mind, he was a young eighty and didn't really feel like he was at risk for the virus. Several close calls over the years, most notably from prostate cancer, had taught him to be wary—and he was. The image of being in intensive care with a breathing tube jammed down his throat keeping him alive was enough to scare him straight.

He was also a realist and knew he wasn't as spry as he once was. If things got "interesting," he would only be a burden on Mac, Mel, and Pamela. There were ways that he could help, and staying back here to figure out the relationship of the players was one.

This wasn't the first time the mob had worked with the government. Operations Husky and Underworld were two collaborations that had benefited the Allied forces in World War II. The association fizzled after several failed attempts to assassinate Castro.

After meeting his grandson, it was no surprise to see Lucky Luciano's name tied to everything related to the mob and the CIA. Though Lucky had been in jail at the time of the war, after his cooperation with the Navy and other intelligence organizations, his fifty-year sentence was commuted in 1947. He was exiled to Italy, but Cuba didn't care about the American deal, and he soon found a home in the Caribbean—where he was able to renew his occupation.

Ned looked up and rubbed his eyes. Computer screens were not as friendly to his sight as books, and he needed constant breaks. He sipped his scotch and looked around the room. The decoration and pictures still reflected his old friend Wood's life, and he reminisced about many of those adventures. Most of Ned's research was about long-lost wrecks and people who had perished centuries ago. He might be too old to be out there in the middle of the action, but he could still contribute. With a renewed vigor, he turned his attention back to the screen and started to read.

The Mafia's involvement in the planning and execution in advance of the Allied invasion of Sicily had been named Operation Husky. Mussolini was no friend to the mob, and the families readily cooperated with the Allies in drawing maps, providing photographs, and advising about terrain. It wasn't physically possible for Luciano to play a major role in the operation, but he was rumored to have provided the contacts.

As Ned read about Operation Underworld, his skin started to tingle. He'd done enough research in his time to know when he had struck gold, and he had that feeling now.

During World War II, Meyer Lansky and Luciano both were personally involved in the operation to aid the government in controlling the docks on the Eastern seaboard. Using Lansky as a conduit, the Naval Intelligence Service and Luciano worked several sides of the problem, from stopping the entrance of German and Italian saboteurs to the American docks, to controlling the labor unions. Once Luciano and the State of New York agreed to the deal, there were no more dockworker strikes through the end of the war. It might have been bad for business at the time, but both gangsters were smart enough to know that if Hitler won the war, fascism would not be their friend.

Ned's searches revealed little more until the mid-fifties, when both men resurfaced in Cuba. The intelligence agencies had been transformed and renamed after the war, but the players remained the same.

What Ned needed was to find the CIA connection.

37

STEVEN BECKER

A MAC TRAVIS ADVENTURE

WOOD'S
HOPE

Little Whale Cay

PAMELA HAD REGAINED MOVEMENT IN HER EXTREMITIES BY THE time they had landed, but it was of little help to her: she and Luciano had been restrained. As she shuffled down the stairs from the small jet, she glanced around. She could see the island as they approached, but there was little to identify it. A small housing development sat on one end and an airstrip ran down the middle of the boomerang-shaped island.

Once she had regained her ability to speak, Taggart had prodded her for information. Despite his efforts, Pamela knew the tricks of the trade and provided vague and elusive answers. A big help was that she really had no idea what was going on. Her phone had been taken, and she had watched a man sitting just aft of the cockpit plug it into his computer. She felt relief that there was nothing on her phone that could help. It didn't take her long to figure out that Luciano already had provided them with everything he knew. Watching the gangster and the CIA man, all she could think was that a pile of gold certainly made for strange bedfellows.

Two gas-powered golf carts awaited them on the runway. Taggart led Pamela to one, with the other agent pushing Luciano along behind them. With her and the gangster loaded, the CIA man walked back to the second cart. Her cart took off in the direction of a small building next to the airstrip, the only structure in sight. Pamela's senses were on full alert now that she expected she was looking at her prison.

Before they reached their destination, Pamela saw Taggart's cart head toward a docked ship. She watched as he got out of the cart and walked purposefully toward a man wearing a Royal Bahamas Defense Force uniform. He presented his credentials and was led aboard.

Just as the CIA man boarded the ship, the cart stopped. She and Luciano were led into the small metal building, which appeared to be a workshop. A table and chairs were in one corner with two locals waiting beside it. Pamela was directed to sit and Luciano was pushed into one. The difference in their treatment ended there, as they were quickly tied to the chairs.

The Berry Islands

Mac had been watching the boat racing toward them on the radar screen. It was still several miles away, but he had determined it was the RBDF cutter. The reduced signature of Rudy's boat due to his countermeasures was significantly different from this blip on the screen that said, "We're coming for you."

"Is there any way to play this to our advantage?" Mac asked. The last few minutes had been spent reviewing every option he could think of. Pip's boat was probably faster than the cutter, but making a run for it wasn't the answer. With the Bahamian's ability to call in a chopper, they would be easily apprehended before they could reach Bimini. Surrendering and hoping for mercy might save them, but Luciano still had Ned.

"Smoke screen," Pip said. "Instead of running from the bullets, we'll run into them."

"They'll corner us if we head into Chub," Mac said.

"Maybe he's onto something," Mel said.

"All ears."

"What we need is a dead drop. Rudy's divers haven't produced, so he's likely thinking there's nothing down there but the plane. We walk away with what we've got, ditch enough to satisfy him someplace that he can recover it, and get Ned back in the process."

"Got just the place," Pip said. "We head back to Green Turtle Cay. What are they going to say if I'm just heading home? All we have to do is avoid being boarded, and we're in the clear."

Mac wasn't convinced the RBDF was going to let them go that easily. He was worried that the Abacos weren't the answer. The hundred-mile ride would give the Bahamians too much time to plan, and he figured they would still be considered as running away. Mac doubted they would reach the island without being searched. That would mean the loss of the gold—and Trufante.

"Nassau," Mac said.

"That's craziness," Pip yelled, though they could easily talk over the engines. "So, here's the thing. We just pull in and hand them the keys to the boat, then give 'em Trufante and the gold?"

"No. But they're more likely to sit back and observe, rather than board us, if we appear to be heading toward their base."

"It does make sense," Mel said.

Mac glanced back at Trufante. He knew the Cajun was well aware of their position. A course change would have to involve him. Mac called him to the helm.

The Cajun took two long strides and stood behind them with a death grip on the leaning post. "Seen the course change. Nassau?"

Mac explained their plan.

"Sure as shit, I can disappear better there than out at Pip's. I'm game." He dropped back to the seat by the transom, but not before pulling out two more beers.

Mac turned to Pip. "Do it."

Pip wasted no time, and before his passengers could even brace themselves, the boat was on plane and heading south. Mac and Mel were on either side of Pip at the helm, both staring intently at the radar screen for any indication the RBDF cutter would follow. Trufante sat by the transom with a beer in each hand. Mac was well aware that his deckhand stood to lose the most if their ruse failed, but there was no other way.

Pip set a waypoint by the Nassau harbor. Trufante's assessment might be right on in normal times, but with the population all at home and with no vehicle or boat traffic, the largest city in the Bahamas would be the same as the smallest. There was no way to blend in if there wasn't anyone to blend in with. The lockdown had leveled the playing field.

The exhilaration from recovering the gold was gone. In its place, Mac's mind focused on everything that could go wrong. Their course was clear, and Mac expected the cutter would turn any second. He'd already decided that if it appeared the RBDF intended to board them, he would ditch the gold. If a trail of ingots on the bottom of the sea was the cost of the freedom he needed to find and rescue Ned, it was worth it, and despite the loss, the millions stashed in the fish boxes was pocket change compared to what remained aboard the plane.

"They're coming."

All eyes were on the screen as the cutter seemed to pause, then slowly, the dot seemed to reverse its course. The movement would have been negligible if they hadn't expected it. After a few minutes, it became clear that the boat had turned. Now the question was if they would pursue.

"What if we led them to Rudy?" Mel asked.

Mac thought for a minute. "If we knew where he was. And what about Ned?"

"The locals are better equipped to deal with a hostage situation than we are."

The idea had merit—if they could find the smuggler. Mac shifted his focus to the chartplotter, trying to figure out where he would go if he had a pair of fouled propellers and a hostage aboard. The range would be limited, and Mac doubted he would have gone into Chub Cay. As Trufante had pointed out, unless the entangled line had damaged the lower units, the repairs didn't require a mechanic or specialized tools.

Mac panned and zoomed the chartplotter to show the smaller islands in the area. A glance at Mel sitting on the other side of Pip showed she was doing the same on her phone.

"First thing we need to do is change our course to the larger channel to the east of Chub." The cutter probably wouldn't chance the cut between Whale and Little Whale Cays, where they were currently headed. Pip made the adjustment. Mac knew the radar would be a lagging indicator of the cutter's reaction, and continued to concentrate on figuring out where Rudy would be.

"You know he's on one of them beaches," Trufante said.

The Cajun was standing behind the leaning post, peering over their shoulders. "Once we're through the channel we can get eyes on him." If Trufante was correct, the shallow bottom leading to the beach areas along the coasts of Bird and Whale Cays would allow the smuggler to make his repairs.

Mac noticed the attitude of the boat change as they exited the channel, and he could see waves breaking on the beaches. The shoreline on the lee side of the island was rocky, leaving Rudy little choice but to make his repairs in the surf.

"Looks like they're coming," Pip said.

Mac instinctively glanced back, but saw nothing. "Might want to give us a little breathing room so we can find Rudy before the cutter's through the channel." Pip smiled and clamped down on the cigar in his mouth. His hand slowly pressed down on the throttles, and the boat seemed to lift out of the water as it accelerated. A glance at the chartplotter showed the speed at over fifty knots. Despite their situation, Mac paused to appreciate the moment. It was the fastest he'd ever traveled on the water.

The Freeman blazed through the channel and in minutes they were on the leeward side of the islands. Ahead, miles of pristine beach stretched to the northeast. There were several boats anchored on the reefs just offshore, and a few more right by the beach, but they were too far away for Mac to tell if one was Rudy's.

Pip reached up, opened the electronics box, and pulled a pair of binoculars out. Mac took the glasses and scanned the water. Despite the smooth ride, the wave action was enough to disrupt his attempts to focus on the beach. "Might slow down a bit and give the locals a chance to catch up."

Pip cut the RPMs in half. The boat settled enough for Mac to focus on the boats ahead. He panned the binoculars across the sandy shores, stopping at each boat. Rudy's was the last.

"Got him."

Pip slowed to a fast idle and zoomed in on the area ahead to check the soundings. The radar showed the RBDF cutter just approaching the channel. Its speed had increased, showing a direct response to their own actions. With Rudy in their sites, that was good news. Now he needed to lure the authorities to the smuggler. Pip turned to parallel the beach and added enough speed to ensure the cutter wouldn't catch them before they reached Rudy.

"This might work," Mel said, as she pecked a message in her

phone. She finished and looked up. "That was Ned. He's out at the island and okay. Apparently Pamela went Rambo and took out some gangster Rudy had left Ned with."

"No shit, that's my girl." Trufante reached into the cooler and cracked a celebratory beer.

"What happened?"

"I'm not sure. He's emailing, so it's taking a while, but somehow Pamela's headed here with a mobster and a CIA guy."

That was good news, and the mood lightened. If they could lead the RBDF to Rudy, this was going to end without the need to jettison two million in gold or risk Ned's life. Mac tried not to show his concern. He knew things never worked out smoothly and was getting the distinct feeling it was too easy.

They approached the beach where Rudy was anchored. Mac no longer needed the binoculars and set them back in the electronics box. He could clearly see the smuggler's boat anchored bow out, with the two port engines tilted out of the water. The divers were huddled around one. Mac couldn't tell how close they were to removing the line, but it wouldn't matter, as a glance back told him the cutter was only a half-mile away.

Mac knew exactly how to provoke the smuggler, but he needed to wait for the cutter to close the distance. With the current situation in hand, his concern turned to Pamela and her present company.

38

Little Whale Cay

"WE HAVE TO MAKE IT LOOK LIKE HE'S THE BAD GUY," MAC explained.

Pip glanced back to check the position of the RBDF cutter. "Shouldn't be too much of a stretch."

They were a little over a quarter mile off the beach and the smuggler's boat. On their starboard side, the cutter was still a half-mile behind. "Maybe we ought to try the fishing gig again."

"See that. First you laugh, then you steal. Y'all got no love for brilliance." Pip switched the radar screen to the bottom finder and started to circle the area.

The word "fishing" had Trufante instantly alert. Hearing the plan, Trufante sprung up and started removing the rods from the T-top and placing them in the rod holders on the gunwale. "Bait?"

"What the hell are you two doing?"

"Thought we was fishing." Trufante continued to check the terminal tackle. "Got a cast net? Bait's busting over there."

"Just so we're clear here. This is a show."

"And so is that." Pip pointed to the display.

A dark red line with several bumps and ledges scrolled along the bottom of the depth finder. Multicolored arcs littered the screen above it. Higher in the water column was a colorful cloud of bait. Fishermen often covered miles of bottom looking for indicators like that. Mac felt the excitement too and had to fight it down.

"Fine. Anchor on it, but keep the scope short in case we have to run." He would have normally deployed at least a hundred feet of line to comfortably anchor in the fifty feet of water. The extra line, or scope, allowed the boat to swing with the wind and current, as well as to provide a shock absorber for the waves. Even more scope, up to a seven- or eight-to-one ratio, was recommended for an overnight anchorage.

Pip and Trufante organized the fishing-slash-decoy operation, while Mac worked out the logistics. He looked over at Mel, who was on her phone, and wondered if he was the only one with his head fully in the game. In truth, he knew that the more realistic their fishing setup appeared, the less likely the RBDF was going to be interested. Anchoring and setting their lines over the sandy bottom closer to the beach would be noticed. The only difference, as Trufante continued to harp on, was that they were fishing without bait.

Mel set her phone down. "That might help."

Mac gave her a questioning look.

"Reported Rudy's description and location to the RBDF headquarters. He's got to be on some kind of watch list."

"Good idea." Mac still held his plan close. Counting on a desk jockey to relay the information in time was a crapshoot. Mac looked back at the cutter. It had slowed, probably in reaction to their anchoring. He couldn't help but look over at Trufante, who was frantically jigging one of the rods. Suddenly the tip bent over and the Cajun revealed his thousand-dollar grin. A minute later he reeled in two small fish.

"Great. Now ditch the rig." Mac didn't want to have the dozen razor-sharp hooks attached to the bait-catching rig dangling anywhere near him.

Trufante removed the two fish, tossed one to Pip, and placed the other on a heavier rod, which he sent immediately to the bottom. Mac couldn't take his eyes off the rod tip as the line dropped. Often the strikes happened instantly.

Pip's rod bent first, and Mac watched as he gently lifted the rod tip while he reeled. The circle hook set and the rod doubled over, almost causing him to spit out the cigar butt. There was something about a fish on the line that attracted everyone's attention. It was so magnetic that boats out trolling for dolphin and tuna could sense when a nearby boat had a fish on. Within seconds the angler's boat was often surrounded by the others trying to draw the school away.

Mac could see the strain on Pip's face as he tried to wrestle the fish from its attempt to hole up on the bottom. These types of fights were often won or lost in the first few seconds. Beads of sweat dripped from his brow as he struggled to pump the fish higher into the water column.

"Take the rod, Travis, I'm having a heart attack."

Even though he knew it was drama, Mac almost went for it, but his attention was drawn to the activity on the RBDF cutter. The ship was holding offshore and deploying a RHIB from a davit on the stern. Once the small inflatable moved off, the captain maneuvered the ship to allow a clear line of sight for its bow-mounted fifty-caliber gun. The only problem was that both Pip's and Rudy's boats were in range. He still didn't know who they were after.

"We're gonna have to stack the deck," Mac said.

Mel glanced over at Pip and Trufante, who were each

hauling a fish over the gunwale. "Those two aren't going to be much help."

"Maybe for the better. We couldn't look any more convincing."

"What do you have in mind? We're kind of stuck here."

Mac calculated how long it would take him to swim to the beach. "You hold them off for five minutes and I'll take care of the rest." Mac moved quickly to the bow, where he removed the dive gear from the hold, leaving the fish bag holding half the gold in clear view. The RBDF was the only military arm of the Bahamian government. Mac could only hope that didn't also include whatever version of a fish and game department they had.

Moving the gear away, Mac slid several yellowtail snapper Pip and Trufante had caught into the box. The slime and blood quickly covered the bag, and Mac expected only the most zealous search would reveal it. Removing a tank from the opposite side, he instructed Trufante to fill the boxes with fish and dragged the gear back to the stern. The tank felt light, but he only needed enough air to get him to the beach unobserved.

Mac quickly assembled the gear. "What do you have for firepower?"

Pip looked back. "Flare gun's your best bet if you're getting wet."

Mac left the gear and reached into the console, where he found an orange case. He set it on the leaning post and removed the gun and several cartridges, then returned to the stern and loaded them into the pockets of the BC.

Geared up, he checked the situation. Rudy's boat was still at the beach. From the course of the RBDF inflatable, it was clear they were heading toward Pip's boat. He had to act quickly.

Mac dropped into the water on the opposite side of the approaching boat and immediately turned toward the beach. As he finned, he descended enough to eliminate the surface current. Within a minute he felt the telltale restriction in the regulator. He had no need to check the air gauge. The needle had been only a hair above the peg.

Slowly, the bottom started to rise and Mac felt the surge of the waves above him. Visibility decreased as he entered the soupy water where the waves were breaking. Stopping for a brief second, he removed his fins and released them. His bare feet searched for the sandy bottom but found only water. He had misjudged the depth.

Without his fins for propulsion or any extra weight to take him down, Mac was stuck in the purgatory between the surface and the bottom. At the mercy of the waves, he felt his body tugged back and forth. It took him a second to realize that the buoyancy of the empty tank was part of the problem. Mac removed the flare gun and cartridges from the vest's pockets and released the straps. He wiggled out of the shoulder harness and was free of the gear.

Exposed, Mac's only chance was that he was close enough to the beach to look like a swimmer. He rose to the surface and extended his arms in front of him. Waiting for the next wave, he kicked hard, and felt the rush as the water's energy took his body with it. The surge of the wave hurled him toward the beach.

Body surfing didn't allow you the same freedom of bailing out of a wave as a surfboard did, leaving Mac stuck for the ride. Mac had no choice but to go with the flow and waited for the backwash of the previous wave to slow him down. When he felt the water change, he set his feet down, hoping he had timed it correctly.

Instead of finding his footing, the energy of the breaking wave brought him to his knees. Mac lifted his head and blinked the water from his eyes. As soon as his vision cleared, he adjusted his grip on the flare gun and dropped to his belly, leaving only his eyes and nose out of the water. The breaking waves mixed with sand clouded the water and provided Mac the concealment he needed to scope out the beach.

Rudy's boat was to his left, but a little farther away than he expected. For his plan to work he needed to be closer. Mac resisted the urge to look offshore. He would have to trust Mel to handle the RBDF.

Mac needed to move to a position where he was close enough that when he stood, Rudy could see him. That forced him to creep along the shoreline with only his eyes above the water. Hoping the sand didn't bugger up the flare gun's trigger mechanism, he stayed low in the water and used his hands to walk along the surf line.

As Mac approached the boat, he noticed the three men aboard were looking offshore. He risked a glance and saw the RHIB only few feet away from Pip's boat. A man's voice broadcast over a hailer. The wave action made it difficult for Mac to hear what was being said, but it wasn't necessary. They were about to be boarded.

Mac had to move fast. Rising to his knees, he judged he was about a hundred feet from Rudy's boat. He lifted the flare gun and fired a shot in the air, hoping it would be enough to attract the attention of the RBDF. As the flare reached its apex and started to fall, Mac reloaded the gun.

Mac dropped back in the water and waited as Rudy paced the deck of his boat. Rudy had obviously seen the flare, and the paranoia that had kept him alive this long warned it had something to do with him.

Mac needed to ensure the RBDF had the same opinion. That meant putting himself at risk.

Mac waited until Rudy was on the nearest side of the boat. He rose again, this time to his full height. With the flare gun pointed directly at the smuggler, he waited for Rudy to recognize him. A second later, the gangster's eyes found him and Mac fired, this time just over Rudy's head.

Even though he expected the retaliation, Mac was almost too late. He jammed the flare gun back into his pocket, and dove into the water just as Rudy fired. He stroked hard into the waves until he was sure the water was deep enough to submerge. If it wasn't, he would be a sitting duck. With the waves breaking on and around him, it was hard to know if more shots were fired, and he waited for the burning pain that would tell him he'd been hit. After several minutes, he reached deeper water and turned back to the beach.

The initial phase of the plan had worked, but there was no time to celebrate. Rudy had done his part by allowing his anger to overcome his sense. Now Mac needed the RBDF to react. There was no doubt they had seen the flares and heard the gunshots. Whether they deemed that action more important than boarding a fishing boat was yet to be seen.

STEVEN BECKER

A MAC TRAVIS ADVENTURE

WOOD'S
HOPE

Little Whale Cay

TAGGART WAS FUMING. HE HAD HEARD THE GUNSHOTS AS WELL, but his focus was on Travis. He could care less what was going on at the beach. The RBDF captain had completely ignored his "suggestions", and made the decision to divert the inflatable to investigate the gunfire—he knew the captain was within his rights to do so. Using his credentials, Taggart had been allowed onboard the RBDF boat as an observer. It was a bluff, though; as far as his superiors at the agency knew, he was on vacation. Had he been on assignment, he might have been more cavalier about pressing the captain for the agency's interests, but he couldn't risk a call to his superiors. Crossing the line would only lead to trouble.

Gunshots were a big deal in the Bahamas, and Taggart knew the captain was making what for him was the correct decision when he radioed the RHIB to leave the fishing boat and investigate the activity at the beach. Taggart had done his best to advise him that the fishing boat was not actually fishing, but with yellowtail snapper coming over the rails at a frantic pace, his argument fell on deaf ears.

At least the Freeman was anchored, and as the captain and crew focused on the beach, Taggart watched the boat. He had to give Travis credit, it was a brilliant ploy. With the RBDF redirecting their attention and resources to the beach, Taggart moved off to the starboard rail, away from any prying ears, to call Luciano.

He dialed his man who was stationed at the airfield. A minute later the vile-filled voice of Luciano came on the line.

"Now you need my fucking help! First you tie me up like a freakin' pig, and now you need me. I'm supposed to beg for treats, is that it?"

"We're both in this together." Taggart knew he had the upper hand and wasn't about to let Luciano gain any leverage over him. He held the phone away from his head while Luciano continued to rant. When he finished, Taggart calmly explained what was happening.

"Sounds like Rudy, the sorry-ass smuggler. He's of no consequence," Luciano said,

"You're sure?"

"To us, he's worthless. The old man he was holding hostage is out at that island Travis lives on. Let the locals have him, they'll be doin' us a favor."

"You let him go?"

The line went silent.

"It's in the middle of freakin' nowhere."

Frustrated, Taggart disconnected the call. There had to be a reason that Luciano had freed a hostage, but he had no idea what it was. Leverage was the game, and Luciano had lost theirs. Fortunately, he still had the woman. He breathed deeply and called back his associate.

"Make sure the plane's fueled and ready. We're heading

back." He paused, thinking this might be a good time to get rid of the gangster. "Might be time for our Italian friend to feed the sharks."

Between the old man's being released and the attitude of the Bahamian captain, he needed a win, and Luciano's demise would satisfy him. But it wasn't time. "Never mind that shark bit. We might still need him." Even if it was just for cannon fodder.

A glance across the water showed the crew escorting three men to the RHIB. A minute later they pushed off the beach and started toward the cutter. Taggart figured the captain would be satisfied with apprehending the men who fired the shot. Travis and his knowledge about the plane and the gold were free.

At his wits end with the locals, he turned toward where the Freeman had been fishing—only to find it gone.

THE MINUTE the RHIB altered its course, Mac dove into the water and started swimming toward the Freeman. He hoped the attention of the crew on the cutter and the beach would be focused on Rudy and the divers. The gunshots had probably sealed the deal. There was no way that authorities were leaving the beach without seizing the weapon—and its owner.

Once clear of the beach surge, Mac was able to settle into a rhythm. Living on the island, there were few opportunities for land-based fitness routines. Mel did her bootcamp workout, but Mac was not one for burpees. He stayed in shape by paddling and swimming. Those hours on the water paid off as he made his way to the boat.

"Pull those freakin' poles in," he called as he approached the transom. It was disturbing, but not surprising, that no one was watching for him. Pip and Trufante were fishing, and Mel was on her phone—pretty much the same as when he had left.

Mac clung to the motor mount while Trufante placed the

ladder in its bracket. The water flashed gold around him as the snapper, emboldened by the chum floating in the water—no doubt cut pieces from some of their smaller cousins—swarmed around him. Mac knew this was a recipe for disaster. It wasn't a question of if but when the sharks would sense the activity.

He was aboard seconds after the ladder was set in place. "Pull the anchor. We gotta go." A glance across the water showed the RHIB still beached by Rudy's boat. This was their chance if they wanted to escape.

Finally, Pip reeled in his line and stashed the rod. He made his way to the wheel and started the engines. Mac went to the bow to assist with the anchor. While he waited for the windlass to bring in the line, he checked the beach again. Rudy and the divers were aboard the RHIB now. In seconds they would be underway and the focus of the crew aboard the cutter would shift back to the Freeman.

"Go, go, go, go, go." Mac reached over the bow and started pulling line aboard. The windlass was a back saver, but lacked the urgency he needed now. Mac called Trufante to feed the line through the windlass, and into the anchor locker, while he pulled the anchor aboard. Seconds later they were on plane, but without a destination.

"Where to?" Pip asked.

"Nassau."

All eyes were on Mac, wondering why he would head to the largest city in the Bahamas.

"We need to disappear." On a normal day, he knew the island and its adjacent waters would be busy. With the carousel of cruise ships that stopped there, there were always a slew of tour vessels. Snorkeling, diving, fishing, sailing, and sunset charters were plentiful when the ships were in port. He hoped that despite the virus there would still be enough local traffic coming and going that they could blend in.

Pip moved the chartplotter's cursor back to the spot outside the harbor he had set only an hour ago. "Got a plan from there?"

"Working on it. But we're going home."

Mac glanced back again and saw the cutter pulling into the harbor at Little Whale Cay. A few minutes later, he heard the roar of a jet engine and looked up to see a private plane take off. It turned and performed a low circle just above them, before setting a course to the west. He had to think whoever had been working against him here was heading to Marathon. It was the logical place to find him. Both parties were aware that this business was only going to be settled without the authorities.

Turning toward the waypoint in Nassau, Pip adjusted the trim, and the ride evened out. Trufante started to rinse the deck of fish blood from the slaughter-fest. Using the raw-water washdown and a brush, the boat was soon clean.

Mel looked up from her phone. "Might seem petty, but any of you know if there's a limit here?"

"Twenty fish, but we're screwed if they check licenses," Pip said.

"Ditch 'em," Mac said, then thought about it. They had been seen fishing, and the snapper in the box was good camouflage for the bags full of gold. "Wait. Ten each box. Make sure they're legal."

Trufante started sorting through the fish, throwing every third overboard. He didn't measure any, but Mac knew he had calibrated eyeballs. His deckhand had seen enough fish to know if they were legal by simply looking at them.

Moving at fifty knots had advantages, but it forced Mac to make a choice. With the tip of Andros Island approaching, he had to decide whether to turn into the Northwest Providence Channel, the most direct route to Bimini and the United States, or follow the Tongue of the Ocean. The Tongue would take them down the east side of Andros and force a crossing of the

Great Bahama Bank. The Channel was the simpler and most obvious route, which made Mac examine the other option.

Running down the TOTO and cutting to the south of Andros Island would cost them a hundred and fifty miles, with most of that in Bahamian waters. But in the Freeman, the additional mileage would take only three hours. To Mac, if they were caught and detained in the Channel where they might have been expected, the additional time was irrelevant. They needed to get back to Marathon and Ned.

"How much range do you have?" Mac asked Pip. The digital engine displays were showing the engines were sipping instead of gulping fuel.

Pip pressed a button on the display, which changed to estimated range. "Might oughta fill in Marathon, but we can get there."

Mac nodded and stared, adding waypoints down the Tongue and across the bank. At that point, he couldn't avoid noticing that they were closer to Cuba than the Keys. Adding a few more waypoints to run north of the Cay Sal Bank, he selected the points and created a route. The thick purple line showed their path of travel, and the display showed that at their current speed they would reach Marathon in five hours.

The last few miles would be run in the dark, which, if he had guessed correctly, worked well for his plan to take back his island.

Mac was satisfied. "Guess it's sushi for dinner."

40

Wood's Island

IT HAD BEEN A QUIET DAY—ALMOST TOO QUIET, AND WHEN NED heard a boat, he ran down to the beach. Outside of the two days of lobster mini season, Harbor Channel didn't get a lot of boat traffic. Only a small percentage of visitors headed that far into the backcountry without a guide. Ned had done the same for every boat he'd heard since noon.

Mel hadn't answered her messages, which, considering they were across the Gulf Stream, wasn't all that surprising. He figured the odds were stacked that the boat was headed to the island, and fifty-fifty if this was good news or bad.

Standing on the dock, he studied the water to the south. A small dot was visible on the horizon, clearly moving through the channel. It took a few minutes for him to decide that if it wasn't friendly, he was vulnerable where he stood. Using the Surfari seemed the logical choice. He could hide aboard in the cabin and observe the approaching boat through the windows.

Stepping onto the motorsailer, he made his way to the cockpit and then moved forward into the salon. From the bench by the table he could see most of the channel. He waited as the boat grew larger. When it was a quarter mile away, he ducked back against the bulkhead. Pamela was clearly visible, as was the gangster. He didn't recognize the two figures by the helm, but he was certain they were not Mac and Mel.

Ned cursed himself for not bringing the shotgun to the dock. Defenseless, he crept deeper into the cabin. The engine noise dropped as the boat slowed, and the wake found the motorsailer a few seconds later. He could hear someone talking aboard the approaching boat, but was unable to make out what was being said. Ned crouched deeper into the space between the bulkhead and the bed.

All he could do was listen and wait. If Pamela hadn't been aboard, the sound of the lower unit slamming into the rock at the entrance to the channel would've be easy enough to explain. With her on the boat, it was indicative of what was going on. By not pointing out the obstacle, he knew she was in trouble.

The unmistakable crunch was followed by several loud curses. Wood's old defense system had worked again. With the boat at least crippled, Ned took a chance and moved aft to a position he could better observe the intruders. As he watched the boat idle down the channel on its remaining engine, he wasn't sure at this point if the twin engines were a blessing or curse.

Several quick commands were called out, followed by another crunch as the boat crashed into the dock. Ned could tell right away that although the man at the helm was used to giving orders, he was not any good on a boat. Even on one engine, with no wind and little current docking should have been relatively easy. Instead of using the one good engine to accomplish the task, he had plowed into the dock, where he dropped the other man. Once the bow line was secure, the captain tossed another line by the stern. The man on the dock tried to pull the stern toward the dock, but was restricted by the bow line, which he had tied too tightly. Ned would have had a good laugh if he hadn't been able to see the distress on Pamela's face. The man finally had the lines adjusted and the captain stepped onto the dock.

"Wait here and keep an eye on them. I'm going to have a look for the old man."

It wasn't a large island and the man returned in a few minutes. Now that their intentions were clear, Ned knew his only chance was to escape.

"He's not here," he said to the captain.

"Take them up to the house and then hide the boat."

Ned saw the pistol as the second man nodded to Luciano and Pamela. They exited the boat without a struggle and started walking down the dock toward the trail that led to the house. The man followed behind.

Ned was alone now and wasted no time. Wood had always kept the keys to his boats hidden by the battery switch. He suspected that Mac followed the tradition and moved toward the hatch to the engine compartment. He found the switch behind a small access panel. The key chain seemed to stick on something when he pulled it, but a hard tug released it.

Ned moved back to the helm. Just before he inserted the key into the ignition, he felt a distinct gust of wind. He paused, wondering if he could sail the boat out. It would be to his advantage to slip away without the sound of the engines to alert the men. Another, stronger gust followed the first, and he decided to try.

With a decade of summer-break research trips to the far corners of the globe, Ned was an experienced sailor. Some of the places he'd been were best accessed by sail, but those ships were much larger and managed by a full crew. He had watched Mac work the Surfari's controls on the way up from Key West, and had no doubt he could do the same. The only problem was that damned rock.

Weighing the risks, sail power won hands down. With a powerful engine, he would have risked it, but with the motor-sailer's limited power, stealth was his friend. Taking a quick glance to familiarize himself with the controls for the engine in case he needed it, he moved his attention to the sails.

Ned glanced at the trail, and seeing no one, turned back and released the catch on the self-furling jib. The sail, assisted by the increasing wind, bellowed out. Just as it caught, Ned closed the lever, allowing just a fraction of the jib to be released. The wind quickly filled the small triangle and the boat strained on the lines. Ned left the helm and released the boat from the dock. Powered by the wind, the boat drifted quietly but quickly into the channel. Ned waited patiently for a large enough gap to open that would allow him to add more sail. He started to worry as the Surfari started to crab toward the shallow water at the edge of the channel. Ned spun the wheel, but it failed to alter the course. To get enough steerage to clear the rock, he would need more power—and fast.

Ned had been out to the island many times over the years that Wood had worked on it and knew the channel well. That only made matters worse as the boat slid toward the shallow flats. He had no choice but to raise the main, and he activated the control. The sail started to extend from the mast and caught a gust of wind. Slowly, the boat started to turn, but it was too late. Ned braced for the inevitable crash.

Just as he expected contact, another gust heeled the boat over, and the keel slid over the rock. Ned knew how lucky he had been, and he said a quick prayer to the gods of the tides. If it were any time but high tide, the boat would be sinking instead of cruising down Harbor Channel.

Marathon

The crossing had been uneventful, giving the crew enough time to wind down and decompress. Mac had been watching their progress on the chartplotter, but was still relieved when Trufante spotted the light above Sombrero Key. The lighthouse allowed Mac to orient himself and within a few seconds he had located the lights of the Seven Mile Bridge and the three red blinking lights on top of the radio towers that he suspected still broadcast propaganda to Cuba. Pip was studying the chartplotter, and Mac looked ahead to see if the markers for Moser Channel were visible.

They reached the bridge a few minutes later and slowed. After spending the last five hours running at fifty knots, it took them all a few seconds to acclimate. From having a gale blowing in his face to now a light breeze was a change, and it took him a few minutes to realize that it was coming out of the west. Pip had turned down the gain on the radar to remove most of the clutter and only show the signatures of boats large enough to be a problem for them. Just as it registered that he had failed to check the local weather, he felt a tinge of cool wind coming from the north, and saw the approaching storm on the radar screen.

Fronts generally came from the northeast, and even though it was late in the winter season, it didn't mean a storm wasn't going to be severe. The night sky showed nothing of the coming threat, but as the wind increased, Mac suspected that if it were daylight, he would be looking at a dark line of clouds on the horizon.

"We've got weather coming. What do you want to do about checking in?" Mac asked. The question was more for Pip than anyone. It was his boat that was at risk.

Trufante's smile gleamed brightly now that they were back. He was finally out of the reach of the Bahamians. Mac had no idea if Tru was wanted for anything locally, but he could swim to Pigeon Key from here in a matter of minutes if he needed to. From there, the mainland was only a mile or so away, accessed by a section of the old railroad bridge. It was currently closed for renovations, but Mac didn't think that would stop the Cajun if he needed to disappear.

"I'd make the call. It's eight o'clock at night, and with the virus, they'll let us go without a face-to-face."

"Unless they flagged the boat. We might have gotten out of the Bahamas, but the RBDF could have called ICE," Pip said.

"If they had, we would have had company several miles ago." State waters reached out three miles from land. Mac knew ICE preferred to operate past the state's reach.

"Shit, y'all. Sitting here ain't solving nothing," Trufante said.

"We get this gold somewhere safe, they can have this old boat. I'll be looking to upgrade." Pip laughed.

"What's the fuel situation look like?" The last thing Mac wanted was to make it this far and run out of gas before reaching the island.

"I'd say we got about fifty gallons left."

For a car, that sounded like a lot, but a boat could drink that faster than Trufante could down a shot. "It'll work. Too risky heading into Boot Key. We should pay Jesse a visit." Mac had lost count of how many boats Jesse had crammed into his boathouse.

"Roger that." Pip clamped down on the cigar butt and pushed the throttles forward.

It was a relief to see the bridge fall behind them. If the authorities were interested, they would have made their move by now. That left the CIA man and the gangster to deal with. Mac didn't have to guess where they had gone. He started planning what amounted to an invasion of his own island.

"We're gonna swing back by the Content Keys and see if McDermitt's around."

Each person's reaction was different at the mention of the former Marine. Pip had a man-crush on him after Jesse had flown them out of the Bahamas last year. Mel nodded her approval—Mac didn't need to tell her that there was a good chance they would be outgunned when they faced the men, and need Jesse's help. Trufante slunk back to the transom in an effort to disappear.

"Reckon we can pick up some firepower?" Pip asked.

"I'm hoping for that and some backup if this goes south. Hoping we don't need any of it." Since seeing the private jet take off from Little Whale Cay, Mac had guessed at what they would face when they reached the island. As each obstacle was removed from their path, he went farther down the rabbit hole of ways to approach the island and now, with the RBDF hundreds of miles away and ICE showing no apparent interest, he was ready. He glanced again at dark sky, hoping the storm would hold off long enough for him to implement his plan.

Wood's Island

After securing Pamela and Luciano in the house, Taggart started to search the island. If this were a legit operation he would have called in backup long ago, but since he wanted the gold, he was on his own. Armed with only his pistol and the .410 he had found in the house, he started to search.

After going through the house, he moved downstairs to the shed. The butt of the shotgun made short work of the padlock, and he unlatched the hasp and stepped inside. Taggart found the light switch and turned it on. Knowing that Travis was at least a few hours behind, he wasn't worried about giving away his position or intentions. By his calculations he had at least a couple of hours to fortify his position. From everything he had learned about Travis and the Woodson woman, he knew they would be coming for the hostages.

It was unsettling that the old man was not here, but it didn't really worry him. Neither did the coming confrontation. He had plenty of time to prepare, even if the old man contacted Travis that he was safe—he still had the woman.

At first hitting the rock had infuriated him, but Taggart quickly realized why the obstacle had been placed there. As part of his training he had studied warfare, from the time of Alexander the Great to the Viet Cong. It didn't take long to put the pieces together.

When he found the spool of stranded cable, he smiled. It took some digging, but he found a length of cable, a crimper, and the fittings he needed. With supplies in hand, he headed to the dock.

41

The Content Keys

JESSE'S ISLAND WAS DARK. HIS HOUSE, BUILT OVER THE BOATHOUSE, was quiet. There was no sign of any activity from the two detached bunkhouses, either. A quick cruise around the island showed his caretaker Jimmy's house was quiet as well.

Mac knew better than to set foot on land. At the minimum, Jesse would have installed surveillance. Any stored weapons would be well protected and possibly boobytrapped. Mac would have to take on the CIA with what he had.

At Mac's direction, Pip moved into deeper water. There were two ways to get from Jesse's island to his, and both were tricky at night. Mac chose the deepwater route so they would come up on the back side of Wood's Island.

"What's she draw?" Mac asked Pip. He knew the modified twin hulls could handle skinny water.

"Twenty-one inches." He looked around the boat. "Between y'all and the cargo, might add a few more."

Even with the tide at its peak, the Freeman drew too much

water. It would take a boat with half that draft to access the skinny water on the back side of the island. The only way in was a frontal assault.

"Lemme take the speargun and go in the back door," Trufante said.

Mac had expected the Cajun would want to play an active role in Pamela's rescue and nodded his assent. "We'll need some kind of signal."

"Just make some noise and draw them off. I'll take 'em out the back way."

"If it was just Pamela that would work, but I'm not sure if Ned can make it through that flat." There were pros and cons of traversing the flat at high water. The resistance of the extra foot or so of water made the quicksand-like muck even harder to get through, but the deeper water would allow them to float or swim off the flat much sooner than if it were low tide. A glance at the sky showed the moon was well above the storm clouds from the approaching front. The flat would be well lit, and with no backup, he would be a sitting duck.

Mac shook his head. "Better if you draw them off. They'll run for the dock if they can. We'll grab them from there."

"Got any flares left, or did you waste them all on that son of a bitch back there? If it was me, I would have popped him with one and saved the rest."

Mac knew this was all bravado, fueled by the steady stream of blue Gatorade the Cajun had consumed on the way over. "Still got a handful."

Trufante found the gun and remaining cartridges. Loading one into the chamber, he placed the rest in a pocket of his cargo shorts and tucked the gun in his waistband.

Pip had cleared the shallow-water pass, and the boat jerked forward as he accelerated. Though the two islands were less than four miles from each other as the crow flew, the shoal-ridden waters of the backcountry added a few more to the trip.

The Freeman covered the distance quickly. At what appeared to be a random point in the endless flat, Mac directed Pip to slow. The boat dropped off plane and crept forward. Mac moved to the bow, and using hand signals guided the boat through the shallow water.

Mac knew the flat as well as the creases and grooves on his hand, which resembled the terrain below them. Small channels caused by the tidal activity ran through the shallow water, but Mac ignored them.

"Follow that white patch." He pointed at a distinct trail through the seagrass. Hurricane Irma's hand was evident in the unmarked and undocumented passes created by uprooted trees that had been dragged out to deeper water by the storm surge. Pip followed the trail to within sight of the Mac's island, where they dropped Trufante into the water.

The path made by the trees was too narrow for the Freeman to turn, and with the engines tilted so that the propellers were barely submerged, Pip backed out of the channel. When they reached deeper water, Mac glanced over at the flat and saw Trufante slinking heron-like across the open water.

"Let's go knock on the front door," Mac said. "Better take it slow, though. Tru's gonna need some time to reach land." Mac didn't want to point out the fact that they had no idea of their opponents' strength, either in weapons or numbers. He knew he should do a thorough recon first.

As they exited the lee of the island, though, a cool gust kicked up. Mac was counting on the storm to even things out.

The weather continued to work to their advantage. The small gusts turned into a steady breeze, which totally disguised the sound of the outboards. Mac directed Pip toward the channel.

As they entered the first drop of rain hit his brow.

Mac could see the lights in the house between the swaying branches. He smiled, thinking his procrastination in trimming back the banana tree was probably driving the CIA man crazy at the moment as it brushed against the roof. Added to the sound of the waves and other foliage, Mac doubted their approach could be heard.

A few minutes later the noisy leaves became of no consequence. With a crash of thunder and a brilliant streak of lightning, the storm was on them.

The rain blew horizontally into his face as Mac guided Pip toward the channel. Conditions deteriorated by the second as the storm laid into them, but it was all in their favor. His only worry was that Trufante's diversion be effective. Mac shrugged it off. The Cajun had a way of making things work.

"We need to wait for the signal," Mac yelled over the storm.

"Hope that boy works fast. This is getting unmanageable."

Mac noticed Pip was struggling to hold the boat in the channel. On this northeastern edge of backcountry between Big Pine and Key West, there were no natural obstacles to slow the beam seas—the boat was exposed to the elements and paying the price.

They huddled together in the meager protection provided by the center console and waited. The wind seemed to blow the cold rain through their skin, and despite the seventy-degree temperatures they started to shiver. The minutes dragged as the storm beat down on them, and Mac started to worry.

Besides the hurricanes that plagued the tropics, the Keys had two kinds of weather systems. In summer, almost every afternoon thunderstorms formed, grew, and meandered around. They were unpredictable and fickle. There was a Florida saying that it was probably sunny on the other side of the street.

The cold fronts that hit the area were a different animal

entirely. The lines of storms strong enough to reach the south-ernmost latitudes of the state came through like freight trains. They could be every bit as powerful as a tropical storm, but were generally short-lived. Mac knew the stronger the tempest the faster it would pass, and he glanced at the dark horizon wondering how much time they had.

As he prayed to the weather gods, he saw a burst of bright orange in the sky. Even with the storm it was clearly visible. "Go!" Mac yelled.

He grabbed the leaning post as Pip accelerated. Their plan was based on speed. Mac wasn't sure what kind of diversion the Cajun planned, but the flare was a good sign it was going to happen fast. Pip gunned the engines and the boat reacted almost too quickly. With visibility reduced to just a few feet, Mac struggled to see the dock, which would give him only a second's notice before they reached the channel and the rock.

He had expected to see the Surfari's mast, but it was gone, Seconds later, Mac finally spotted a center console and called out to Pip to make the turn. He had no time to speculate about the missing sailboat.

His interest was in whoever had come in the center console. There was a little wiggle room in the channel, and he breathed a sigh of relief as the bow of the boat cleared the rock.

His relief was short-lived when the boat jerked and a grinding noise penetrated through the chaos of the storm. Mac fell to the deck. He was sure they'd had enough room to clear the rock. As he gained his feet, he saw they were sitting in the channel. An old memory came back, but there was nothing to do about it now except call out to Pip and Mel and dive into the water. He knew what was coming next.

Harbor Channel

Ned found the Surfari responsive, and under other conditions might have enjoyed the sail. The sails were trimmed and he was making six knots, a decent speed considering the jib was only a quarter deployed and the main reefed.

During daylight hours he could easily navigate to Marathon, but as the storm descended around him the conditions made any line-of-sight navigation impossible. Aviators called it IFR, or Instrument Flying Rules. With only a general idea of where he was, in an area where staying afloat required precise navigation, he pressed the power button on the chartplotter. The unit refused to respond.

Ned tried the VHF and several other switches, none of which worked, and concluded the ship had no power. Running under sail he hadn't noticed. The odds were stacked against him making it to Marathon without at least the chartplotter, but the autopilot was out as well. Troubleshooting the electrical system would require him leaving the helm.

Deciding that he could as easily ground standing at the wheel as trying to figure out why he had no power, Ned chose action. A natural reaction of inexperienced sailors might be to bring the sails in, but Ned was not about to put the boat at the mercy of the storm-blown waves. Deciding to heave to, he brought the mainsail in and prepared to come about. Turning the wheel to port, he waited for the boat to turn. His headway brought the bow around, and where he normally would have brought the jib sheet over, he waited until it caught the wind in its present state.

Backing the jib in this manner eliminated the Venturi effect that powered the boat, and the boat started to slow. Suddenly, just as the jib backed, the boat shuddered. A few seconds more and the Surfari would have been safe in the middle of the channel. As it ground to a halt, Ned knew it was parked on a sandbar.

Before he could react and pull in the sails, a brutal gust pushed the boat higher onto the obstacle. As the boat heeled over, Ned became disoriented. He grabbed for the wheel and missed, then reached out for anything else to prevent him from being thrown overboard. Grabbing a line saved him from the water, but swung him headfirst into the gunwale.

42

Wood's Island

THE SECOND THE BOAT GROUND TO A HALT, MAC KNEW WHAT HAD happened. The boom was a classic defense to blockade a harbor. Most notably used in the Golden Horn of Constantinople, booms had been in use since antiquity. Generally made from chain link, they had been placed across rivers as toll barriers and used in defense of harbors during wartime.

Many were elaborate affairs. As they were permanent fixtures, they needed to be raised and lowered to allow for boat traffic. Boom towers and other structures were built to create the leverage necessary to lower, then lift the heavy chains. Years ago, he and Wood had set up just such a device to stop an intruder.

The CIA man had set up a much simpler affair. He had simply looped the middle of a wire cable around the rock in the channel and tied the two ends off to a tree.

It had worked to perfection. Mac guessed that the props and probably the lower units of the Freeman's starboard engines were ruined. As Mac swam toward the dock, he now knew the CIA man was a formidable opponent.

Suddenly, shots rang out around them. Without the dark night and driving rain, Mac expected they would easily be dead by now. With almost zero visibility, the man was shooting blind. Mac sought the cover of the dock to regroup. He found Mel and Pip nearby and called over to them to meet under the dock.

Again the storm worked in his favor. Gasping for air, Mac stood in the shallow water below the dock, Mel and Pip beside him. Their breathing echoed off the structure, but Mac was sure they could not be heard from above.

"Bastard wrecked my boat," Pip said.

"That's going to be the least of our problems if you don't be quiet," Mel scolded him.

Mac ignored their bickering and sought a solution. They were safe for now, but with the Freeman disabled and as good as in his possession, the CIA man would be focused on removing the gold to his own boat. Mac had to assume the guy had help; someone had to be guarding Pamela and Ned. It was reassuring there appeared to be only two men. If there was more than one accomplice, they would probably be at the dock with him.

As he waited, Mac tried to ignore the rainwater dripping through the deck boards, wondering why the hard rain earlier had been less annoying than the drips now smacking his brow.

The CIA man had moved to the brush, where he untied the boom cable and pulled it in. Wasting no time, he ran back to the dock and hopped aboard his center console. Mac couldn't see the man, but he could see the water—and the boats. The CIA man started the engines of his boat—or at least the one functional engine. He backed down on the Freeman and Pip winced as he heard the crunch of the fiber-glass shattering. Mac peered out from beneath the dock to see the man tying off a line to the bow cleat of Pip's boat. His intention was obviously to tow the boat to the dock where he would search it. Though the boat had plenty of storage, it would only take the man minutes to find the fish bags full of gold.

Mac ducked back under the dock. "He'll be busy for a few. Let's go." Moving to the opposite side of the structure, the trio left the cover, and waded toward the brush. The mangrove-lined shore on this side was an impediment, but concealed them. Mac went first, moving branches out of the way and holding them back for Mel and Pip.

They reached the clearing unobserved.

"Pip, stay down here and direct them when they come out," Mac said.

"What's the plan?" Mel asked.

"Wait and see what Tru does," Mac said.

"Oh great. He's the plan?"

Mac ignored the barb and squatted down to wait. He knew time was limited, but he needed the Cajun to draw the man out of the house. As they waited the rain started to taper off, but the wind increased. They had to endure branches and leaves blowing in their faces, but at least the bugs were taking cover as well.

Mac was just starting to worry about Trufante when he saw the Cajun burst through the brush on the other side of the clearing. In typical Trufante fashion, he threw caution to the wind and counted on his current set of nine lives to shield him from danger. Mac watched as he leveled the orange pistol and fired at the house.

The hurricane shutters were still in place on the back side of the house, but the ones on the front had been slid back to allow airflow to the living room. There was a fifty-fifty chance that the flare would hit a screen section instead of glass, but this was Trufante, and a second after the shell left the barrel he heard glass shatter. A dull orange glow appeared in the windows. The Cajun's attack served its purpose.

A second after the shell entered the house, the door opened and a man ran down the stairs. He glanced back at the house, then took off down the path to the dock. Figuring it was the CIA man's accomplice, Mac let him go. Once he was past, Mac sprung out from his hiding place and ran upstairs. Mel went for the shed and the fire extinguisher.

A fire had started where the flare had landed. Trusting Mel to take care of it, he moved toward the table and went to work on the ropes binding Pamela. Once she was free, she pulled the gag from her mouth.

"Go. Pip is downstairs. I'll take care of this," Mac said.

"Thanks, Mac Travis," Pamela said, turning to the other man. "Score one for Tru."

Mac glanced at the man. The projectile had burned a hole through his chest before landing on the floor. "Where's Ned, and who's this guy?"

"He was gone when we got here and so was *Sea Runner*. This creep is Lucky Luciano's grandson, if you can believe it. He was in with the CIA guy," Pamela said. "Think he called him Taggart."

"Go. I got this," Mac said, moving his attention to the fire. From the corner of his eye he saw Pamela exit through the door. He took his eyes off the dead gangster and focused on the fire. He'd rebuilt the house twice, and he was determined not to do it a third time.

Without air conditioning, the tropical humidity had permeated everything in the house, and the wood held moisture, helping it resist the flames—at first. But with the chemical reaction in the flare burning at nearly two thousand degrees, Mac knew it was only a matter of time. Just as he grabbed a blanket from the bedroom, Mel appeared in the doorway with the fire extinguisher. Without pausing, she unleashed the foam on the flames. The fire smoldered, then went out, but it took the entire contents of the canister to dull, then extinguish, the flare. Even then, it glowed back to life.

"I got this," Mel yelled. She took the cast-iron pan from the stove and placed it over the smoldering flare.

With Pamela safe, Mac's focus turned to the gold. He ran out of the house. Taking the steps two at a time, he reached the clearing. Pamela had her arms wrapped around Trufante, and Pip stood off to the side.

"I need you," he called to the Cajun. Mac didn't slow down. Half-skidding, half-running, he took on the mud-slick trail. Trufante's long legs closed the distance. By the time Mac stopped at the end of the trail, the Cajun was right behind him.

Slowly, Mac crept forward. The two men had towed the Freeman to the dock and were in the process of offloading the gold onto their center console. Mac immediately noticed that both men wore holstered sidearms. The difference in firepower made things difficult, but Mac already knew what he wanted to do. If the boom worked in one direction, it would work in the other.

"I'm gonna swim out and set the boom back." Trufante gave him a queer look, and Mac realized that the Cajun had missed that part of the evening's activity. "Follow me."

Mac led him to one of the few trees capable of securing the boom. From the scar now running deep around the trunk, as stout as it was, it had barely done so. "I'm gonna swim out and loop the cable over the rock. Look for my signal and tie the ends off."

Trufante immediately made a dropper loop in the cable to cinch it tight. Mac glanced back as he entered the water and saw Trufante secure one end to the tree and feed the remaining line through the loop. Once Mac set the cable over the rock, he would use the loop as leverage to tighten the cable. With that end in hand, Mac took a breath and dropped below the surface.

Moving through the water was considerably less stressful without being fired upon. As a result, Mac was able to maximize his breath hold and reach the rock without breaking the surface. Once there he looped the line around the rock, he took a quick breath, and swam back to shore.

By the time he exited the water, the men had finished moving the gold from Pip's boat to their center console. The Freeman blocked their exit. They set it adrift. The man called Taggart was behind the center console's wheel and called to his partner to release the lines. Mac crawled from the water and stood by Trufante. There was nothing to be done except wait.

43

STEVEN BECKER

A MAC TRAVIS ADVENTURE

WOOD'S HOPE

Harbor Channel

WATER SPLASHED AGAINST NED'S FACE. SLOWLY HIS EYES OPENED, and he found himself facedown against the gunwale of the Surfari. It took a moment to realize that he was held in the awkward position by gravity, and he remembered what had happened. Another wave hit, this time covering his head. After a quick inventory showed all his appendages were in operating order, he started to rise. A wave of dizziness sent him to his knees, and he vomited into the pooling water in the cockpit of the boat.

With his head pounding, Ned fought his way to his feet. He overcame the lightheadedness and made it to the starboard gunwale. The boat was heeled over on the sandbar and taking on water over the port side.

Ned regained his wits and checked his surroundings. The rain had stopped, and the sky behind the front was speckled with stars. To the west, he could see the dark line as it moved toward Key West.

There was no way to tell how badly the boat was damaged,

but Ned was not going to wait for a thorough survey. Moving to the cockpit, he turned on the VHF radio to call for help, but found it had no power. He was sure the boat had flares aboard, but he was reluctant to send a signal. He was only a mile or so from Wood's place where the wrong person might see it, and far enough from the mainland that the flare wouldn't be seen there. Self-rescue seemed his only option.

Ned got his bearings and moved around the cockpit. A loud clanking sound got his attention. It sounded like a clip on the halyard slapping against the mast, and he climbed onto the wheelhouse to check. Reaching the mast, he found all the lines were inside it. The source of the noise was somewhere else. It took a few seconds for him to realize that it was gunshots coming from Wood's place.

Despite his predicament, he was safe, and the noise meant that Mac had returned. Stuck in a position where he was unable to help, he tried to figure out how to free the boat.

Wood's Island

Mac crouched by Trufante.

"What we gonna do?" the Cajun asked.

"Hope they panic. I'm thinking the weight of the men and gold might swamp them. We can take 'em in the water."

They waited as the man released the lines and boarded the boat. Mac smiled as it listed to the port side. In their haste to load the gold, they had failed to balance the weight. Neither man seemed to notice, and the boat started to move away from the dock.

They must have known about the rock to set the boom in the first place, and Mac was counting on them carefully picking their way out of the channel. Idle speed would have done the job, but the man was being overly cautious and bumping the single engine in and out of gear.

He wondered why they were only using one engine. "It's not going to work," Mac muttered.

"What say?"

"Never mind, let's go." Mac left the cover of the brush and started toward the water. The boom was set to take out the port engine when they made the turn, but if they were already disabled, unless the propeller became entangled, the device wouldn't stop them. Mac watched as the boat hit the cable. Instead of stopping, it simply slid over the obstruction. The man at the helm must have felt something and goosed the throttle. Mac hoped it would be enough.

The boat suddenly crabbed to the side and stopped. A low whine was audible and the motors slowly tilted out of the water. To Mac's dismay, the boat floated over the cable. Having originally set the trap, the men knew exactly where the line was and had avoided it. The motors dropped back into the water, and the boat accelerated.

"Come on!" Mac waded into the water. The Freeman was only twenty feet away, its drift stopped by the shallow flat. Trufante was at the boat in a half-dozen strokes. Mac was right behind him.

With the cable in his path, Mac wasted valuable seconds as he avoided the urge to power up immediately. Once he was clear, he pushed the throttle hard and steered around the rock and into the channel. Searching the water, he saw the white wash from the boat ahead.

With both boats down engines, things seemed to be happening in slow motion. Taggart's boat was struggling to get up on plane, and Mac dropped his speed. Even with two engines, the design of the Freeman made it the faster boat.

Knowing he could overtake them was good enough until he formulated a plan.

From this distance, the water was Mac's only advantage. This wasn't his first chase through the backcountry. He knew how to use the narrow channels and skinny water to his advantage. There was a sandbar less than a mile ahead, where he planned to force the other boat to ground. In order to do so, he would have to expose himself, and knowing they were armed, that could be a problem.

Accelerating, Mac took a position to the starboard side of the other boat. His tactic was similar to a sheepdog herding sheep. He would use the deeper water and direct the CIA man onto the sandbar. With the tide just starting to ebb, the boat would be high and dry in an hour. That would buy Mac the time he needed to figure out what phase two would be.

Mac positioned the Freeman to the starboard side and behind the other boat. Seconds later, the men saw them and shots were fired, but the hundred-yard gap and the rocking seas were enough to ensure they went wild.

Mac used the Freeman to gradually push the other boat toward the sandbar. The CIA men appeared to be oblivious to his plan, but as the gap closed, the possibility of a lucky shot from the continuing fire increased.

"What's that?" Trufante pointed into the dark night. "Shit, cut it hard!"

The Cajun could spot a frigate bird from a mile away. Mac had to trust his mate's eyes. He spun the wheel to port and ducked behind the windshield. The small piece of plexiglass gave him a sense of security that he knew was false, but it was better than nothing.

They were close enough now that random shots hit the boat. Mac ducked lower to use the console for cover, but before he did, he saw something looming in front of the other boat.

Cutting the wheel a little more, he added power, hoping the move would push the other boat into what appeared to be a sailboat. Grounded boats were common here, but he didn't recall a boat beached here. Before he could identify it, a loud crack shot through the night.

The mast shattered. Before it gave way, the lines once buried so neatly inside it entangled the men and their boat. Mac wasn't sure if the props were fouled, but everything else was, including the men.

He jammed the throttle forward and braced himself as the Freeman surged toward the wounded boat. Just before impact, he pulled back on the lever and set the boat into reverse. As the bow scraped against the other boat, Mac set the transmission in neutral and ran for the bow.

With Trufante a step behind him, he launched across the void onto the other boat. Trufante took one man and Mac the other. The men, already wrapped up by the lines from the sailboat, now struggled to free themselves.

Mac had Taggart in a grasp when the knife appeared. He had missed the CIA man's attempt to slash the lines and now faced the blade himself. Enraged, the man fought frantically, slashing everything in his path in order to reach Mac. The blade was inches from Mac's face when he felt a steel cable swinging behind him, and with one jerk, grabbed it and wrapped the man's knife hand with it. Taggart tried to free himself, but the knife was no match for the steel cable.

Mac had yielded ground during the struggle and found himself against the gunwale of the sailboat. The man had escaped from the steel cable and now had only one more line to cut before he was free. He pressed forward and swung the knife in a wild arc, hoping to cut the line and reach Mac at the same time.

The knife sliced through the line, and Mac ducked to avoid

the follow through intended to kill him. He avoided the strike, and the blade glanced off the fiberglass of the sailboat. Mac was looking into the man's eyes to try and judge his next move when he saw them flash up and to the left. The man had seen something, but Mac didn't have the luxury to look. The man changed position slightly, as if an attack was coming from a different quarter.

Mac thought the move was defensive, but it proved to be a feint. Realizing too late that the next strike would land, he tried to back away, but there was nowhere to go. As a last resort, he tried to counter by sacrificing his arm to the blade, but even that was too late. Flinching, he waited for the strike.

He felt the blade penetrate the skin on his forehead. Blood sheeted into his eyes, blinding him. Thinking the searing pain was just a prelude, he used his last strength to push the man away. At first he felt resistance, but then—nothing. Blinded by the blood, he fought his invisible opponent.

"Mac!"

The voice was enough to stop him from flailing. Stepping back, he wiped the blood away with his shirt and blinked hard to clear his vision. Ned was perched above him on the gunwale of the sailboat holding a boat hook.

Mac was disoriented. Blood still poured from the wound on his forehead, forcing him to wipe it away again.

"Ought to have that looked at," Trufante said.

Mac turned and saw the Cajun's opponent wrapped like a mummy in the sailboat's lines. "Looks like I got the worst of it."

"Foreheads are bleeders. You'll be okay," Ned said.

"And what about you?" Mac looked past Ned at the wrecked sailboat. He quickly recognized it as the Surfari.

"What about these fools, and the gold?" Trufante asked.

"Leave 'em here. It'll be a cold night, but someone'll come across them tomorrow," Ned said.

"We'll secure them and call Garrett. I'll have Mel come up with a laundry list that should keep 'em off our backs." The deputy was one of the few law-enforcement types Mac trusted.

"There's not a judge down here that'll hold a CIA agent for five minutes."

The three men looked down at the man, who had just regained consciousness. Mac kicked the knife from his reach.

Mac had his offer ready.

"You know where the plane is. How about we keep what we have and the rest is yours, and I can assure you we just made a dent in it," Mac said.

"What's to keep you from going after it before I get there?" Taggart asked.

Mac shook his head. "The fact that we're not you, or like you."

The look in the man's eyes told Mac that he had a deal. Mac knew he was walking away from another fortune, but with the gold they had already recovered, even Trufante and Pamela wouldn't be able to burn through their share. Mac knew he'd have to fight Ned to give him a share, but he'd take it eventually. As for Mel and himself, they'd donate most and hide the rest.

It was settled in his mind, except for the fate of the Surfari. Pamela had told him he'd have a moment of truth with the boat, and he hoped this was it.

Because there wasn't a chance in hell he was going to salvage it.

ABOUT THE AUTHOR

Always looking for a new location or adventure to write about, Steven Becker can usually be found on or near the water. He splits his time between Tampa and the Florida Keys - paddling, sailing, diving, fishing or exploring.

Find out more by visiting www.stevenbeckerauthor.com or contact me directly at booksbybecker@gmail.com.

facebook.com/stevenbecker.books

instagram.com/stevenbeckerauthor

Get my starter library First Bite for Free!
when you sign up for my newsletter

http://eepurl.com/-obDj

First Bite contains the first book in several of Steven Becker's series:

Get them now (http://eepurl.com/-obDj)

Mac Travis Adventures: The Wood's Series

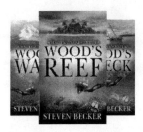

It's easy to become invisible in the Florida Keys. Mac Travis is laying low: Fishing, Diving and doing enough salvage work to pay his bills. Staying under the radar is another matter altogether. An action-packed thriller series featuring plenty of boating, SCUBA diving, fishing and flavored with a generous dose of Conch Republic counterculture.

Check Out The Series Here

★★★★★ *Becker is one of those, unfortunately too rare, writers who very obviously knows and can make you feel, even smell, the places he writes about. If you love the Keys, or if you just want to escape there for a few enjoyable hours, get any of the Mac Travis books - and a strong drink*

★★★★★ *This is a terrific series with outstanding details of Florida, especially the Keys. I can imagine myself riding alone with Mac through every turn. Whether it's out on a boat or on an island....I'm there*

Kurt Hunter Mysteries: The Backwater Series

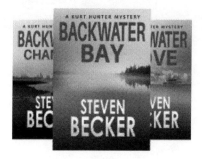

Biscayne Bay is a pristine wildness on top of the Florida Keys. It is also a stones throw from Miami and an area notorious for smuggling. If there's nefarious activity in the park, special agent Kurt Hunter is sure to stumble across it as he patrols the backwaters of Miami.

Check it out the series here

★★★★★ *This series is one of my favorites. Steven Becker is a genius when it comes to weaving a plot and local color with great characters. It's like dessert, I eat it first*

★★★★★ *Great latest and greatest in the series or as a stand alone. I don't want to give up the plot. The characters are more "fleshed out" and have become "real." A truly believable story in and about Florida and Floridians.*

Tides of Fortune

What do you do when you're labeled a pirate in the nineteenth century Caribbean

Follow the adventures of young Captain Van Doren as he and his crew try to avoid the hangman's noose. With their unique mix of skills, Nick and company roam the waters of the Caribbean looking for a safe haven to spend their wealth. But, the call "Sail on the horizon" often changes the best laid plans.

Check out the series here

★★★★★ *This is a great book for those who like me enjoy "factional" books. This is a book that has characters that actually existed and took place in a real place(s). So even though it isn't a true story, it certainly could be. Steven Becker is a terrific writer and it certainly shows in this book of action of piracy, treasure hunting, ship racing etc*

The Storm Series

Meet contract agents John and Mako Storm. The father and son duo are as incompatible as water and oil, but necessity often forces them to work together. This thriller series has plenty of international locations, action, and adventure.

Check out the series here

★★★★★ *Steven Becker's best book written to date. Great plot and very believable characters. The action is non-stop and the book is hard to put down. Enough plot twists exist for an exciting read. I highly recommend this great action thriller.*

★★★★★ *A thriller of mega proportions! Plenty of action on the high seas and in the Caribbean islands. The characters ran from high tech to divers to agents in the field. If you are looking for an adrenaline rush by all means get Steven Beckers new E Book*

The Will Service Series

If you can build it, sail it, dive it, and fish it—what's left. Will Service: carpenter, sailor, and fishing guide can do all that. But trouble seems to find him and it takes all his skill and more to extricate himself from it.

Check out the series here

★★★★★ *I am a sucker for anything that reminds me of the great John D. MacDonald and Travis McGee. I really enjoyed this book. I hope the new Will Service adventure is out soon, and I hope Will is living on a boat. It sounds as if he will be. I am now an official Will Service fan. Now, Steven Becker needs to ignore everything else and get to work on the next Will Service novel*

★★★★★ *If you like Cussler you will like Becker! A great read and an action packed thrill ride through the Florida Keys!*

Made in United States
Orlando, FL
25 July 2024

49521202R00198